A Time and a Season

CHARLOTTE EVERHART

NEVINLY PUBLISHING

To my grandmother, who taught me to love the Spanish language and patiently answered all my questions about her Catholic faith. I thought of you often as I wrote this story. And to my very special aunt. You were such a gift to our entire family. As time goes on, I realize more and more what an amazing blessing you were. Until we meet again ...

Also By

Hope for Tomorrow
books2read.com/HopeForTomorrow

Joy of Today
books2read.com/JoyOfToday

From This Moment
https://books2read.com/FromThisMoment

When Someday Finally Comes — Coming Soon

Sweet December — Coming Soon

Contents

Epigraph

There is a time for everything, and a season for every activity under the heavens.

Ecclesiastes 3:1

Prologue

THEN

There was a time and season for everything, according to Father Tim, who stood behind the lecturn at the front of the church and read from Ecclesiastes chapter three. Seated in the front pew surrounded by family, Leila Molina didn't need to be told that now was the time to mourn. If the painful squeezing of her heart hadn't given it away, the quiet, broken weeping coming from her parents on either side of her surely would have.

She couldn't look at them. She knew what she'd see: quivering chins and watery, red-rimmed eyes. But Leila's hands, resting on her pudgy thighs and folded tightly together in her lap, twitched. She should reach out—touch her mother's shoulder or squeeze her father's hand.

She didn't.

She couldn't.

Somehow, she knew the moment she moved, she'd lose control and split into a million pieces. So, unlike the rest of her family with their outward displays of grief, Leila stared, rigid and dry-eyed, at the small casket at the front of the church. Luca was in there. So quiet and so still.

So *gone*.

Forever.

Chapter 1

NOW

Jackson Lang had grown up on the ice. It wasn't a stretch to say he'd learned to skate right around the time he learned to walk. In the small town of Nicolet on the southern shore of Lake Superior in the Upper Peninsula of Michigan, hockey was a way of life. Parents all over town had big dreams for their sons. They were all going to go to college on full-ride scholarships prior to being drafted into the NHL, and so they dutifully carted their boys and their malodorous hockey bags to and from the rink day in and day out, all year long.

Jackson's father, Philip, had needed a piece of that action. From the moment of Jackson's birth, Philip had placed him firmly on the hockey track. Never mind that Philip knew nothing of the game. His boy was going places.

So, for Jackson, hockey loomed large in life, even at the tender age of two. It was simply good luck that he'd loved it—for a time, anyway. Even when his passion for the sport cooled—something he made sure nobody ever knew—being a hockey player had given him an identity and kept him out of trouble.

Well, mostly.

Jackson spit over the boards and onto the ice before blowing his whistle. Its shrill chirp echoed through the large arena. "Koski, run the play! Either drive the seam or pass to the point already. Let's go!"

"Yeah, Coach," the forward muttered from around his mouth guard as he skated away.

"Run it again!"

Again.

Variations of the same plays. Game after game, year after year. Today, Jackson didn't even have skates on, and he should. The head coach, Sean LaCombe, wasn't there, so Jackson was running the show alone, something that ought to have thrilled him.

He watched the team. Mitch Davis was the obvious star. He was their first-line center. That had been Jackson's position in high school, though he hadn't been nearly as good, something for which his father had never quite forgiven him. Not that Jackson was the one in need of forgiveness. For all he cared, Philip Lang could go straight to—

"Jackson Wilfred Lang!"

He jumped. There was only one person in the world allowed to speak his middle name. Pushing himself away from the boards he'd been leaning against, Jackson turned to greet his mother. With a sheepish grin, he addressed her where she'd stopped, which was well short of the players' bench. She had a strong aversion to the smell she claimed lingered there like a polluting smog.

He sniffed. Nope—he still couldn't smell it.

"Mom!" He moved to close the gap between them and wrapped her in a hug. "What're you doing here?"

"Ensuring that you're still alive," Virginia answered dryly.

Over her shoulder, Jackson noticed Elizabeth making her way toward them. His older sister's turquoise eyes—the only feature they had in common—danced in amusement.

"I'm alive," he answered easily. After planting a swift kiss on his mother's cheek, he moved around her to greet his sister. "Lizzie, how are you?"

She rolled her eyes. "Enormous."

And she really was. As a joke, he made to hug her before pulling back and looking down at her burgeoning tummy. "On second thought, I'm not sure I can get my arms around you. How much longer again?"

Lizzie swatted at him, but she did it with a good-natured smile. "Stop. You know I'm not due until the end of January."

It was only mid October. How in the hell was his tiny sister going to last that long without splitting open? She was pregnant with twin boys, and there was just no way her little frame was going to hold until January at the rate they were growing. It worried him, but he covered it with a playful grin. "Good luck with that."

Excusing himself for a minute, Jackson stepped away and hollered at the guys, telling them to get a drink and take five. Since he knew his mom and sister hadn't come to watch the team practice, he led them around the corner and into the hallway where they could have some privacy.

Virginia wasted no time. With a frown she asked, "Jackson, where have you been?"

She was calling him out as he'd known she eventually would. He knew he deserved it, but he still played dumb. "Here, mostly. Why?"

She planted a hand on her hip. "You're avoiding me."

"What do you mean? I called you back yesterday and left you a message."

She slanted her head and viewed him through narrowed eyes. "True, you finally did, but you called the house instead of my cell when you knew I'd be at work. I called you back, but of course you didn't answer." She shook her head, but the corners of her mouth twitched. His mother could never stay angry with him for long. "Anyway, Elizabeth and I wanted to see you."

He stretched his arms out wide. "Well, here I am."

"Here you are," she repeated, and then mirroring him with her own arms she added, "Here we all are. Finally. And apparently, all I needed to do was ambush you in this ice arena to make it happen."

Her tone was teasing, but behind that small smile she wore, he could sense a profound sadness. Lately, it was there every time she looked at him. Nothing about her outward appearance had really changed, but she looked different to him.

Her dark hair was still pulled back in her perfect signature French twist—or maybe it was an Italian twist, he couldn't remember. Whatever the classy style was called, it was always secured by one of the many decorative combs that had their own special place in her vanity drawer at home. She collected them the way some people collected trading cards.

It was strange, but Jackson took some small comfort in his mother's immutable appearance. He was grateful that at least some things never changed.

Obviously, she was still going to the hair salon every two weeks for a dye job because she'd once admitted she was fully grey. He never would have known it. She was still very much the attractive, youthful, and put-together Virginia Lang, pillar of the community—though she may have fallen a few notches in the eyes of some. It was a small consolation, at least, to know his father's reputation had taken a much bigger hit, and it wasn't likely to recover.

Nicolet was a small town, and people there watched out for one another. They valued loyalty and faithfulness. Philip Lang, while he'd never been all that warm or approachable, had let them all down.

It might be her eyes, Jackson thought as he studied his mother. That was what was different. Her smiles didn't quite reach them now. And that was the real reason he'd been avoiding her. He knew what it meant about him that he wasn't trying harder to be supportive. But he found that right now he just couldn't be there for her the way she needed him to be. He didn't have it in him. He should have, but he didn't. How could he help Virginia with her wounds when he was still—quite literally—nursing his own? Reflexively, he traced the rough scab of the cut on his bottom lip with his thumb.

The women followed the movement of his hand and looked away. They were all struggling, trying to make sense of things in their own ways the best they could.

Jackson's way of dealing with the recent implosion of their family was—well, *not* to deal with it. He'd needed some space, and he justified his retreat by telling himself Virginia could handle Philip on her own the way she'd always left him to do growing up, and if she couldn't, she had Lizzie to lean on. His sister was by far and away the better option anyway. Lizzie was pure goodness and always had been, and she had a strength to her he'd always known he lacked. She could handle their mother. Her grief. She could handle their father too, if it came to it.

Jackson had gotten involved that day two weeks ago when everything had come to a head, and he shouldn't have. The matter should have stayed between his parents, much as he'd felt the need to defend his mother in the moment.

"I'm sorry, Ma. I've been busy, that's all."

She sighed. "With what, Jackson?"

His work didn't take up all that much time, and she knew it. He tried to think of something, but what else was there? His robust love life perhaps, though he couldn't imagine she'd care to hear about that, and anyway, he probably couldn't in all honesty refer to it as a *love* life so much as a *sex* life, and she definitely wouldn't want to know about that.

Elizabeth spoke, saving him from answering. "Jackson, we have something important we need to talk to you about."

A cruel wave of dread crashed over him. It must have something to do with the old man. It had to, but Jackson didn't want to hear it. He'd been doing well the last week by simply pretending Philip didn't exist. He was trying to move on, heal a lifetime of hurts. His black eye had mostly faded, but the cut on his lip was proving to be more stubborn. Every time he smiled too big, which wasn't often these days, it split open again.

The cut was not unlike his invisible wounds. Even though he knew they must be healing, if they were manipulated too much too soon, they'd split wide open again too. He wasn't ready to talk yet. "Listen, is this about Dad? Because I can't—"

Lizzie cut him off. "Partly. It's complicated." Gently, she reached out and touched his arm. "Some of it's good news, Jackson."

He ran a hand through his sandy brown hair. Then, setting his shoulders back and lifting his chin, he said, "Okay. Let's hear it."

His sister shook her head. "Not here. We want to take you to dinner to discuss it."

He glanced at each one of them in turn. They stared back expectantly.

"What, you mean tonight?"

Lizzie nodded.

"Are you free?" his mother asked.

Jackson took in her wool dress slacks and fancy, high-heeled shoes. Clearly, she was dressed for dinner. So was Lizzie, come to think of it. It didn't matter if she was as big as two houses. His sister could never be anything but beautiful. She was soft and feminine, and even the cleft chin she'd inherited from their father couldn't detract from that, though she claimed it did. Her shiny chestnut hair fell to her shoulders in a cascade of curls, which meant she'd spent some time on it in anticipation of an outing, and he was pretty sure she hadn't planned the rink as the final destination.

He was about to disappoint her. He was about to disappoint them both because there was no way he'd be spending his Friday night out at a restaurant talking about his father. Jackson was done with him.

He couldn't go anyway. He had plans with Mindy. "I have a date tonight," he said.

Lizzy pulled a face, wrinkling her nose in distaste. "Please tell me it's not with that same woman you brought home last month."

Ignoring his sister, Jackson looked at his mother, who studied him through sad eyes. Could he blame her for being upset? They'd become close now that those teenage years were behind him, and the distance he'd deliberately put between them was undeniable.

He was hurting her, and he needed to fix it, but something inside him had shifted that day two weeks ago, and he didn't know how to go back to the way things were.

He took her hand and squeezed it. "I really do have plans, Ma, and I can't change them now. Mindy would kill me. She bought a new outfit for tonight and everything."

Lizzie and his mother exchanged a look. They'd met Mindy only once, and that had been at their Labor Day barbecue when she'd shown up wearing a flesh-colored, see-through dress with a bright red thong underneath. It hadn't been the best first impression.

Jackson had to admit, Mindy wasn't doing it for him anymore anyway. After tonight, he might need to cut her loose. It meant he'd be alone for a bit since he didn't have anyone else waiting in the wings this time. He knew why.

Leila.

A few months ago, back in August, he'd bumped into her at a miniature golf course. It had been a gut punch, and he was still reeling from it. Since that encounter, he hadn't been able to muster much enthusiasm for Mindy or anyone else. And he hadn't been able to get Leila off his mind.

She'd barely looked at him that day, but he'd noticed the flush creep into her cheeks as he'd chatted up her friend. He wished he could remember what he'd babbled on about, but he'd gone on autopilot the moment he saw her. She was as beautiful as he remembered, maybe more-so, having completed the transition from girl to woman.

One night post high school, shortly after moving to Canada for hockey, he'd found her on MySpace, and he'd stalked her there for a while until he quit the platform in self-disgust. Having never hopped on the Facebook bandwagon, he hadn't seen her since 2009, her last year of college.

Seeing her again in person, out of the blue like that, had caused his heart to contract in a painful squeeze he could still feel if he let himself think about her. It helped to know she hadn't been indifferent to the experience either. He'd lain awake in bed for hours that night, wondering what it meant. What had she been thinking that would make her go red in the face like that? He supposed he'd never know, and he told himself he didn't care.

He had enough problems to worry about. He felt stuck. He was stuck in his job, stuck in one meaningless relationship after another, and stuck with a father who probably would never speak to him again. And now, it would appear, he was stuck having to meet up with his mom and sister to hear news he knew without a doubt he didn't want to hear.

After Lizzie announced he wouldn't be getting out of meeting with them, they settled on Monday. Jackson was out of town Saturday and Sunday for a weekend of scrimmages with the team, but Monday morning worked for everyone. First, they'd all gather down at Nicolet Harbor for part one of the discussion, and then he and Lizzie would head out on the boat for part two, because why not make it as complicated as possible? Virginia couldn't join them on the boat. She had to work, and whatever his sister needed to tell him required more time than their mother had.

His mother had a job. She was an *employee*.

The thought of her punching in and punching out after all those years of running the show at their family's business—he hated to think of it. At least he approved of her new boss. She was a good woman he'd known well once, even though it rankled that his mother now reported to her and relied on her for a paycheck.

Lizzie stepped toward him. "Alright, that's settled. Now, give me a kiss and get back to work."

Jackson obliged her, once again making a big show of not being able to wrap his arms around her. Her playful annoyance was gratifying, but he grew serious quickly when his mother reached for him. He held her in a gentle hug. She felt smaller, more frail in his arms than she had the last time he'd hugged her. She was losing weight, he realized.

He was about to say something when she whispered, "I love you, Jackson."

He swallowed hard, and he felt some of the wall he'd erected around himself crumble. "Love you too, Ma."

That night, Jackson's date with Mindy was a disaster. She greeted him at the door wearing some kind of go-go dancer getup. If the belted skirt had been any shorter, her butt cheeks would have hung out below the hem. The top, like the skirt, was fringed and looked more like some kind of rodeo bra than anything else. If Mindy had to raise her arms for any reason, her boobs would pop out the bottom. An open cardigan was thrown over the top of the outfit to try to give it an air of respectability.

It failed.

She was a sexy woman with a beautiful body, there was no question, but all through dinner, Jackson shifted around uncomfortably. Anyone with eyes could see that Mindy Moore was looking for some action that night. She'd gone to all that trouble with the new clothes and what appeared to be a fresh haircut and dye job, but try as he might, Jackson couldn't muster up a single ounce of interest. He hadn't been able to for weeks, and by the looks of it, Mindy was growing desperate for his attention.

Maybe he should call his doctor.

Or maybe it was just time.

It was, he decided. It was past time, and even though he knew what he needed to do, he dreaded it. He hated this part. He didn't set out to hurt women, but it always happened anyway. There would be tears tonight, and he'd feel like the scum of the earth, which he knew he deserved. Hopefully, Mindy wouldn't get nasty with him. He could never predict which ones would go a little nuts. He'd been slapped and kicked before. One ex named Jenna—no, Kendra—had taken off a high-heeled shoe and thrown it at his car as he'd driven away.

Jackson glanced at his watch as he pretended to listen to Mindy talk about the latest Kardashian news.

"... and then he just *dumped* her, just out of the blue. I mean, can you, like, even believe he would do that?"

He could.

Another hour. Another hour, and he'd send Mindy packing.

Chapter 2

Seated on a stool behind the checkout counter, Leila Molina looked around her mother's bustling store. Every time she came in here, she felt like that high school student she'd been when her mother had first opened the place just before the holidays during their first year in Nicolet. Just as she was now, she'd been so proud back then. What had started out as a small and quiet little bookshop years ago had grown into a much larger bookstore-coffeehouse combo. Somehow, it had kept its cozy feel while also offering customers plenty of space to browse, read, and sip specialty coffee. It was a successful business by anyone's standards, and Leila knew it had far exceeded her mother's expectations.

"Mama, when are you going to get some more help in here?" Leila asked.

Carmen Molina, crouched on the floor over a box she had just opened, didn't look up.

"Mama," Leila persisted as she languidly spun the display case of personalized bookmarks that rested on the counter near the register. She scanned the *L*s. Still no *Leila* after all these years. But there was a *Libby* now, so maybe there was hope. "When are you going to hire for that manager position we talked about?"

Carmen lifted a pile of books out of the box and rested them on the back counter below the large display case. She sighed and brushed her long locks away from her face. They were thick as ever, but her once black strands were now completely silver. Leila was proud of how her mother was embracing the aging process. The combination of silver hair and the youthful complexion of her face was actually quite striking. Thanks to their heritage, their skin would age well, just as Leila's *abuelita's* had, God rest her soul.

"As a matter of fact, I did hire someone," Carmen finally answered.

Leila stilled her hand as her eyes found her mother's. "When?"

Carmen fidgeted with the pile of books. "Oh, about a week ago."

"That's great news!" Leila narrowed her eyes. "Why didn't you tell me?"

Carmen's gaze shifted to the box on the floor, and she reached for more books to unpack. "I just forgot, I suppose."

Leila hopped off the stool to help, grabbing an armful of books and setting them on the counter beside the pile her mother had started. "Well, who did you hire then? Someone good?"

"She's lovely, and she's very experienced. She's actually owned her own business, so she can help me with payroll and all kinds of other things."

"That's awesome, Mama!" She reached for her mother and hugged her. Carmen smelled like lavender, as she always did. "You've needed someone like that for so long. Now you can have a little rest from all the craziness."

Carmen chuckled, giving Leila a small squeeze before stepping back. "You know I love the craziness, *mija*. It keeps me busy."

"Busy is good, but so is rest," Leila said firmly. "*¿Equilibrio, no? Es muy importante.*"

Her mother leveled her with a stare. "I agree. Balance is important. You remember that the next time you work a sixty-hour week in that hospital, hmm?"

"*Touché.*" Leila grinned and reached down for the remaining books in the box. She slowly inhaled. She loved the smell of books—the earthy, woody fragrance of the pages mixed with the scent of the glues used to bind them. She loved all the smells in the shop. Books, combined with the enticing aromas of lattes and cappuccinos and even the faintest scent of cigars from the display case behind the counter, created an instant feast for the nose of any customer who walked through the door.

Glancing around, Leila took it all in. A handful of patrons quietly perused the rows and rows of books, while two little kids giggled in the back children's nook from one of the plush sofas as their mother read to them. Two baristas, Hattie and Mackenzie Jones, were busy grinding beans and serving up coffee drinks. They were identical twins, juniors at Nicolet State University, and they were probably the reason that four young college boys now occupied two tables at the front of the coffee shop. An elderly gentleman sat alone at another table and read the newspaper, seemingly oblivious to the attention-seeking boys and the young couple occupying the last table in the corner.

It wasn't that it was terribly busy at the store, but Leila knew that business was steady like this all day long, every day of the week. It didn't leave her mama much time to have a personal life, develop a hobby, make friends. Leila took a moment to study her overworked mother. She'd be fifty-six at the end of the month and widowed these two years now.

Luca's Book Cafe, named *Luca's Books* originally, had been a lifesaver for her mother after they'd moved to town. It had been a time of great upheaval in their family. Carmen could have fallen into a sinkhole of depression and never climbed back out again, and nobody would have blamed her if she had. Instead, she'd done the brave thing and reinvented herself.

The shop had given her renewed purpose back then, and it had kept her busy since Leila's father had passed, but it was time for Carmen to slow down now. Taking on a full-time manager would allow her to set a new pace—one she could keep up for the next several years if she wanted.

Maybe she could even travel. Carmen had always wanted to see the rest of the United States and explore Europe, but she never had. Leila couldn't remember the last time her mama had gone on any type of vacation. With no living relatives remaining in Puerto Rico, Carmen didn't even go on her biennial trips there anymore. She hadn't for years.

Since Leila had returned to Nicolet from Lower Michigan five months ago, she'd been nagging at her mother to slow down. But whenever Leila would suggest Carmen take a little time for herself, her mama would ask, "Who would run the store?"

"I'll do it," Leila had offered once. She still knew how to ring up a book and do basic inventory. It had been years, but she was fairly certain she could figure it out.

Carmen had laughed at that. "Oh, right. My grown daughter, a doctor, is going to come and work my cash register like she did as a teenager. I don't think so."

Leila smiled now at the memory of her teenage self in those early days of the business. The shop had opened just in time for Christmas during Leila's senior year, and she'd been there helping out from the very beginning. It had been a mad scramble for her mother to get everything up and running in time to benefit from even a fraction of the holiday sales boost. As it was, they'd missed Black Friday, but it had been a tremendous feat to begin a business from scratch and have it up and running in just over five months, so it was an overall win.

Leila had helped as much as she could, and she'd loved every minute. After finishing up her school day at Nicolet High, she'd head over to the store where her mother would have a snack waiting for her. Usually, the snack consisted of carrots and an apple, at Leila's request, but occasionally a treat from Trader Truffles, the chocolate shop across the street, would greet her instead.

"An occasional chocolate splurge makes life worth living, *mija*," Carmen would say. Leila smiled as she remembered. Never again would she be able to eat a chocolate truffle without thinking of her mother.

Every week, from the time of the grand opening until the day she left for college, Leila spent hours helping out at the store, and each week it seemed like half the town would stop in to say hello and buy some book or another.

The downtown's charm, with its historic redbrick buildings and quaint cobblestoned sidewalks, attracted locals and tourists alike. Even today, in the age of online shopping and social media obsession, it drew people, and Leila knew why. Being in the downtown was like stepping back in time. It was refreshing to loll away an afternoon in a place where the storekeepers were on a first-name basis with most of their customers, and strangers passing on the streets still greeted one another.

As if on cue, old Mr. Trader, second generation owner and operator of Trader Truffles, knocked on the window pane and waved. Leila smiled and waved back, watching him continue on down the sidewalk towards the art gallery his granddaughter owned.

Times had definitely changed, but not here on Main Street. Briefly, Leila had been concerned about the future of her mama's store, especially when the ebook market had really taken off. She needn't have worried. Carmen's store had never been in any real danger, but even if it had been, the decision to expand to include the coffee shop would have staved off any trouble.

Part of the expansion had included the addition of several small nooks with comfortable easy chairs where patrons could relax and read, and she'd also created a children's section even bigger and more enticing than the local library's.

Behind the counter, Carmen now carried ebook gift cards along with an impressive variety of cigars, pipes, pocket knives, and trinkets. Locally made jewelry filled the display cases on either side of the register. There was something for everyone in her shop.

Leila's mama might be busy, but she was doing alright. For a woman who had lost a son and a husband, she was getting by just fine, and with a manager coming on board, things for Carmen Molina were about to get even better.

Leila was asking the name of the new hire when the bell on the door jangled violently as it was ripped open. A willowy, mousy-haired girl blew in on a Lake Superior wind gust.

"Nadia! Hello dear," Carmen called out in greeting.

The young girl was out of breath and looked ready to drop. She wrestled the door closed as she turned her head to address them in her thick, southern twang. "I'm so sorry I'm late, Carmen! I'm dog sittin' again, and Marvin the Mastiff ran clear after a squirrel soon as I opened the door. It took me more than a hot minute gettin' him back inside. And where did this wind come from? My car near to careened off the Steele River Bridge on my way here."

Carmen grinned. "I do love your Marvin-made-me-late stories."

Nadia approached the counter looking stricken. "But they're all true," she insisted. "Every one of 'em. Cross my heart!"

"Oh, I don't doubt it." Carmen gave Nadia a reassuring pat on the arm before taking a quick glance at her watch. "Brings back memories. We had a crazy dog once, just ask Leila. And you're not really all that late, but I do think you should plan to leave earlier when you're dog sitting."

"Yes, ma'am." Nadia flushed pink.

Carmen smiled kindly. "Alright now. Go ahead and put your stuff away, and we'll go over a few things. Tonight I need you to flip the books and face-out some new ones. I have a list."

"Okay, thanks y'all." Nadia headed to the back room where the office was located and where they kept their belongings during work shifts. "Hiya, Leila," she called over her shoulder in belated greeting.

Leila smiled. "Hey, kiddo. How's your sister?"

Nadia turned and continued to walk backward through the Self-Help section on her way to the back room. "She's good. Busy teaching and bein' in love and all that."

Chuckling, Leila shook her head. "Sounds pretty great." Sarah Josten, Nadia's older sister, was an English teacher at Nicolet High School and a new friend of Leila's. Sarah had been dating another high school teacher since the summer. Apparently it was still going well.

Leila really liked Brian Beninger, or Benny, as he liked to be called. He was good to her friend. She made a mental note to reach out to Sarah soon. It had been too long.

Leila turned to her mama. "Where do you want to go for dinner?"

"How about 906 Pizza? I've been dreaming of their deep dish Mediterranean for weeks."

A geyser sprang open in Leila's mouth. That place had the best pizza in the entire world. No other pizza came close, and now that Carmen had mentioned it, Leila had to have it. Deep dish would add an unspeakable number of calories to an already rich dinner, but it would be worth it.

"Deep dish it is," Leila agreed. "It's actually fitting because as soon as we sit down in one of those old booths, *you're* going to dish. I'm done waiting."

Carmen made a disapproving noise. "*Paciencia.*"

"Mama, this *is* me being patient. I've been patient for days. You tell me you have news, and then you make me sit in suspense for *three* whole days."

"Yes. And you never stopped badgering me. I will tell you over pizza. Now, be a good girl and zip it, hmm?" Her lips curled as she eyed Leila up from beneath lowered lids before turning and lifting the empty box. "I need to run this to the back door. Once I go over things with Nadia, I will be ready."

Leila sighed, but she did it with a smile. "Alright. I guess I'll wait a little longer." She grabbed her coat, which was draped over the back of the stool in front of the register, and watched her mama walk away.

She turned her attention to the window. Pedestrians on the sidewalk were moving quickly, bracing themselves against the wind. A storm was blowing in, there was no question. Leila smiled. Luca had loved a good storm, especially at night. He'd climb into her bed, and together, they would listen to the wind and rain and—if they were lucky—the rumbles of thunder.

It happened like this for Leila not infrequently. Her little brother popped into her head all the time. So did her papa.

Now it was just herself and Mama. Well, the two of them and her cousin, Elena, who had just moved to town a few months ago. Still, it was jarring to think they'd started out as a family of four. They'd been *complete* all those years ago. It was odd how sometimes it all felt like a dream. Like none of it had ever really happened.

After Luca died, nothing had ever been the same again. Even something small, like going to a restaurant and telling the host or hostess they needed a table for three, was just *wrong* somehow. Almost always, they'd be led to a table set up for four people, which was even more wrong. Throughout dinner, the three of them would try to ignore the empty chair, but Leila watched, and she knew her parents' eyes were drawn to it just as much as hers were. For a time, they'd stopped eating out altogether.

Today, she and her mama would go to dinner and ask for a booth or table for two.

Only two.

Sometimes it scared Leila to think about it. She knew all too well from her own personal experiences how fragile life could be and how quickly things could change; how a loved one could fall out of your life in an instant, with no warning whatsoever.

Professionally, she saw it almost every single shift in the Emergency Room. Her patients in the ER started out their days as they always did. They drank their coffees, started a load of laundry, fed their pets ... never suspecting that catastrophe was lying in wait just around the corner. She was there for those people and their families when the sky fell down on them, and as exhausting and gut-wrenching as the job could often be, she was grateful to be in a position to help them in their time of need. It fed something in her soul.

Chapter 3

Within minutes of mother and daughter sliding into their booth at 906 Pizza, their young waitress was handing them menus.

"I don't believe we will need these, do we Leila?"

The pretty blonde's name tag read "Claire," and Leila shot her a smile. "We're stuck in a hopeless rut, Claire."

Retrieving the menus, the girl nodded in understanding. "I get it. You like what you like, right? Do you guys want to order everything now then, or do you want to get your drinks first?"

Leila looked to her mother for the answer.

"Let's get our drinks first, prolong the evening, hmm?"

That sounded perfect to Leila. They didn't go out together like this enough. Speaking to Claire, she said, "Sure, I'll have whatever amber ale you have on tap."

"We've got Floating Harbor from the Nicolet Brewing Company," she offered helpfully.

"Oh!" Leila exclaimed, taken aback.

"We just started carrying their line. I don't like beer usually, but I sorta like theirs," Claire offered helpfully.

"Alright, I guess the Floating Harbor will be fine."

"Got it." Claire wrote down the order. "And for you, ma'am?" she asked Carmen.

Once Leila's mama had completed her drink order, she reached across the table, palms up, in an age-old invitation. Leila joined their hands, and Carmen gave hers a brief squeeze.

"You ordered a beer from the Nicolet Brewing Company," Carmen noted.

"Yeah, so?"

"So this would be a perfect lead-in to one of the things I need to tell you."

Leila lifted her eyebrows and waited.

"You asked me who I hired earlier." Carmen paused again, and Leila wondered if she was waiting for a drum roll.

"And?" she prompted.

Carmen's words tumbled out in a rush. "I hired Jackson's mom, Leila."

Leila's mouth fell open. "You hired Virginia Lang?"

Carmen gave one final squeeze of Leila's hands before letting go. "I did."

Leila was speechless for several seconds. "I don't understand." She shook her head. "Virginia Lang is your new manager?"

"You haven't heard then?"

Leila stared at her blankly.

"Obviously you have not." Carmen lowered her voice and leaned forward. Leila mirrored her from her side of the table. "Philip has been carrying on an affair with Marjorie Taylor these last several years."

"No! The mayor's wife?"

"The very one."

Leila jerked back from the table. "Years? That's disgusting! How could Philip do that to sweet Virginia?"

"How could Marjorie do that to poor Robert?" Carmen countered. "He's a good man. I talked to him just the other day when he came in to order a book."

Leila shook her head, dumbfounded. "I'm sorry, I'm still processing all this."

"It's quite the scandal," Carmen agreed. "But Virginia is strong. She'll be okay."

Leila's thoughts were a tangled mess. She felt awful for Virginia, obviously. She had always deserved better than Philip. Back when she'd known them well, Leila had wondered what Virginia saw in him. How did two people like that—so different in every way that mattered—get together in the first place? Where Virginia was warm and nurturing, Philip was cold and callous.

As sorry as she felt for Virginia, Leila couldn't help thinking about the implications of this new arrangement at the store.

"Have you ... have you seen Jackson?" she asked, not looking at Carmen.

"Of course, it's a small town."

She met her mother's eyes. "You know that's not what I mean."

Carmen did know, and she reassured Leila with a smile. "No, he doesn't come into the store. And no, Virginia and I don't discuss you kids."

Leila nodded slowly. "Okay, then."

Carmen leaned forward again. "Have I done a bad thing, *mija*?" She rushed on before Leila could answer. "I had to do it, though. I just had to hire her. When I heard that she left Philip and that he was retaliating by trying to cut her out of the company—"

Leila made a surprised choking sound.

Carmen nodded sagely. "Oh, yes, *mija*. It is in his name, you see? The furniture stores. Everything. Not hers. All that money and all her security ... poof." Carmen clucked her tongue. "She should have insisted things be done differently, but she must have trusted him. I'm sure I don't know why. Anyway, when I heard that, I reached out to her. I wasn't sure if she would be looking for work." Carmen shrugged. "But she was, and we are now becoming friends, Leila. Fast friends."

Lifting a hand, Leila massaged her right temple. She felt a headache coming on. "Of course you are. Virginia's a good person, and you're a good person. I could see where you would be friends."

"Leila, what happened between you and Jackson ... it was so long ago. You were only children."

Leila knew that. It shouldn't still sting. The fact that it did was embarrassing. Normally, she wasn't prone to dramatic and theatrical responses to things, but then again, Jackson had always been able to stir up intense emotions in her. Instead of denying it, she spoke honestly. "I know. I've hung onto it too long, but I am trying to let it all go."

"To let *him* go," Carmen clarified.

"Sure, whatever."

Carmen sank into the back of the booth and smiled. "You're already well on your way. A year ago, you would never have ordered a beer made by Jackson's sister's brewing company. To have anything at all to do with him, even a tiny bit, would have been too much for you. Tonight you have taken a step. And I believe seeing Virginia at the store, hearing me talk about her, that will help too. It's too small a community for grudges, Leila."

Leila pressed her lips together before forcing herself to say she was sure her mother was right, although she rather felt that the constant reminders of Jackson, of what they once had, would be more like picking the scab than letting it heal. She'd had to get off Facebook for that very reason. She had the self-control of a gerbil. How many times a week had she tried to look him up only to find he still had no profile? On MySpace, she'd looked at his profile picture at least two or three times a week. Then one day, he was gone.

"Enough about the Langs," Leila said, changing the subject. "What was the other thing you needed to tell me?"

Chapter 4

"Good morning," Elena Torres greeted in a raspy voice as she stumbled into the kitchen. Without looking at Leila, she headed straight for the pot of hot coffee.

Leila grinned. Her cousin looked as though she'd been tumbled in the dryer on low all night long. Having experienced countless sleepovers with Elena growing up, Leila knew that she never settled down, not even in her sleep. A dreaming Elena was far more dangerous than any boxer in a ring, and Leila would wake up with the bruises to prove it.

This morning, Elena's hair had escaped her single braid in a cloud of inky curls and tangles, evidence of a particularly active night of sleeping. Leila's smile grew. "Happy Saturday."

"I thought the week would never end."

"You're up early." Elena was up, but it was debatable whether or not she was awake. She turned and looked at Leila through heavy-lidded eyes and mumbled something incoherent in Spanish.

She'd give her cousin another minute.

The sky wasn't fully awake yet either, though the emerging light visible through the east-facing window hinted that a glorious sunrise would soon start the day. Last night's storm had brought a downpour of rain, but today was forecast to be all clear and still unseasonably warm for October in the Upper Peninsula. Today would hit sixty, which was impressive since the thermometer mounted on the other side of the window read a mere forty-one degrees at the moment.

The small table for two where Leila sat rested under the single window of their itty-bitty kitchen, which overlooked the sparse backyard of their duplex. Devoid of trees, the tiny square patch of lawn had needed a little something, so Leila had hung two shepherd hooks side by side. A fern in need of some watering hung on the left one, and an empty bird feeder hung on the other. She made a mental note to buy more birdseed, even though she fed far more squirrels from that feeder than she did birds. At least it was wildlife.

Leila glanced at the digital clock displayed on the microwave above the stove. It was only seven-thirty. Normally her cousin slept in on the weekends, and she wondered what had motivated her to tumble out of bed a full three hours earlier than usual.

Reading her mind, Elena spoke in a low and scratchy voice, again in Spanish. "I'm pampering myself and using my gift certificate this morning at that day spa."

"The Dancing Sun?" Leila asked. "Mama will be happy you're using it. You'll love it there."

Elena switched to English, her accent thicker than usual as her brain continued to awaken. "I have a manicure at ten-thirty, then a facial, then a massage ... so I need to start getting ready."

Leila fought a smile. Only Elena would "get ready" to go to a spa. Everyone else would just throw on some sweats and call it good, but Elena dressed for any outing.

In Leila's opinion, her cousin looked most beautiful at times like this when her olive skin was natural and unadorned by makeup. Her rumpled yellow cotton pajamas revealed a soft, feminine figure underneath, and wisps of hair curled around her face and brushed against her bare shoulders. She was earthy and innocent—the Latina version of the Greek goddess, Artemis.

But every morning Artemis would enter the bathroom, where an arsenal of products awaited, and an hour later, Aphrodite emerged.

Nothing Leila said to Elena could make her soften her touch with a makeup brush, but it didn't really matter. With or without it, her cousin was a bombshell. Next to her, Leila sometimes felt like a bumpkin.

Erin Hennings—principal of Nicolet High School and a friend of Leila's—had put it best after meeting Elena for the first time when she interviewed her for a teaching job. "How can your cousin make cotton chinos and an Oxford button-up look sexy?"

Leila tried not to be jealous. Elena could eat whatever she wanted and maintain her perfect figure. She didn't even exercise. All Leila had to do was *look* at a potato chip, and it converted itself into a wad of cellulite. She ran nearly every single day, and she still carried five extra pounds. It didn't matter what she did or how many compliments she got, she'd always be a fat girl inside. Some childhood experiences could never be fully overcome.

Elena's voice was stronger when she spoke again, and ironically, she brought up her boss's name herself. "After Erin's evaluation of me yesterday, we need to go out and celebrate that I made it through the week. I was so nervous! What should we do?" She finished pouring and returned the coffee pot to its burner, where it made a low sizzling sound. She turned with her *World's Hottest Teacher* mug in hand and rested her hips against the counter.

"I might have to work. They asked me to take call."

Elena pulled a face. "You work too much."

Leila took a small sip of her coffee and shrugged. She *did* work too much, but she didn't mind. It was how she was wired.

"How about just dinner then?" Elena persisted. "No dancing, no drinks."

"Dinner might be okay." Especially since she was in a cooking rut. When Leila did cook these days, she wound up making some variation of the same uninspired meal. She needed to rediscover her creativity in the kitchen, but who had the time for that? "So long as you know I might get paged," she warned.

"I can deal."

"I ate pizza last night with Mama, so I'll have to get something a little lighter tonight. Would you want to check out that new place on Second Street? I hear they have fantastic salads."

Elena scoffed. "You and your salads. Leila, you haven't been fat since Luca died."

"And freshman year of college," Leila reminded her.

"Everyone gains weight freshman year."

"*You* didn't."

"Whatever, eat your lettuce. As long as I can get a good, strong Margarita, I don't care where we go." At Leila's lifted brows, she scoffed. "What? Am I not allowed to drink, either? I'm not the one on call, and I need to unwind and have a little fun. I came close to a mental breakdown this week."

Elena was exaggerating, but not by much. Her cousin had been edgy for days.

"I *hate* being observed in the classroom, and my principal is nice, but she's hella intimidating." Elena set her mug down and moved to the fridge, where she began rummaging around for the creamer.

"It's in the door," Leila offered before breaking into an amused grin. "And are we talking about the same Erin?" Erin Hennings was feisty, Leila would give Elena that, but she was barely five feet tall, and that anyone would find her intimidating was hysterical.

Elena rolled her eyes. "I know, I know. She's your friend, but you don't know what she is like at work. She clicks those high heels all over that building, walking around like she's got a giant rod up her *culo*."

That, Leila could believe. She was one of the few people who knew Erin was unhappy at work. The truth was, Erin had already locked in a transfer to the elementary school, beginning the following year. Disciplining teenagers had taken its toll on the high school principal, although she was a pro at masking her feelings. Erin was eager to trade in the surly teenagers for a younger batch of kids who would adore her and bring apples to her office instead of attitude.

"Anyway," Elena worked the cap on the small bottle of vanilla-flavored creamer, "I have to meet with her after school on Monday and hear about all the things I did wrong. The woman has no hairs on her tongue."

Leila giggled. "That doesn't translate. In English, it's 'She has no filter.'"

Elena waved a hand. "Whatever."

Leila fought a smile and lifted her mug to her lips. The hot liquid went down nice and smooth. She'd recently discovered the specialty coffee from Copper Harbor up in the Keweenaw Peninsula, and she'd never drink anything else ever again. It was bold, rich, and smooth as butter. "Well, I'm sure you did great because you're an amazing teacher," Leila murmured. "Don't worry about Erin. She might say exactly what's on her mind, but she's a lot softer on the inside than she lets on. We'll get you all loosened up tonight, alright? And I'll tell you some stories about your scary pint-sized boss so you can get over your Erin phobia. Does six o'clock work?"

Elena grinned. There was nothing she liked more than a good night on the town. "*Perfecto.*"

"Good." Leila gestured to the empty seat across the table from her. "Now sit down, because I have something to tell you."

Elena paused in the act of stirring her coffee and raised one eyebrow in question, but she didn't budge from her place near the counter.

Leila pointed to the chair. "*Siéntate.*"

Elena sighed, but she placed the spoon on the counter and joined Leila at the table. "Alright, but be quick or I'll be late. I can *not* miss my manicure. Look at these nails!"

Elena had what Leila jokingly described as "hooker hands." Her nails were too long, too bright, too *much*. Leila eyed them up briefly and then held out her own hands for comparison. "They look better than mine," she lied.

"I keep telling you, you need to get yourself some acrylics. It will make your nail beds look less *stumpy*."

That her nails were "stumpy" was news to Leila, but she supposed if she had to choose between stumpy and the red claws Elena pressed onto her fingertips every month, she'd choose stumpy every time. "That's never going to happen."

Elena pulled a face. "Suit yourself, but I'm telling you, men like polished nails."

"Yeah, well, patients don't. Back to what I was saying. Mama told me a few things last night, and one of them kind of affects you."

Elena leaned forward, all ears.

"The short version of the story is that Mama is selling the house."

Elena sat back in her chair, gobsmacked. "No!" she cried. "She can't!"

Leila understood the reaction. She'd had the same one. "She's going to put it on the market Monday. She says it's just too much for her to keep up with now that Papa's gone."

"But that's in two days! And that Victorian is one of a kind! Leila, you can't let her."

Leila was glad her cousin felt that way. "That's why I wanted to talk to you. I know you just got settled in here with me—like, *just*—but Elena, I'm going to buy it. I have to. On some level, I think I've always planned on this. I need to live there."

Her cousin's eyes widened. "Are you pulling my hair?"

Leila burst out laughing. "What?"

"I'm asking if you're being serious."

"Ah, you mean am I pulling your leg."

"*Ugh!* Stop correcting my idioms. They work just fine in Spanish. Leila," she continued earnestly, "where will I go?"

Leila stared at her a moment, puzzled. "What do you mean? You'll come with me, of course. I mean, if you want to. I *hope* you'll want to because—"

"I want to, I want to."

Leila studied Elena. She could see the moment the sudden tension eased. Looking her cousin firmly in the eye, she said, "Elena, you will *always* have a place with me and Mama. We're a family."

Elena nodded and looked out the window. Knowing her cousin would need a minute, Leila stood to top off her coffee. On her way to the pot, she stopped to plant a kiss on the top of Elena's head, and with her back turned, she poured and wondered if Elena would always fear being left behind. It was possible, she decided. If she herself would always be some version of the ugly fat girl, Elena would probably always see herself as someone who could easily be discarded and abandoned. More and more, Leila was of the opinion that childhood wounds could never be completely outgrown, only managed.

"Can you afford it? Do you have enough money?" Elena spoke from behind her.

Leila turned and grinned. Her cousin had already moved on to the practicalities. She'd never been one to beat around the bush. "Sort of."

Elena studied her a moment, holding her mug in both hands. "But honestly, can you *actually* afford it, Leila? What about that five-year plan you always go on about?"

"I'll have to make some adjustments," Leila admitted, sitting down again. "The bottom line is that, with those adjustments, I have the money, and I can always pick up extra shifts here and there if I need to."

"Work *more* than you already do now?"

"Elena, I need to do this."

"Does my *tía* know you're buying her house?"

Leila frowned. "Not yet." There were some things to work through, but she'd made up her mind. She loved that house, and it couldn't belong to anyone else. It held her last memories of her father, and it had been a grand gesture of love and sacrifice when he'd bought it for them. It was where they had healed as a family. There was no way she could let go of it.

She'd done the math last night, crunching numbers well past midnight while the wind howled outside her window, and it was a relief to find that she could, in fact, afford it. She'd have to ease up on her loan repayment strategy, which was much more aggressive than what the rest of her colleagues were doing anyway. She'd pay off her student debt in ten years instead of the five she'd planned, but with interest rates at 3.1 percent, she could swing it without much risk. Especially if Elena remained her roommate to offset the monthly mortgage payments.

With her slippered foot, Leila gave Elena a small nudge under the table. "Your rent amount won't change."

Elena blew out a relieved breath. "I didn't know how to ask that. You know I can only pay—"

"I know."
Elena grinned. "When do we move?"

Chapter 5

For Leila, the rest of the day was a flurry of activity. She called the bank and made an appointment with the mortgage lender for Monday morning. She was a live wire, energized by her excitement of things to come.

Over their pizza dinner the night before, Carmen told her she'd already put in an offer on a condo near the lake, over by the community ice arena. Her offer was contingent on the sale of the house, of course, and she was eager to sell it.

Leila felt another surge of adrenaline. At this rate, she'd make herself sick. But she couldn't help it. On Monday, Carmen would have a full-price offer—if Leila could wait that long—and she imagined they could all be moved into their respective homes in a matter of a month.

One month!

To burn off the excess energy, Leila cleaned the house, did two loads of laundry, made some phone calls, and went for a five-mile run. She, Carmen, and Elena even squeezed in the three o'clock mass at their church, the Cathedral of St. Paul, since Leila had to work the following day and would miss Sunday service.

By the time the evening came around, she was ready to have some fun. It wouldn't be the kind of "letting loose" Elena loved—with tequila shots and dancing into the wee hours—but it was better than sitting at home on the couch watching *Friends* reruns, which is what they would have done otherwise.

Leila hoped her cousin wouldn't kill her, but she'd invited a few people to join them, including Erin Hennings. Leila smiled as she waited by the door for Elena to come down from upstairs. Elena was about to see her school principal in a new light.

As the hostess led them to their booth, Leila experienced the smallest thrill of anticipation. She was about to see her friends after a long stretch of everyone being too busy with life to get together. Her running partner and colleague, Heidi Lakanen, had introduced Leila to the group of women over the summer, and she'd taken to them instantly.

It was time for Elena to make some connections and put down some additional roots. Not only would it be good for her, but she'd also need some very good reasons to stay once she experienced a string of Upper Peninsula winters. Having only experienced two U.P. winters during the short time she'd lived with Leila's parents after her mother died, to Elena the idea of fluffy white Christmases and beautiful, snowy winters for the rest of her life was still a novelty. But by the end of March, after four months of the stuff, she was bound to question the sanity of her decision to move permanently to such a wintry place. Come March, while the rest of the country sipped their lemonade on patios surrounded by crocuses and daffodils, Nicolet would be bracing itself for another six or seven weeks of freezing temperatures and blizzards.

Since two of Leila's new friends wouldn't be joining them tonight, she'd have to organize another get-together soon. Heidi was probably on an airplane somewhere over Kentucky or Ohio, on her way home from a cruise with her fiancé, and Olivia LaCombe hadn't been able to find a sitter for her one-year-old daughter. Olivia's husband, Sean, was head coach of the Nicolet State hockey team, and they were out of town for games.

Only Erin and Sarah Josten were meeting them, and Elena was already somewhat acquainted with both through her work at the high school. Sarah was an English teacher who was as sweet and gentle as they came—a product of her southern upbringing, most likely.

"You started without us," a voice accused from the head of the table.

Leila looked up from her menu to see Erin Hennings standing above them with a mock scowl. Elena, who had just taken a sip of her margarita, nearly choked.

"Oh!" she sputtered, drawing her napkin to her mouth.

Leila grinned. She probably should have given her cousin at least some warning that she'd be eating dinner with her scary boss tonight, but she hadn't wanted to deal with the complaints. After standing to first hug Erin and then

Sarah, who stood behind her, Leila met the narrowed eyes of Elena from across the table.

If looks could kill.

Feeling the corners of her mouth twitch, Leila quickly looked away.

"Am I ever glad you called," Sarah said after she and Erin had greeted Elena. She hung her purse over the back of her chair and sat. "My sister's havin' some friends over tonight, and with Benny gone for the weekend, I did *not* know what I would do with myself. I was just goin' to hide in my bedroom until everyone cleared out."

"I just saw her yesterday at the bookstore," Leila informed her. "She looks good."

"She's so happy these days. This was such a good move for her. Oh, and she just loves your mother all to pieces."

Over the top of the menu she held in her hands, Elena looked back and forth between Leila and Sarah, clearly trying to make the connection.

Leila flashed Elena a sheepish grin. "Sorry. You've met Nadia, but I guess you didn't know she's Sarah's younger sister. Nadia just moved to town and in with Sarah a few months ago."

"Ah." Understanding registered on Elena's face. "She's been putting in a lot of hours at the bookstore. Sweet kid."

Erin snorted, but she followed it up with a good-natured smile.

"We had a rough go of it there for a while," Sarah admitted.

They paused their conversation so Sarah and Erin could put in their drink orders.

"I'm not sure what I want," Erin muttered as Sarah was putting in an order for a glass of Cabernet. Her eyes scanned down the length of the drink menu. "What are you drinking, Leila?"

"Diet Coke. I'm on call."

Erin crinkled her nose. "Bummer for you." She turned to the waitress and ordered herself a mohito.

Sarah turned her attention to Elena. "How's teaching?"

Elena looked like one of those bobblehead dolls when she answered, "It's good, it's really good. It's going really well."

"What else would she say, Sarah?" Erin joked. "Ask her sometime when her boss isn't sitting at the table."

Elena blushed as red as the blouse she wore.

"Ignore her. I do." Sarah turned to pull her phone out of her purse. "Sorry, I just got a text." After swiping the screen, she broke out into a cheerful smile. "Olivia's on her way. She got a sitter."

The women requested another chair and delayed ordering their food until Olivia arrived. They spent the next twenty minutes making small talk. Leila noticed that Elena did more listening and observing than the rest of them, but she looked a little more relaxed with each passing minute, and Leila could tell she was enjoying herself. As usual, her cousin looked gorgeous. People often said the two of them looked alike, and sometimes Leila could almost see it.

Although they may have shared some resemblance to one another on the outside, their confidence and attitudes about their looks didn't match. For one thing, Leila didn't walk around the way Elena did—strutting her stuff, *knowing* she was pretty, but then her cousin had never gone through an ugly duckling stage.

Elena had been born beautiful and her beauty had only steadily improved with time, whereas Leila had spent most of her formative years with the terrible knowledge that she was truly ugly. Growing up, she'd been pimpled and overweight with very few friends and certainly no boyfriends.

Until Jackson Lang.

By the time Leila had met him, the transformation was complete. No longer was she the pimple-faced *whalephant* who hid packages of double-stuffed Oreos and Twizzlers under her bed, pulling them out only under the cover of darkness and stuffing them down—along with her feelings—to the soft glow of a flashlight, her only company. But in the months following Luca's funeral, she'd become the proverbial butterfly, making the full transformation from "hideous" to "hot" in a matter of months—at least according to the boys in her school.

She hadn't been "that fat girl with the retarded brother" for a long time, but cruel words lasted long after they'd been spoken.

"—Leila knows what I mean, right Leila?" Elena looked at her expectantly.

"Oh, sorry. I missed that."

"She was faaaaar away," Erin teased.

Sarah's eyebrows drew together in concern.

Elena waved a hand. "She was probably just going over a medical chart in her head. She does that a lot."

Leila took in Elena's wide grin. Tonight, her cousin wore bright red lipstick to match her cap-sleeved top.

Leila didn't even own red lipstick. Or a red top. She looked down at her attire: jeans and a tee-shirt. On her forehead, she might as well write in red Sharpie: *Not Interested in Snagging a Man, So Stay Away.*

She needed to do better.

With a sheepish grin Leila admitted, "I totally missed what you were saying. I was thinking about ... butterflies."

Elena stared at her blankly.

"Huh?" said Erin.

"Butterflies are ... nice," Sarah offered.

Ignoring the strange confession with a quick shake of her head, Elena explained, "They asked if we speak more English or Spanish together, and I told them we sometimes start out in one language and then switch to the other without even realizing it."

Leila nodded her agreement, quickly reentering the conversation. "Or sometimes one of us speaks in Spanish and the other in English."

"How fun would that be? I want to speak another language," Erin said in wonder. "The only thing I can say in Spanish is *Mas cerveza, por favor.*"

Elena giggled. "Then you know the most important thing. That and how to ask a guy to dance."

Leila couldn't keep the smile off her face. Her cousin was having fun, and her cat eyes sparkled as she explained how to say this or that in Spanish and the funny mistakes her students made as they learned her native language. With the smallest mispronunciation—even of just one letter—an otherwise innocuous word could take on a whole new and very colorful meaning.

"Take *cajones*, for instance," Elena instructed. "*Cajones* are drawers. You know, like dresser drawers. But change that *a* to an *o*, and you've just said something really funny." The four of them laughed long and hard as Elena went through other examples.

Leila observed those same eyes continue to dance as they all listened to Erin share a story about her mother. Apparently, this evening she'd called, and Erin told her about the plans to help renovate her boyfriend's small house on the Steele River Basin.

"I don't know what her problem is," Erin complained. "I'm going to live there one day anyway. I mean, Ethan and I *will* get married someday, even if he might not know it yet." She laughed. "There's no way he's getting rid of me now, not after everything we went through."

"So, what did she say about it?" Sarah prompted.

"She didn't really *say* anything."

Sarah pressed further. "But how do you know she disapproves if she didn't say anything?"

Erin was stubborn in her answer. "I just know."

"But how? It was a phone call. It's not like you could read her body language."

Erin set her jaw. "Because she … sniffed at me."

Sarah tilted her head, and after glancing at Leila and Elena to see if she was missing something, she let out a small laugh. "What?"

Erin doubled down. "She sniffs, okay? It's what she does when she doesn't like something I've said. She's been doing it forever."

Sarah sniffed. "Like that?"

"Shut up."

"No really, I want to learn this skill. All this time, I've wondered how to get the upper hand with you. To think I could have managed it only by using my nose!" She gave two more sniffs, flaring her nostrils dramatically each time.

Elena dissolved into a fit of laughter. Even Erin had to smile.

The banter between the two close friends continued, and Elena looked even more at ease. By the time Erin spilled her drink trying to move over to accommodate the additional chair the waitress brought over, Leila knew her cousin would never find her boss intimidating again.

"Shitty, shit, shit!" Erin exclaimed, jumping up to avoid getting wet as the contents of her glass poured over the edge of the table like a waterfall.

The rest of them sprang into action, mopping up what they could with their napkins while the waitress ran to get more. It was at that moment Olivia LaCombe chose to arrive.

She glanced at Erin, who was wiping at her pants, which were soaked at the crotch. "We just can't take you anywhere, can we?" she teased.

Erin scowled. "Technically, this is your fault," she informed Olivia.

"Of course it is," Olivia said easily. She kissed Erin on the cheek before taking a seat and greeting the rest of them. She wore her red hair pulled back in a thick ponytail, and her face was bare of makeup. Leila liked that about Olivia. She never tried too hard to be anyone but herself.

To Elena, Olivia said, "When I heard you'd be here, I called half the girls in the senior class to find a babysitter. My usual sitter was tied up, but I've been hoping to get to know you better, so I put my stubborn streak to good use tonight."

Elena smiled, her pleasure obvious. "I'm glad you found one."

Immediately, they launched into a conversation about a shared student.

Distracted by the waitress, who'd returned with additional napkins and another mohito for Erin, Leila lost track of Elena and Olivia's conversation and tuned in instead to Erin and Sarah's, but after a few minutes of listening to them talk about Nadia's college plans, she took a sip of her soda and let her thoughts roam.

A feeling of well-being settled over her as she enjoyed the sound of friendly chatter around their table. This was her crew now, and it felt nice. She'd never really had a close friend-group before, and even though she was still getting to know the three women who had joined them tonight, she liked them immensely.

Heidi was the one Leila knew best. She was more than ten years her senior, but the two of them had the most in common, and she saw Heidi more frequently than the other women since they worked together at the hospital. Heidi Lakanen was one of three radiologists in town, and they'd often meet up for lunch or a cup of coffee in the cafeteria. They also ran together after work and on the weekends.

Leila missed her running buddy. Her friend had been away for more than a week now, living it up in the Caribbean, and Leila had gone alone on her last eight runs. Nobody else in their circle enjoyed it the way they did. Briefly, earlier in the summer, she and Heidi had gotten Erin to join them, but after training for a race that had since come and gone, Erin had declared that she'd rather camp out tentless in the deep woods in the middle of June with no bug spray than run another mile with them.

No offense.

Leila grinned at the memory. She really was content. She had friends who cared about her, a job that fulfilled her, and a mother she was close to and talked with nearly every day. And then there was Elena, the sister of her heart. Soon, they'd be moving into the blue Victorian together.

It wasn't how she'd originally dreamed it would happen. From the moment Leila had set foot in that house, she'd dreamed of raising her own children there when the time came for her parents to downsize. But now Samuel was gone, leaving Carmen alone in the world to grandparent the grandchildren that might not ever come to be.

Leila never discussed it, but she longed for a family of her own in a way that pulled at her heart so powerfully she sometimes thought it might split right in half. And sometimes, if she was honest, she experienced a creeping dread at the thought that it might not ever happen. Because to have a family, she'd need a husband, and that seemed more and more improbable as time went by. She was almost thirty-one.

Tick-tock.

She'd thought she'd met him once, the man of her dreams. But a girl wasn't supposed to meet the love of her life at seventeen, so she should have known better. She'd been so sure, so naïve, and it still hurt. Worse, it had made her skittish, reluctant to put her trust and faith in anyone else.

But her mother was right.

It was time to let go and move on. Leila just didn't know how. During her waking hours, she could control her thoughts—mostly—but at night, in her dreams, she saw his face. Jackson Lang, with his startling turquoise eyes and dazzling smile, had ruined her for all other men.

She hated him for it.

Chapter 6

Drinking caffeine late at night had never worked out well for Leila, and Sunday morning came far too early. She'd downed three sodas at the restaurant before they'd called it a night, and she'd lain awake until two a.m. staring at the ceiling.

Now here she was, only three hours into her ER shift, and she already needed more coffee. Stifling a yawn, she pressed the big square button to open the double doors leading out of the Emergency Department. Just as she stepped out into the brightly lit hallway, she heard a familiar voice call her name. Turning in surprise, she saw Heidi walking briskly toward her from the opposite end of the hall, the hem of her unbuttoned white lab coat streaming behind her like a tail.

"Heidi! What are you doing here?"

"Living the dream, just like you," Heidi called back. When she drew close enough, Leila reached out and pulled her in for a hug. "Why are you working? Didn't you just get home? How was the cruise?" Leila didn't let Heidi answer any of her questions. Instead, she held her at arm's length and studied her. "You look nice and tan, and I loved the pictures you shared. I can't believe you swam with sting rays!"

Heidi sighed. "I'm moving to the Bahamas."

"Does Steven know?" Leila joked. Steven was Heidi's fiance and very much tied to Nicolet through work and his two college-aged children. "And why are you here?" she asked again. "I didn't think you were coming back in until tomorrow."

"That was the plan. Take Sunday to unpack and rest a little, but I got called in this morning to cover for Jordan again," Heidi rolled her eyes.

Leila scoffed. "Sick cat?"

"No, it's one of the dogs this time." She gestured toward the ER doors. "Has it been as crazy down here as it's been upstairs?"

"A zoo," Leila confirmed. "The warm weather has people out doing stupid things."

"We're supposed to get snow next week."

"Quiet," Leila commanded. "I don't want to know." She pointed toward the hospital cafe. "I'm grabbing some coffee. Want some?"

"Please! It was one in the morning before I climbed into bed. My suitcase isn't even unpacked yet, and I swear this pair of clean underwear I pulled out has bits of sand in them." She completed a stealth panty adjustment.

Leila laughed. "That can't be comfortable."

Heidi gave one final wiggle. "It's not."

Together, they walked down the hall that led to a common area that housed the cafeteria and coffee shop.

"Anything new in your life since I left?" Heidi bumped her with her hip.

Leila knew what she was asking. "I still haven't called him."

"Why not? I thought you liked him."

"I do. He's nice."

"He hasn't called you?"

"No, he did."

"Well?"

Leila shrugged. "I sent him to voicemail."

"Leila!" Heidi stopped to scold her. "Gina and I worked hard to set you two up."

Gina was a radiographer who worked with Heidi. Together, the two of them had hatched a plan to set Leila up with Gina's brother, Austin. To say that Leila had been reluctant was an understatement. She'd never been set up with anyone before, and it had made her feel like a total loser. Next, she'd be joining one of those dating sites begging for someone to love her.

But she'd done it. She'd gone out with Austin, and it had been a perfectly pleasant evening, and at the end, when he'd gone in for a kiss, she'd thought fast and given him her cheek instead. That had been over a week ago.

One of the hospital administrators passed, and after they both said hello, Heidi grabbed Leila by the arm and they continued on their way to the coffee shop. "I'm just curious," Heidi said in a lowered voice. "What's wrong with Gina's brother?"

Leila hesitated. "Nothing's wrong with him, really."

"Then what's the problem?"

"Nothing!"

Heidi leveled her with a look.

"Okay, fine. You'll think this is stupid, but he's a little too ... *pretty*."

Heidi grinned. "Gina hinted at that."

They'd reached the counter of the little coffee shop, and Heidi ordered for them both. They liked the same thing: dark roast with room for creamer. "I got this one. You get the next."

"Deal," Leila answered promptly as she adjusted her pager on the waistband of her blue scrubs.

They waited in silence, and then, after carrying their coffees to some open seats in a small lounge area between the coffee shop and the cafeteria, Heidi spoke again. "So back to Austin ..."

Leila settled into an oversized leather chair and groaned. "Please, stop."

Heidi was undeterred. "Okay, so you don't like good-looking men. I'm sure that's perfectly normal."

"Not when they're prettier than I am! Heidi, you should see how he dresses. A cashmere sweater? Really? It was a size too small, probably on purpose, and he wore these super tight designer jeans with polished shoes. No hair was out of place, and the guy is *fit*, and I mean fit. His muscles are sculpted, but almost like they're for show, and not for, I don't know, chopping wood."

Heidi failed at suppressing a smile. "If it's a lumberjack you're looking for, you moved to the right place." She craned her neck to look through the doorway and out into the busy cafeteria. "I bet I can find you one right here."

Leila chuckled in spite of herself. "He doesn't have to be a lumberjack, just someone who doesn't spend more time getting ready for a date than I do. I don't trust guys like that."

"Fair enough." Wisely, Heidi moved on. She filled Leila in on the trip, and Leila filled her in on the house. Earlier that morning, she'd spoken to her mother on the phone. It wasn't the sit-down visit she'd planned, but Leila hadn't been able to wait. At first, Carmen had been uncomfortable with the idea of taking money from her, but after Leila laid out all the reasons the arrangement would be best for them both, Carmen had come around, and now she was as excited as Leila was. Together, they'd be taking inventory of the house and deciding what should stay and what should go.

Heidi was thrilled for Leila and had just asked when the move-in date would be when an incoming Trauma One was called over the PA system for the Emergency Department. They exchanged a quick glance.

"Duty calls." Leila leaned across the small table between them, careful not to upset their drinks, and gave Heidi a one-armed hug. She scooped up her nearly full to-go cup and rose. "Talk later."

Heidi blew her a kiss. "We'll settle your love life over the next cup," she called after her.

Leila laughed and waved in response as she headed back to the ER to prepare for the incoming patient. Heidi thought she could settle her love life over a single cup of coffee? Yeah right. They'd drink a hundred cups before they even scratched the surface.

All resources for the trauma patient were in place by the time Leila got back to her department, but another trauma came in not long after, and Leila found herself tending an elderly gentleman and his wife who had crossed the center line in an area of town known as The Outcrop on Harlow Road, a road that connected the small, unincorporated community of Harley to the city of Nicolet proper, just five miles away.

It was a dangerous stretch of road, and people in the community had been clamoring for years to get the issues addressed. Usually pooled water or slippery ice were the culprits, but on a day like today she couldn't imagine what would have caused the sweet old man to drift into oncoming traffic.

The Outcrop's most recent victims had originally been placed in separate rooms, but they'd called out for each other so loudly that she'd finally had them put in one of the unused trauma bays together. They had serious injuries, but they weren't life threatening, and they would both be okay in time.

Along with some nasty cuts and contusions, the woman had a hairline fracture of her pelvis and two broken ribs, and her husband had a subdural hematoma that would need to be addressed surgically along with a wedge fracture in his thoracic spine that Leila hoped would heal on its own. Before the transporters took the wife to the neuro-ortho floor, and her husband to surgery, the woman, Maude, took Leila's hand and thanked her. "God bless you, honey," she said in a voice made soft and slurred from her intravenous pain medication.

Not long after the sweet couple moved out, a little girl was brought in by her parents. She'd swallowed a nickel that had become lodged in her esophagus. After that, a young motorcyclist came in with such a terrible head-to-toe road rash that he looked like a burn victim. Not wanting to pass him off mid-care to someone else, Leila stayed an extra two hours at the hospital.

Having worked straight through lunch and dinner, Leila was running on empty and her stomach let her know it had waited long enough to be fed. So before heading out, she stopped in the cafeteria and picked up a chocolate milk and a square of dried-up lasagna since she knew nothing was waiting for her at home. It was definitely time to get back into cooking.

Elena didn't know how. She couldn't even boil frozen corn. She'd tried the other day and burned it because she'd forgotten to add water to the pot, and it had taken two whole days for the house to smell normal again.

Messenger bag slung over her shoulder and tray in her hands, Leila headed to the seating area. Thinking it would be empty this time of the day since it was well past the dinner hour, Leila blinked in surprise to see Heidi at a table in the far back corner. She was alone and scrolling through her cellphone with a small, whimsical smile on her face. On the table in front of her rested her own plate of mostly untouched lasagna.

"Hey," Leila said in greeting as she plopped her tray down on the table and slid into the seat across from Heidi. "Fancy meeting you here."

Heidi jumped and quickly clicked off her phone's screen.

Leila blinked. "What were you looking at?"

Heidi met her eyes guiltily. "Uh ... nothing?"

"Nice try. Come on, what were you looking at? Your face looked all dreamy."

"Just ... pictures from the trip."

Leila stabbed a fork into her lasagna and worked to break off a piece. "Can I see? She brought the bite to her mouth and chewed. It crunched.

Heidi observed her with an amused smile and gestured to her own square of lasagna. "Careful, you'll break a tooth."

"No kidding," Leila agreed, after washing it down with a sip of milk. She set the small carton down on the table. "So, can I see these pictures?"

"Mmm, not right now." Heidi's cheeks flushed red.

Leila felt heat creep into her own face. She shouldn't have asked. Now she felt like some kind of meddler or gossip demanding to know her friend's private business.

Heidi groaned. "Okay, okay. Listen"—She looked around the cafeteria, empty except for a few employees wiping down tables and sweeping the floors—"I'll tell you, but only because I know you won't tell anyone else."

Leila leaned forward and lowered her voice. "Tell me what?"

"We got married on the cruise," Heidi whispered.

Leila's mouth went slack. "Are you serious?"

Heidi bit down on her lower lip and nodded vigorously, unable to keep the bright smile from her face.

"This is huge!"

"Shhh!"

Sheepishly, Leila pressed her lips together.

"You can't tell anybody, okay?"

With a nod, Leila agreed to secrecy, but in a low voice, she asked, "Why, though? I mean, I won't, but why?"

"It was a little impulsive," Heidi explained. "We're not sorry, but we do feel bad that the kids weren't there. Now we're trying to figure out what to do about them."

Mitch and Anna, Steven's children, both attended the university in town. They also happened to be Heidi's niece and nephew. Steven had first been married to Heidi's twin sister until she'd died tragically when Anna was just a baby. Things got complicated for a while, but now the four of them were very close, and Leila could understand why this might be exciting yet difficult news to share with the kids, if they hadn't already done so.

"You haven't told them yet, I'm assuming."

"Not yet."

Leila regarded her friend, who was absolutely radiant with happiness, and absorbed the news. Heidi was *married*! She and Steven had been planning a grand summer wedding, and Leila had already saved the date in her calendar. "Wow, this is just so amazing! I'm so happy for you guys."

With a glowing smile, Heidi thanked her.

Out of curiosity, Leila asked, "But what about Mackinac Island and the Grand Hotel dream wedding?" She knew all the big plans for that wedding had been set in motion months ago.

Heidi shrugged. "I canceled almost everything while we were still on the ship."

Leila fell back in her chair. "Man!" she protested in mock complaint. "I was really looking forward to going to that wedding."

Heidi grinned. "Maybe you'll have your own there one day."

It was as if her friend had poured an ice cold bucket of water over her. "Maybe, but I won't hold my breath." Leila stuck her fork into the center of her lasagna.

It stayed upright.

Later that night, covered by her heavy down quilt, Leila listened to the rain gently fall outside her window. As usual, the sound ushered in memories of Luca. He would be nearly twenty-one now, if he'd lived. Leila tried to imagine him all grown up and couldn't. To her, he'd always be just six years-old with baby-fine hair and an impish little smile.

But it wasn't her brother's smile she saw as she drifted off. Her traitorous subconscious opened the gates to memories she kept carefully locked away during her waking hours, and she found herself staring into the face of the boy she'd met near the river that day long ago.

As soon as Leila gave herself over to sleep, those turquoise eyes haunted her every dream.

Chapter 7

Jackson worked the cover off the boat and stopped for a moment to look up into the heat of the sun. The weather was unreal. If someone had told him it was the middle of July instead of the third Tuesday of October, he would have believed them. Only the changing colors of the leaves gave away the season. It was even slightly muggy out, thanks to the rain from the night before. With his eyes closed, he inhaled slowly and deeply. The scents mingled in his nostrils: wet pavement, fresh water, and the slightly musty smell of the boat's blue cover. He couldn't wait to get out on the water.

Lizzie had canceled him yesterday. She'd woken in the night with contractions that had turned out to be some no-big-deal type with a two-word name he couldn't remember. Even though she wasn't in labor and the contractions were considered normal, the doctor had advised she take it easy for the day, which she'd done, but only because her husband, Matt, had insisted upon it. She'd told Matt she'd give him one day of bed rest, and that was it.

Matt Maki towered over most men, but he was no match for his head-strong wife and her giant-sized will, and even though he was less than thrilled that she'd be out on the lake today in her condition, he was wise enough not to challenge her decision. He wasn't above going behind her back and calling Jackson, however.

Fifteen minutes earlier, as he'd pulled into the marina parking lot, Jackson's brother-in-law had called him.

"Listen, man, I need you to take it nice and easy today," Matt had pleaded. "Just low speeds, and stay near the harbor in case she needs to get off fast. And whatever you do, *don't* tell her I called you."

"You got it, brother."

"Thanks, man."

The idea of his sister going into early labor—or any kind of labor—within two feet of him was enough to make Jackson feel faint. He'd stay south of the breakwall that protected the harbor and keep the conversation as brief as possible, but it would help to know what she wanted to talk to him about. "Hey, how about a heads up?" he'd asked. "What's this all about? Ma wouldn't tell me Lizzie's news yesterday at our picnic, just her own."

"Oh, no you don't. She'd have my head. They both would."

"Give me a clue."

Matt had sighed over the phone. "Alright, since you're doing me a favor, I'll just say this. It's about the future, it's exciting, and you're a part of it."

"That's it? That's all I get?"

"That's it. Have fun, man. Oh, and hey, I'm sorry about your parents. It really sucks that Philip is pulling this crap, not that I'm all that surprised."

"Yeah, I know."

"Virginia will be just fine. She's got us."

"I know," Jackson repeated. "Listen, man. I gotta go, but I'll catch you later." Jackson had dropped his phone into the cupholder and stared at the harbor through the windshield of his Chevy Blazer.

He hadn't wanted to talk about his parents just then, not with Matt or anyone else, and he still didn't. He didn't want to think about them and their train wreck of a marriage. He'd much rather just enjoy the sights and his time out on the water.

Now, looking out into the smooth expanse of Lake Superior from his spot in the boat, Jackson thought it resembled the ice the way it always appeared right after the Zamboni had its way with it. He'd always viewed that process symbolically. The Zamboni took all that hacked up ice and smoothed it out again. It made him think of fresh starts.

Man, did he ever need one of those.

He worked another snap on the cover. Undoubtedly, the topic of their parents would come up when Lizzie got there—he knew that—but he'd deal with it then. "At least this news will be good," he muttered to himself as he popped the next snap, uncovering the boat one painstaking inch at a time. Yesterday's news from Virginia hadn't been good. Not at all.

Out of nowhere, the heaviness of the situation wrapped itself around him like a python and squeezed the air out of his lungs with one great *whoosh*. Jackson collapsed into the captain's chair and tried to catch his breath. It was too much all of a sudden. He didn't want to have to deal with any of it, but he knew he had to. There was no getting around it.

Jackson relented and let his mind go back to yesterday morning and the things his mother had told him. It seemed he needed to process the conversation whether he wanted to or not, and he was tired of fighting against it.

He and Virginia had still met at the harbor, even though Lizzy hadn't been able to join them. His mother had packed a small breakfast of bagels and fresh fruit for them, and Jackson had brought two fresh coffees from a local coffee shop. Never one to do something halfway, Virginia had included a red and white checkered tablecloth in her picnic basket, and she'd carefully laid it out over the wooden picnic table that rested just feet from the water's edge.

"Ma, by the time you get this all ready, you'll have to leave for work," he'd complained. But she wouldn't let him help, and she wouldn't cut any corners, and as he'd watched her graceful movements, he'd wondered again how his father could have stepped out on her. Virginia was all class, and she could still turn heads. Marjorie Taylor was cheap, a poor man's Virginia. It was a mystery how Philip—a man who always had to have the best of everything—had missed that key detail.

When Jackson had found out that Philip was having an affair with the mayor's wife, he'd raced to his parents' home to confront his father, and all hell had broken loose.

Things had escalated quickly, and they'd come to blows as Virginia screamed hysterically for them to stop. A lot of things had come to light that day, including that Virginia had known about the affair for nearly a year and had been turning a blind eye instead of confronting Philip. It still made Jackson sick to think about that, just as he could barely think of how it had felt to smash his fist into his father's face. Twice.

He wished he could say Philip had lost the fight, but Jackson had shown some restraint. Philip hadn't. Jackson ran his tongue over the cut on his lip. It had been an ugly scene, and after it had all played out, there was no going back.

Virginia filed for divorce the next day. Philip had been absolutely furious, and he'd been retaliating ever since.

Yesterday, Virginia had sat across from Jackson at the picnic table and confirmed what he'd already suspected. "Honey, Dad still says he's selling the store."

Jackson had been prepared for that. He'd known selling the store was Philip's plan, and that he might succeed in his vindictive agenda against them, but hearing the words still left him feeling a little sick. That was the store he and

Lizzie were supposed to run together first. Philip had planned to hand them all over one by one as he eased into retirement.

"And there's already a buyer who wants them all," his mother added.

She'd shocked him.

He was selling *all* the stores? The entire business?

"Yes," Virginia had confirmed. And he was actively trying to cut them all out of the proceeds.

Jackson had been speechless. The business was always supposed to be handed down to himself and Lizzie. Eventually, all of Lang Furniture was supposed to be theirs.

"Can he do that? Can he actually sell everything without your consent?" he'd asked.

His mother was still waiting on answers from her lawyers, but she warned him that things were getting ugly.

Without thinking about his words or their impact, Jackson had told her it was never all that pretty to begin with—that their lives had been like a shiny red apple with a rotten core. Immediately, he'd been remorseful.

Virginia had gone white, but she'd accepted his apology and added that Philip and Marjorie were moving south once everything was settled in Nicolet. That's when she'd cried.

"Ma, I'm so sorry," he'd said. "I can't imagine how you must feel."

She'd told him that she was the one who was sorry. That she'd never wanted a broken family for her children.

Jackson might not have understood a lot about the intricacies of his parents' marriage, but he did understand his mother's need to keep their household together. She'd come from a broken home where her parents had used her as a pawn and a weapon, and she hadn't ever recovered from it. She'd wanted to protect her own children from that.

"I'm not really blaming myself, Jackson," she'd admitted. "Not exclusively. I don't want you to think that. But if there's one good thing to come from all this, it's that I've been able to step back and see things more clearly. I'm looking at the choices I've made. Taking stock of my mistakes, my passive nature all through my married life, and I need to say this to you. I need to acknowledge this out loud. Jackson, you have every right to be angry—with your father, yes, but also with me. I didn't protect you from him. I should have been there for you."

That pronouncement had left Jackson feeling much as he did now as he sat in the boat and tried to regulate his breathing. He'd known he wasn't ready for that conversation. He'd imagined having it with her for years, but as the opportunity to point a finger at his mom finally stared him in the face, he hadn't been sure what to do.

An all out war had broken out in his head in that moment. One side needed to make it easier for her; she'd suffered enough, and he wanted to protect her, but the other wanted her to answer for how her actions—or rather her inactions—had caused *him* to suffer through his childhood in a way no kid should ever have to.

He'd searched his mother's eyes, and seeing the sorrow there, the virtuous side of his mind had won out. In that moment, he focused on helping her. He had intended to tell her she'd done nothing wrong. Absolve her of any guilt. Jackson had been carrying his resentment so long, he'd known he could handle its weight a little longer.

But his mother knew him well, and she'd put a hand up to stop him before he could speak. They both knew he could say the words, but it wouldn't have made them true.

"I need you to know one thing, though." She had looked him in the eye and held his gaze. "I was not aware of your father's history of getting physical with you. As your mother, I should have known—it was my job to know—but I didn't even suspect it. If I had, I wouldn't have stood for it, Jackson. I wouldn't have, and I need you to believe that."

Slowly, he'd nodded, accepting what she said as the truth. She'd been naïve, but she wasn't a liar. "It only happened a handful of times," he'd told her.

"A handful too many," she'd said, and then she'd used her fingers to count all his black eyes and excuses for them: a hockey stick through his facemask, running into a door. Once he'd even told her he'd gotten into a fight with Peter from his team.

Regret made her eyes shine, and she'd squeezed his hand.

With his hand held firmly in his mother's, Jackson had swallowed hard several times. Grown men didn't cry, at least not according to Philip.

"I just hope with time you can find it in your heart to forgive me," she'd said. "Maybe your father, too, someday. He's a broken man, and I don't know if he'll ever change. If you decide to forgive him, don't do it for his benefit. Do it for your own sake. For your own peace."

Jackson had worked to digest her words. He was still digesting them. Forgive his father? Could he really do that? It would take some kind of superhuman strength to accomplish it, if it was possible at all.

There was still so much left to say, a lifetime of things, but he would let those words spoken between himself and his mother yesterday be enough for the moment. They were a start, and even though he was fairly certain he'd forgiven her already, he wanted to be certain before he told her so.

Towards the end of their breakfast, after he'd forced down half of his bagel, Jackson asked one last question of Virginia. It was the question he'd been dying to ask and loathe to ask all at the same time. Was Philip going to make good on his threat to close out his and Lizzie's trust funds?

Jackson shouldn't have been surprised by the answer.

His mother tried to soften the blow. "I know this feels like a betrayal," she'd said, "and I don't know what will happen now, but please believe me when I tell you that one good thing could come from all this. It will be a clean break for you. He won't have any more power. Nothing left to use as leverage. Then, if you ever care to reconcile with Philip, it will be on your own terms."

It had taken all of Jackson's willpower not to react. He'd wanted to scream. He'd wanted to punch something. Instead, he'd said, "He sure likes to dangle that carrot, doesn't he? Always just out of reach, so he can get his jollies watching me chase after it. You know, he's always had all the power, like you said." He had shaken his head. "Not anymore, because you know what? I don't want it. It's only money, and I don't need it. I didn't know that before. I do now."

As he'd spoken the words, Jackson found he meant them, and it was freeing.

Virginia had smiled then, the way she always did when he said something she liked, and it crinkled the corners of her eyes. "You're stronger than you think you are, Jackson."

He'd smiled back. "So are you."

The sound of sirens in the distance competed with the shrieks of seagulls close by and brought Jackson back to the present. The idiot birds hadn't had the good sense to get out of town yet. They'd been lulled into staying put by the unseasonably warm weather, but they'd be sorry next week when the temperature dropped. They'd be sorry they hadn't planned their lives better, just as Jackson was now.

As he sat, waiting for his sister in a boat that wasn't really his, he admitted to himself for the first time that he'd always had a love-hate relationship with the idea of running a furniture business. It certainly wasn't his lifelong passion, but there would have been security in it. Financial security and prestige. He'd planned for the trust fund to be his retirement account. Without that, and without the store, he was royally screwed. He was an underpaid assistant hockey coach with no college degree and a skinny savings account.

Jackson checked his watch. Lizzie would be there in less than ten minutes. He stood and finished removing the cover, and when he'd stowed it away, he lifted his face to the sun once more. Out of nowhere, amid the mess of his life, he experienced a brief flash of contentment. It was the simple things in life, like the feel of the sun on his face, that made life worth living. With all the crap going on with his family, he took the moment for what it was—an unexpected gift. And it was enough to remind him that life had been good to him once. A long time ago, he'd known what it was to be truly and completely happy. Maybe, just maybe, he could have that again.

Chapter 8

Elizabeth arrived a few minutes early, and Jackson hopped out of the boat when he saw her white Jeep Cherokee pull into the space next to his. He jogged back up the dock and along the sidewalk to meet her just as she was opening her door.

"You're already here," she greeted.

"I wanted to have the boat ready."

Elizabeth took his proffered hand and hoisted herself out of her seat and onto the blacktop. Already, the heat was radiating off it. "It feels amazing out here. Can you believe this time next week we'll be buried in snow?"

"Now why'd you have to go and bring that up?" Jackson replied with a laugh as he closed her door.

She moved to the back of the Jeep and opened the hatchback.

Jackson was right behind her. "What can I get for you?"

"Just that bag there," Elizabeth said, pointing to a large, red-and-white striped beach bag. "I packed that blanket, too, but I don't think I'll need it."

Jackson grabbed both the bag and the blanket. "Might as well. You never know what you might need out there. All it takes is a small wind shift and the temperature can drop twenty degrees."

Elizabeth nodded. He wasn't telling her anything she didn't already know. Everybody in Nicolet knew about the capricious whimsy of their weather. One of their beloved meteorologists for the local news channel liked to say, "If you don't like the weather in Nicolet, wait a few minutes—it'll change."

They fell in step beside each other as they walked toward the boat, and the dock creaked under the combined weight of them. "How are you feeling?" Jackson asked.

"No different than the last time you checked," Elizabeth joked.

Jackson threw an arm around her shoulders. "Can't blame a brother for worrying."

"You're right. Every grown woman wants her little brother texting her once every hour to see how she's doing."

Her tone was teasing, but Jackson responded in all seriousness. "I was concerned."

Elizabeth stopped walking and lowered her sunglasses. "Jackson, I'm fine, really. I promise."

"I just feel like this is dangerous," he admitted, "You're so small, and you're carrying not one, but *two* babies, and let's face it, if they take after their dad, they won't be petite."

Jackson could still remember his reaction when Lizzie had started dating Matt Maki, a guy he'd looked up to his whole young life. Matt had graduated three years ahead of Jackson, and at six-foot-five, he'd commanded a universal respect. Lizzie had claimed that Matt was as soft and gentle as a teddy bear, and while Jackson had come to accept that as truth, it didn't change the reality that the enormous, two hundred twenty pound teddy bear had impregnated his tiny sister with not one, but two boys who were quickly running out of space within her small frame.

Lizzie took a step back to better view him and removed her sunglasses. Her turquoise irises fixated on his. "Hey, you really *are* worried!"

"I said I was."

She shook her head and smiled softly. "It's sweet that you care so much about me, but listen to me now. Really hear my words, okay?" At Jackson's nod, she went on. "I'm doing great, and the babies are doing great. If something should change, my doctors will be on it. They're very seasoned and very, very good."

Jackson tried to look convinced. He must have failed because she reached out and pulled him into a hug. "Aww, honey. Thank you for worrying about me, but here's a word of advice. Don't let anyone see this side of you, okay? You'll have more women lining up to date you than you already do."

He let out a brief chuckle, and they continued walking to the boat. His slip was the second one to the last, and when they reached it, he helped Lizzie get on. "Speaking of women, I broke things off with Mindy."

Elizabeth plopped herself down into the passenger chair and looked up at him. "Well, hallelujah. Maybe you're finally getting some sense."

He grinned. "Don't count on it."

It didn't take long to get settled into the boat. Jackson started the engine and removed the moorings, and within minutes, they were on their way. He was an expert at backing the boat's long body out of the narrow slip and navigating it forward out of the harbor. As he did, he looked around and experienced another flash of contentment.

He loved this town. He loved this lake that was so clear, he could see straight to the bottom of it out here in twenty-plus feet of water.

As he turned to look behind him, Jackson saw Lizzie was taking it all in too. The houses that sat above Nicolet Harbor were old, stately Victorians, many of them one hundred years old or more and surrounded by mature maples, cedars, and quaking aspens. The trees were full and lush, and the houses and lawns were well tended.

It was a quaint little scene made complete by the crisp, white masts of the half-dozen sailboats standing tall and bobbing to and fro over the glistening surface of the water. The vibrant yellows, reds, and oranges of the autumn leaves were icing on the cake.

Jackson experienced a small prick of pride for his town. How many people got to live in a place with so much natural beauty and such variation in scenery and terrain? Any direction he turned right now, an outdoor paradise would reflect back at him. One thing he knew: Whatever job he took next—and he wasn't foolish enough to think he wouldn't have to start looking soon—it had to be here in Nicolet. His family was here, and it was home. He wasn't leaving his home.

They'd only just made it out of the no-wake zone when Elizabeth cut to the chase. "I know you talked to Mom yesterday, and I'm sure you'll want to talk about all of that—I know I need to—but what would you prefer, a rehashing of all the ways Dad sucks, or a discussion about a business proposition I have for you?" She'd tried to be funny, but they both knew there was nothing funny about what their father had done.

"I can't do Dad right now," he said quietly.

She stretched her legs out in front of her. "Yeah, me neither. Let's talk business then, shall we?"

"Let me guess. You guys want to hire me at the brewery as the new taste tester. I'll be a professional beer drinker."

Lizzie and Matt had started a brewery with Matt's best friend. What had started out looking like a dubious business enterprise had taken off in a way Jackson never could have predicted. Not only was Nicolet Brewing Company an instant hit in their small community, but it was gaining recognition throughout the Midwest.

"There's a thought, but no, and you don't drink anymore anyway," Lizzie pointed out.

"That's because alcohol and the Lang men do not mix." He'd figured that out early in college after a night of drinking had left him sicker than he'd ever been in his life, before or since. That horrendous experience—and the fear of becoming like his father—had put an end to it then and there, and it had been non-alcoholic beer for him ever since.

She laughed. "Lucky for me, the Lang women do just fine. Anyway, this is something unrelated to booze and right up your alley."

Intrigued, Jackson put the boat in neutral and gave Lizzie his full attention.

"We want to open a sporting goods store."

Jackson lifted his brows. He hadn't seen that one coming. Lizzie wasn't exactly an athlete and never had been, unless he considered tap dancing and ballet a sport, which he did not. His brother-in-law had played football for a few years in high school and had dabbled here and there with mountain biking, but that was about it. "Well, that's interesting."

"Yeah, yeah, I know what you're thinking: I don't know anything about sports, blah, blah, blah, but look, there's a need. Since RT Sports closed last year, we don't have anywhere for people to buy their kids cleats, mitts, and skates in this town. They either have to order online and hope stuff fits, or they have to drive three hours to Green Bay."

That was true. There wasn't even a place to sharpen skates in town anymore. Nicolet State had purchased its own equipment to do the job for their team, and Jackson had needed to learn in a hurry how to operate the four thousand rpm wheel. He was a master now, but he'd damaged a few blades in the process. A sporting goods store wasn't just a good idea, it was necessary in a community their size.

Jackson felt something stir inside him, a thrill of excitement he hadn't felt in a while, but outwardly he was cautious." Is this still just an idea, or do you have a whole plan already?"

Lizzie bobbed her head from side to side. "Somewhere in between, I guess. We've developed the business plan and inquired about the loan, and we've found a tentative location, but no money has exchanged hands yet. I wanted to talk to you first."

"Why?"

"Because I want you to be a part of this."

"Why?" he repeated.

She laughed again. "Because, dummy, you're talented and well-connected in the sports world up here. People have a lot of respect for you in the realm of athletics. It just makes sense that you would lead this."

Was she saying what he thought she was saying? "Do you mean as a partner?"

Briefly, she picked at a piece of lint on her pants. "That would be my preference, yes."

Jackson's heart skipped a beat, but he forced himself to suppress his excitement. This couldn't be an emotional decision. "Lizzie, I don't know. If it went under …"

She shook her head definitively. "It won't."

Her confidence was encouraging, at least. She'd grown up in the business world, just as he had, and she'd already successfully started one business, so it wasn't like she didn't know what she was talking about.

"How would it work?"

"Well, we'd set it up as a limited partnership to start and then move into an LLC down the line."

Jackson was out of his depth. "Talk to me like I'm five. You know I'm a moron when it comes to this stuff."

"Stop it. You are not."

He grinned. "Fine, but I still don't know what it means."

"A limited partnership means that only one partner is liable for the debts of the partnership. That would be us."

"You and Matt."

"Right. Technically, you'd be the limited partner, and we'd be the general partners. That protects you more, financially. But those are just names on paper. In practice, we'd be more like your silent partners." She flashed a smile. "More or less. You know I couldn't stay silent to save my life, but you get what I mean. If the business does well, and we believe it will, we would look at forming a corporation at that time. But for now, a partnership makes the most sense."

An uncomfortable tightening bloomed in Jackson's chest, and he pulled at the collar of his shirt. He didn't even have an associate's degree, only a high school diploma. "Lizzie, I have no experience with this. I don't even know what questions to ask."

"You're already asking all the right questions, but all I really need to know is if you're interested. The rest can be sorted out." She leaned forward onto the large ball that was her stomach. "Jackson, we want you to run this. That's the bottom line, so whatever it takes to make that happen, that's what we'll do. I can walk you through the plans, spell it all out so that you're completely comfortable—"

He turned off the engine. He needed it quiet. "What about Dad?"

She pressed her lips together and stared at him. "What *about* Dad?"

He turned his gaze away from hers and looked out over the bow of the boat. The breakwall was straight ahead, and he could see people walking on it.

He turned back to Lizzie. "I guess I just wonder what he would think."

His sister scootched to the edge of her seat to be closer to him. "Listen to me, Jackson," she began, pausing to search for words. "I know it's hard to shut off a lifetime of habit, but you need to stop worrying about what Dad will think. Have you ever been able to please him or make him proud, ever?"

Jackson shrugged.

"He's incapable of feeling those things, and that's on him. He'll have nothing to do with this. This would be yours. Ours."

It was appealing, that was for sure. Still, the pressure remained. "He'll say my sister handed me a job."

"Maybe," she conceded. "Who cares? We'd be partners. Us. Only *we* would know the terms. He'll only know as much as we tell him. And honestly"—she reached out to touch under his eye, tracing the spot that still had a yellow tinge—"he won't be hearing much of anything from me ever again."

Jackson reclined against the back of the captain's chair and rubbed both hands roughly across his face. "I can't believe everything that's happened."

She sat back, too, watching him. "I know."

"Mom is just—She's ..." He couldn't finish. Suddenly, he had the horrible sense that he might cry. He cleared his throat and turned his head away, looking out over the water on the starboard side this time.

He felt the boat shift slightly before Lizzy grabbed his hand. "She's going to be okay, Jackson. She's got the three of us."

"Yeah, I know."

Virginia had them, it was true, but that wouldn't bring back her lifestyle—the one she'd become accustomed to over the years. The one she deserved. The one she'd earned. What if she had to move into an apartment?

A thought stopped Jackson cold. What if she had to move in with *him?*

"My sweet brother, I can't imagine what it must have been like for you all these years. At least for me, he pretty much left me alone. That did its own damage, you know. Left its own scars. But you ... It was different for you." Elizabeth gave his hand a squeeze. "I'm sorry."

He nodded, letting go of her fingers after a moment. "I understand why you left. Going to college seven hours away was a good excuse not to have to come home a whole lot."

"But I should have. You needed me."

He forced his father from his thoughts and allowed his mood to take a turn. "So, what is this then, Lizzie? Matt, the local success story is offering a pity-job to his wife's degenerate brother?"

Sitting up straight, she was vehement in her denial. "Absolutely not, and knock that off right now. I told you that you'd be a full partner, and we would want you to run the show. It has nothing to do with pity or anything else. My whole life, I thought we'd eventually be in business together, and I always knew we'd be a success."

Oh, how he wanted to believe that.

Perhaps seeing he needed more convincing, Lizzie repeated, "You're a big name in the sports world around here."

"You already said that."

She threw up her hands. "Because it's true, you moron!"

Jackson's mouth twitched. "You just got done telling me I'm *not* a moron."

Her expression was mutinous, but she moved on. "You have the expertise we lack, especially with hockey, which is the biggest sport up here. Plus, we're looking for some passive income. The brewing itself keeps Matt busy, and he loves it. I'm behind the scenes running everything, and I love that. Both of us love the business world, and we love our town. And we love *you*," she added. "We see this as a win for everyone."

"I'd have to quit coaching."

The look she gave him was deep and penetrating, as if she could see into his soul. "Yeah." She nodded once. "You would. Is that so bad?"

No, it wasn't, and she knew it. He'd never told her, but somehow she knew just the same. He wanted to be done. He'd wanted out for a while. But he wanted to finish things the right way. "I'd need to complete the season."

She gave a careless shrug. "If you want to."

He nodded. He didn't want to, actually. But he would. He owed it to the team. To Sean.

He hated to ask, but he needed to know. "What, um, would I be making, roughly?"

She reached into her bag and pulled out a folder. Removing a sheet and handing it to him, she said, "It's all estimates at this point, but as we have it structured, we figure between fifty-five and sixty thousand for the first two years or so. This may be a cut for you, but it would only be temporary. Easily, I think you could see another fifteen by the third year. I know it's a risk, but … I feel really good about this, Jackson."

He contemplated the numbers on the sheet. They were projections by year. His eyes were drawn to the column furthest to the right. He tracked the figures down to the bottom of the page and his eyes grew wide. He might start at fifty-five grand, but that's not where he would end up. And even though these were only projections, Lizzie knew her stuff. She had a business degree, and she was sharp. If she thought this was what a sporting goods store could do for him—for them—he believed her.

It was embarrassing that his sister thought fifty-five or sixty grand would be a cut for him. There was no way he'd ever tell her that this would be a giant step up from the salary of an assistant hockey coach at the college level.

Ideas presented themselves to Jackson as they sat in the drifting boat. The water slapped at the hull in a soothing rhythm as he mulled it all over. Lizzie might be the one with the degree, but Jackson knew he was no dummy. Over the years, he'd learned quite a bit about running a commercial business. He'd worked at the store all through high school and during his brief stint in college, not that his dad had ever let go of the reins. He hadn't evened loosened his grip.

Still, Jackson had done a little of everything. As a result, he knew how to run inventory, deal with suppliers, and build vendor relationships. He knew the basics of human resources: payroll, hiring, firing, and all that stuff. He knew about displays and marketing. His knowledge, a mile wide, may have only gone an inch deep, but it was more than some people had before jumping into a business venture. Plus, he'd have Lizzie and Matt as partners, and everything they touched turned to gold.

Jackson had always known he could do a good job with the family business. What he hadn't known was if his father would actually follow through and hand it over. Now, for better or worse, he had his answer.

But if he'd been confident in his ability to sell furniture, a commodity he didn't really feel any connection to, how much better would he be at selling athletic equipment and apparel? Sports was a world he'd been immersed in since the beginning of time.

"I can see your mind working," Elizabeth said with a satisfied smile. "Is this a yes, then?"

Jackson chuckled. "I'm excited at the thought, you've got me there."

"But you need some time."

"Time and information," he agreed. "I'd like you to walk me through the business plan, and I'll need to take a look at my finances. I should have some skin in the game, and I don't know if I have what I need for the startup. I can't have you and Matt fronting all the money."

"Fair enough."

He chuckled again and shook his head.

"What?"

"Dad. This is really going to piss him off."

She grimaced. "There you go again. Does he ever leave your head?"

"Rarely."

"Give him the boot, Jackson. Evict him. He doesn't belong in there."

Jackson would love nothing more, but it was easier said than done.

Lizzie tipped her head. "You know, Mom was the only thing keeping him real, and without her, he'll become the worst possible version of himself. He'll sink even lower than he already has."

Yeah, straight into a pit of money, Jackson thought to himself. To Lizzie, he pointed out, "He'll get a few million with this sale if he goes through with it."

"Oh, at least, but Mom's going to get some of that. Her lawyers will make sure of it. She gave her family and that store her life. She won't walk away empty-handed."

Jackson felt an enormous surge of relief at Lizzie's take on things. "You think? I don't know diddly about this kind of thing."

"I'm no expert either," Lizzie admitted, "but I've been researching, and I talked to my friend Shayna—she's a mediator down state. It doesn't matter that the house isn't in Mom's name, and maybe not even the business. It's considered 'marital property.' He won't be able to stiff her, but it'll take time to sort it all out."

She paused and shifted gears. "Are you disappointed?"

Jackson didn't pretend not to know what she was talking about. "A little. It's almost like my future's been erased. The one I always pictured."

She shifted in her seat and kicked her legs out in front of her again in an effort to get comfortable. "You would have enjoyed the money, Jackson, but that's about it."

He knew she was right.

⁓

By the time Jackson dropped Lizzie back off at the harbor a little after one o'clock, he knew he was in. How could he not take an opportunity like this and hold on to it with both hands? Elizabeth was right. He was made for this role. And really, being from a family of entrepreneurs, it was a no-brainer. He'd always assumed he'd enter the business world eventually anyway. He was just making a little lane change along the way.

After helping his sister disembark from the boat, he promised to call her later on and pushed off for another ride. He wasn't ready to be off the lake yet. They'd gone for a nice and slow putt-putt ride, which was pleasant enough, but Jackson found the need to really open her up out there.

He needed some speed.

He needed to feel the wind whipping through his hair as he cut through the mirror-calm waters of the largest freshwater lake in the world, a lake he admitted he sometimes took for granted.

The Cigarette boat, with a supercharged four-stroke V8 Mercury Racing Powerhead, was his father's pride and joy, or at least it had been until an inner ear issue had made it impossible for Philip Lang to enjoy it any longer. The change in his equilibrium wouldn't allow him out on the water comfortably, but not wanting to part with it, he'd temporarily loaned it to Jackson, mostly for the boat's benefit. It needed to be run and tended to regularly, something Jackson enjoyed doing.

Philip hadn't bought the boat with sea-worthiness in mind. He'd bought it for speed, and for a short time, it had been the fastest boat on Lake Superior. He'd entered it into enough races to know. Probably, his father would sell it along with the business, Jackson realized. It had ceased to be useful to Philip and could no longer make him look good. If anything, having a boat he couldn't use would make his father feel old, which was why he'd wanted it out of the garage and in Jackson's care. There was no way Philip would keep something like that around as a reminder of his has-been status.

Jackson accelerated once he was out of the no-wake zone, and he chased his thoughts away as he planed out over the flat water. On second thought, maybe he wasn't so much chasing those thoughts away as he was running from them. Either way, he wasn't moving nearly fast enough.

He bumped the throttle a little further.

And then again.

And again.

Jackson was flying across the water's surface now. He'd never had it this fast. Usually Lake Superior had at least *some* wave action to slow him down.

Not today.

The wind rushed against his face and sucked the air from his nostrils. Jackson hunkered down further behind the windshield for protection. The adrenaline rush he felt was unreal. His body was enervated. Alive. Glancing at the throttle, he saw he wasn't even maxed out yet. How much faster would this baby go?

And then a thought entered his mind. Philip had won the Lake Superior Grand Prix three years ago with a personal record of eighty-seven knots, which was a little more than one hundred miles per hour. The next year, he'd taken fifth, an outcome with which Jackson had found secret satisfaction. Try as he might, Philip had never broken his own record. Now he never would.

But Jackson was going to do it. Slowly, he pushed on the throttle.

Seventy-five knots.

Seventy-six.

He let out a *whoop* as he raced along the surface of the water.

Seventy-seven.

For fun, just to play, he made a brief, tight turn and threw out a wall of water, letting out another *whoop* as he straightened out. This was what it was to live, to be alive.

Seventy-eight knots.

Seventy-nine ...

Something was wrong. Jackson sensed it before he heard it.

The engine seized, and the boat's speed dropped precipitously. The roar of the motor was replaced by a deafening silence with an immediacy that was jarring. In what felt like slow motion, he turned his head in time to watch the massive stern wave crash over the boat, filling the cockpit.

Shocked from the swamping and shocked from the cold of the water, Jackson found himself unable to move, unable to think. Slowly, he gathered his wits and looked toward shore. He had to be a mile away, at least.

He cranked the engine.

Nothing.

He flipped the switch for the bilge pump.

Nothing there either.

He reached into his back pocket for his cellphone and patted at emptiness.

Shit.

His phone was still in the cupholder of his car. How did a guy leave his phone behind in this day and age?

A quick scan of the horizon told him what he already knew. Nobody was out there. Most people, the smart ones, had already taken their boats out for the season.

But wait!

He had flares! Hopping up and out of the captain's chair, he waded through the frigid water and flipped the seat cushion at the bow of the boat. Up there, the water only reached his shins, where at the back it had been almost up to his knees. He tried not to think about what that meant.

Quickly, he grabbed the waterproof kit and let the cushion fall back down, using it as his working surface. Opening the kit, he took inventory of the four cartridges resting beside the gun.

Four.

He had four chances to be seen, and he liked those odds. On a clear, warm day like today, people were out walking and biking along the shoreline. Someone was bound to see at least one of his signals. Encouraged, he loaded the first cartridge.

For the next fifteen minutes, Jackson sent up flare after flare. And then he sat in the bow, feet pulled up in front of him, and waited.

Nobody came.

With each passing minute, he watched the stern sink lower in the water. A rising south wind was kicking up waves now and blowing him further out. More and more, those waves were lapping over the back of the boat.

Jackson made several more attempts to turn over the engine and work the bilge, but with no success. Time ticked by, and he grew cold down to the marrow of his bones, both from the rising water in the boat and from the dread that cut through him like cold razor blades as he accepted that nobody was coming for him. "Stay with the boat," he said out loud, his voice splitting the silence. "Stay with the boat."

That was the first rule of a marine accident. But the shores of Nicolet were growing further away, and some three hundred miles of Lake Superior stretched out between him and Canada. At the rate things were going, the boat would sink long before he reached their northern neighbor.

"Think, Jackson, think!" Hearing the panic in his own voice did nothing to calm him. This was a life-threatening situation, there was no denying it any longer, and he could only think of one course of action that might save him.

He shook his head.

No, he'd die of hypothermia. Swimming was not an option. He was already wet past his knees, and the water temperature couldn't be more than fifty degrees. On the other hand, he'd never be closer to shore than he was right now, and even at this distance, he wasn't sure he could make it. If he blew even further out, he was done for. A goner. And one thing was certain: The Cigarette *would* sink. Waves rolled over the stern freely now.

He'd been working off adrenaline since the engine had stalled, but for the first time, Jackson experienced a real and sickening fear. The kind that clawed at his belly and raked over his insides. The kind that signaled the nearness of death.

Quickly, he flew into action. Life jackets!

He put on two.

He kicked off his shoes. Pulled off his socks. Stepped out of his jeans. He was done thinking. It was time for action.

Not wanting to risk the shock reflex of gasping for breath when jumping into cold water, he eased himself in off the stern instead.

And then he prayed. For the first time in his life, he really prayed. He didn't even know to whom.

And then he swam.

Chapter 9

S leeping in was not a luxury Leila typically indulged, but that warm Tuesday morning, she must have needed the extra rest. She hadn't even heard Elena get up and get ready for work, which was so unlike her. Normally, on a day off, she'd be back from her morning run in time to see Elena off.

Not this morning.

This morning she lingered over two cups of coffee before paying some bills and making some phone calls that would keep the ball rolling on the purchase of her mama's house. The realtor, an older gentleman by the name of Miles Hayes, was "tickled to be a part of such a sale." He'd said it twice today, once each time she'd spoken to him. After promising her that all was going according to plan, she moved on in her mental list of tasks and logged into the hospital's system from her computer to finish up a couple of charts.

By three o'clock, Leila felt more than a little stir crazy, so she changed into a pair of leggings and a lightweight green tank top, and fifteen minutes later was trotting down the hill of her quiet street towards the bike path that paralleled the water. Without thinking, she turned to the left once she hit the lakeshore. Normally she ran the other direction, towards Nicolet Harbor, but today she headed toward Sable Rocks. She wasn't really sure why. It hadn't been a conscious decision, but she was glad she'd done it. It was nice to see some different scenery for a change.

Oddly, not many people were out on the path, but then Leila supposed all the kids were back in school, and most adults were still at work. With only a few exceptions, she had the path all to herself. There'd been a lady with a yippee dog on a long leash she'd had to circumvent and then an elderly gentleman, who tottered along pushing a walker. She'd congratulated him on getting out, and he'd smiled sweetly back at her before wishing her a good day.

I should probably turn around, Leila thought, after a look at her watch told her she'd been running for an hour. If she headed back now, she'd have run for two hours, which was a lot longer than she normally did. She might pay for it tomorrow, but the day was so beautiful and the pounding of the pavement so cathartic, she told herself she'd only go a little further.

The shoreline towards Sable Rocks was not sandy like the rest of Nicolet's shoreline. It was rocky, partially from nature, but also as a result of the city having to build up the shoreline to keep the lake from eroding the road during big storms in the fall and winter. Eventually, they'd have to move the road further inland. There was already talk of doing so, and even though she knew it needed to happen, Leila would be sad to lose the feeling of driving—or running—right on the edge of the water.

As she ran, she let her mind flit wherever it wanted. She did her best thinking on these runs. Sometimes she'd catch herself coming to some profound realization or another without even knowing how she'd gotten there; without even realizing she'd been processing something important.

Today she was letting herself imagine what she might do to improve the house. The first large-scale thing she'd do was replace the wooden siding. Although it was lovely and authentic, and she'd definitely do her best to match the color, painting it was a real pain and not something she was willing to do herself. And unlike many of the neighbors, she would not be paying out the nose to have it professionally seen to every few years.

And it needed it. The last time it had been done was before Samuel had passed, and now it was peeling. It was funny. It seemed more likely that the house would have been her mother's pride and joy, given that it had been *her* dream, but it had actually been her father's. He'd loved its character and what it represented: his great and enduring love for his wife. The love for his family.

It was beautiful and unique, just as they were, and just as they had been when Luca had been alive. "Newer homes simply don't have a whole lot to say," he used to remark. "They haven't had time to tell a story. Now older homes, they have character in spades. And the stories they tell!"

He loved the creaks of the staircase and the nooks and crannies throughout, including a cushioned window seat in the living room where many an evening Leila would curl up with a blanket and a good book, selected from the library with care to guarantee a happy ending. She'd been lost those first few weeks in town. The move hadn't been easy for her. Leaving Luca had felt terribly wrong, and she struggled with it long after the last moving box had been broken down and recycled.

Aware that she'd begun tensing her shoulders, Leila dropped her hands to her sides and shook them out. As she did, she eyed a tree, a large and stately willow that was performing a slow dance in the breeze. A dark wooden bench sat underneath it, and Leila was filled with a longing to sit underneath that willow with her father and listen to him share another one of his nuggets of wisdom. He used to love to quote verses from the book of Proverbs. He'd say things like: "A tranquil mind gives life to the body, jealousy rots the bones," or "In his mind, a man plans his course, but God directs his steps." That passage was one of her favorites.

Out of the corner of her eye, a movement caught her attention, and Leila shifted her gaze to look out over the water.

There it was again—a splash roughly two hundred yards out. She slowed to a walk and cupped a hand above her eyes to reduce the glare.

She squinted and observed the repeated disturbances in the water. What would make those kinds of splashes?

A seagull?

A bald eagle?

And then she knew. It was no bird catching a fish. Someone was out there! And they must have been crazy because, even though it was a nice day and the air was warm, it was almost November and the lake was definitely too cold for swimming. But the distance from shore was too great for this to be an ordinary swim, she reasoned. And the splashing looked like the type caused by uncoordinated movements, not the efficient strokes of the front crawl.

No, this wasn't just a leisure swim being taken by some idiot in the too-cold water. She could feel it in her bones—this was an emergency.

Leila ran across the graveled shoulder and climbed over a large boulder, yelling as she made her way to the rocky beach. The swimmer continued to splash with slow, sloppy movements. Turning back to the empty road, she saw nobody to call out to for help, and a quick sweeping of the shoreline with her eyes revealed no emergency stations and no life rings. She had no help from shore, she had no rope, and she had no flotation device.

She shouldn't go in.

She knew that.

Rapidly, Leila kicked off her shoes and ripped off her tank top, socks and leggings, tossing her phone on top of the heap. Then, in her sports bra and underwear, she raced into the water. Although it had been years now since her job at the YMCA pool, all her lifeguard training from her college years kicked in.

Forcing herself to remain calm as she swam a smooth breast stroke through the icy chill of the water, she kept her head high above the surface. Further and further out she swam, and when she was close enough to be heard, she let the swimmer know she was there. It went against instinct, but she made herself tread water for several seconds as she assessed the situation. She knew all too well how quickly the rescuer could become the victim in situations like this.

The swimmer, a male, appeared to be wearing two life jackets, and they were still buoyant enough to keep him above the water. It was still a risk, what she was about to do, but less so with life jackets to help them both with flotation. "Hey!" she shouted.

The splashing stopped, but he didn't look up.

"I'm here to help you get to shore. I'm a trained lifeguard and doctor, so just stay calm and don't fight me." She swam forward, closing the distance between them.

"L-Leila?" The swimmer lifted his head, and she saw his face. His skin and lips were blue-tinged, and his eyes lacked focus.

All the breath was sucked from her lungs in one big *whoosh*. It couldn't be! *"Jackson?"*

"L-Leila," he slurred again. "You came. I prayed ..." His weak voice trailed off, and his face dropped into the water.

Leila sprang into action, swimming up alongside him. It took three tries, but she managed to flip Jackson onto his back before wrapping one arm around his chest and swimming the sidestroke back to shore. He didn't fight her, something for which she should have been grateful, but which instead filled her with such terror she could barely breathe. What was he doing here? What had happened? Whatever it was, judging from the look and feel of him, he'd been in the water a good, long while.

What would have happened to him if she hadn't come along? What if she'd run her usual route or had turned when she'd had a mind to?

For the second time that afternoon, Leila recalled her father's words. *In his mind, a man plans his course, but God directs his steps.*

This was no coincidence. Everything that had happened that day, all the choices she'd made that had placed her at this exact spot at this exact time ... It wasn't just happenstance. It had been orchestrated.

Don't think. Swim. Get him to shore. Get him warm.

When Leila's foot touched the rocky bottom, she could have cried out in relief, but instead she kept up the steady stream of one-sided conversation she'd started to keep Jackson awake. "Almost there, Jackson. We're going to get you out of this water and all warmed up. You're really cold, buddy. Really cold. You stay awake now, okay? Listen to my voice, Jackson. Are you listening to my voice?"

"Leila," he slurred again.

"Stay awake; don't close your eyes. Don't you go to sleep, Jackson, okay? We're nearly there. Can you stand? We can touch here."

He tried, but he couldn't make his legs work.

"That's okay, I've got you." And she did. She gripped him by the blue lifejacket tightly with both hands, but as the water became more and more shallow, she found she could no longer carry him. After stumbling twice, she knew she needed help.

Before she could think of what to do, she heard the noise of an engine. A red truck was approaching! It was one of those souped up trucks with no muffler some of those young boys liked to drive.

Leila began shouting at the top of her lungs, flailing one arm to get the driver's attention while hugging Jackson's body close to hers with the other. The passenger window was down, and she saw the moment the driver noticed her. His eyes went wide and his jaw dropped. Immediately, the truck stopped, and a beefy teenage boy jumped out of the driver's side. He rounded the front of the truck at a run.

"Call 911 and ... come and ... help me!" she yelled breathlessly.

He did as he'd been told, reaching into his pocket for his phone and dialing as he continued to run down to the shore and into the water. God bless him, he hadn't even stopped to take off his shoes.

"Here," she said, reaching for the phone with a wet, shivering hand. Her teeth chattered uncontrollably. "Can you ... lift him ... and ... carry him the rest of the way ... to shore?" She was breathing hard.

He nodded and effortlessly lifted Jackson over a shoulder in the fireman's carry. Thank goodness for linebackers in trucks with cellphones! "Gentle now, okay?" she called after him. Just for a moment, Leila rested her hands on her knees and tried to catch her breath. "Lay him down ... as carefully ... as you can. He's probably bradycardic. We don't ... want to throw him into ... an arrythmia."

The beefy kid turned to look at her for a moment without blinking. Clearly, he had no idea what she'd just said.

"Just be gentle," Leila simplified. Following behind them, she spoke into the phone. "Hi, sorry, this is Dr. Leila Molina. I've just … completed a water rescue … at the rock beach along Lakeshore Boulevard … near that big willow tree. The victim is suffering from … hypothermia, and he's in and out of … consciousness. Please send an ambulance. I'm going to pass the phone back to a … passerby and tend to the patient."

The linebacker carefully lowered Jackson down to the pebbled rocks.

She handed the phone back to the boy. He accepted it looking completely unfazed, as if he did this kind of thing every day. She knelt beside Jackson, and before the boy turned away, she heard him tell the dispatcher, "Yeah, dude's pretty cold …"

Jackson lay on his back, unmoving, but she could see the rise and fall of his chest through the two lifejackets. Leila worked the buckles on the first one. "Jackson, can you hear me?"

He mumbled something incoherent.

"Open your eyes, Jackson."

He slowly obeyed, and she could see his pupils were dilated. She placed her fingers on his pulse and counted.

Not good.

His heart rate was way too low. She needed to warm him up, and fast. "Hey, linebacker!" she hollered to the boy who had walked a few paces away, still speaking to the dispatcher.

The kid, nonplussed, turned to face her. Pulling the phone away from his ear, he raised his eyebrows.

"Can you help me get these life jackets off?"

Speaking into the phone, he said, "I'm gonna put down the phone a sec, okay?"

Once he'd come up beside her, she asked, "Can you lift him up under the armpits really carefully to sit him up? We don't want to jostle him too much, but we need to get these life jackets off. His shirt too."

"Okay, I got him," the kid said, lifting Jackson as she'd asked. Together, they worked to get everything off before laying him back down again.

Leila knelt down beside Jackson, the tiny pebbles pricking at her knees, and looked up at the kid. "Alright, now take off your clothes."

He flushed red. "Uh, what?"

She saw the situation through his eyes. A mostly blue, half-naked man lay on the beach while a sopping wet Latina, in her purple Snoopy underwear, knelt beside him. Now he was supposed to strip down too? It probably *was* a little much. "Okay, well, take off your shirt at least," she implored, showing him a little mercy. "We need to lay with him between us, skin to skin."

He took a deep breath. "This is weird."

"I know, but please," she pleaded. "He needs our body heat, and this is how it's done."

Dutifully, the kid took off his shirt. And again, to his credit, he pulled down his sweats. He grabbed his phone off the ground, asked the dispatcher to hang on another minute, and then awkwardly, he laid down behind Jackson, spooning him, as she pressed against him from the front.

"Nobody's gonna believe this," the kid muttered, phone back against his ear. They lay quietly like that for a minute or two. The only sound was their breathing, the lapping of the water, and the scrape of rocks as they each made tiny adjustments to their positions in a futile effort to get comfortable. A faint voice broke through the relative quiet.

"What's the dispatcher saying?" Leila asked.

"He asked for his heart rate."

She felt again for Jackson's pulse. Ah, that was a little better. And he'd begun to shiver. Also a good sign. "He's up to forty-three beats per minute now."

The kid repeated the number into the phone and listened briefly. He looked at her. "The guy says an ambulance should be here anytime."

"Good. Okay." The hospital wasn't far from there. In fact, Leila could hear the sirens now. After another minute or two, Jackson shivered uncontrollably, and she felt herself relax. He was going to be alright. She pulled her head back from his and let her eyes linger on his face, indulging herself for just a moment. It hurt her to look at him. It actually physically hurt. Even blue and half-frozen, he still did it for her. But even after he recovered, all nice and warm, his heart would still be ice cold. Some things never changed.

She looked at the teenager then, stretched out dutifully on the other side of Jackson, an arm wrapped around him. He was probably the age she and Jackson had been when they'd first met.

She spoke over Jackson's shivering body. "So, linebacker, what's your name?"

"Uh, Grant. And I don't play football."

She treated him to an apologetic smile. "Well, Grant, you just helped save a life today. How does it feel?"

He grinned. "Pretty good."

A few minutes later, the paramedics arrived with a backboard. The four of them—the two paramedics, Leila, and Grant—carefully carried Jackson up to the ambulance. Once they'd lifted him in, she shook Grant's hand and thanked him. She wanted to hug him, but they weren't wearing enough clothing for that.

She watched Clancy, a paramedic she'd gotten to know pretty well through her work at the hospital, get Jackson ready for transport.

"You riding along, Doc?" he asked.

"If it's okay."

"Climb on up. I'll give you these heat packs while I get the Mylar blanket. You know where to put 'em?"

"Armpits, abdomen, groin."

Clancy shot her a thumbs up. "You got it."

Leila went to work, and Clancy shut the doors. She continued to help the older paramedic as they set off for the hospital with the sirens blaring. Jackson's eyes followed her every move as she worked, and after she and Clancy had the blanket tucked around him, he tried to speak through shivering lips. She couldn't make it out. He was still slurring.

She *shushed* him. "You're going to be okay. We're getting you all warmed up."

Jackson licked his lips and tried again. "You f-fed ... you fed survever."

"Hush now, and save your strength," Leila murmured, resisting the urge to reach out and push away a lock of hair that had fallen across his brow. He wore it longer now than he had when they were kids. She'd noticed that when she'd bumped into him earlier in the summer. It suited him.

"You fed ... survever," he repeated before closing his eyes again.

Looking at him, Leila felt her eyes sting. He looked so helpless and vulnerable. It wasn't the first time she'd seen him that way.

"What's he sayin'?" Clancy asked.

She cleared her throat and busied herself with smoothing out the creases in the foil of the space blanket. "I don't know. I don't think *he* knows."

Together, they monitored Jackson's vitals back to the hospital. Leila checked her emotions as best she could and put on her doctor's hat, but it was hard not to look at his face. He was so beautiful to her. So dangerously beautiful.

She shivered again, and although she was definitely more than a little cold, she knew that wasn't the reason.

"Here, Doc," Clancy said, opening another pouch with a folded Mylar space blanket inside and handing it to her. That's when Leila remembered she was still in her wet underwear. Her clothes and phone were back on the beach.

Face flushing, she thanked Clancy, and unfolded the blanket before wrapping it around herself.

A few short minutes later, they arrived at the entrance to the Emergency Department. Barefoot, Leila stepped out onto the warm, rough concrete and waited for Clancy and the other paramedic to get Jackson out on the stretcher. There wasn't really much she could do dressed as she was and without shoes, so she clutched at the blanket and stood to the side.

Once Jackson was out, Leila took one last look at him. His eyes were open, and they stared into hers.

"You said forever," he whispered.

Chapter 10

THEN

"I'm sorry, Sam. I don't recognize this at all," Carmen Molina said as their car crawled slowly forward through the thick fog.

"What's to recognize? I can't see a thing." Leila's papa, Samuel, stopped the car and checked their surroundings.

It wasn't an auspicious beginning. According to the car's brand new OnStar system, they'd now arrived at their new home in Nicolet, Michigan, but the thick trees stretching along the two-lane road on either side of them, uninterrupted by mailboxes or driveways, told a different story.

Leila peered out her backseat window. She squinted into the dark while her papa pushed repeatedly at the OnStar button on their Buick Lucerne with one of his giant thumbs. The Lucerne was a full-size car, but Samuel was a full-size man, and seven hours was a long time for him to sit folded between seat and steering wheel. He was getting cranky.

"This stupid thing doesn't work. Stupid over-engineered car. It thinks this is Ridgewood Street, but it can't be. It looks nothing like I remember."

At least he knew what he was looking for. Leila had never been here before. She'd seen the new house only in pictures. The beautiful Victorian home looked like something out of a postcard, and it was supposed to give them the "fresh start" her mama insisted they needed.

Leila didn't want a fresh start. She wanted to stay in their old shoebox of a house, the one she'd lived in since she was just a year old. Already she missed the four confining walls of her pink bedroom, where she'd accumulated hours upon hours of listening to music while staring at her ceiling.

She missed her room, and she missed Luca. They'd left him there in that cemetery all alone. Who would place flowers over his grave each week? Who would sit there and talk to him and tell him how much they missed him?

Her parents had cried as they'd left Grand Rapids behind. Leila hadn't. She couldn't make the tears come even when she tried. She was too numb. Honestly, she didn't feel much of anything these days. She loved her parents, and she loved her new dog, Atticus, who sat beside her in the back of the car—thumping the seat with his tail. But other than that, she just couldn't muster up much emotion—happy or sad. Robotically, she'd finished her junior year in Grand Rapids. Robotically, she'd packed her things and said her goodbyes to what few friends she'd had.

No, she hadn't cried when they'd left home, not even when they said goodbye to Luca at the cemetery. Her mama had covered his headstone with lilacs that had been so fragrant, the car still smelled of them. Luca would have loved them. He'd always loved good-smelling things.

Father Tim said there was a time to laugh and a time to mourn. Lately Leila wondered: *How long?* How long would they mourn this way? Would it ever get easier? Would anything ever be the same again?

Luca would have loved this trip up north to the Upper Peninsula of Michigan. He would have loved the sense of adventure brought on from driving over the Mackinac Bridge, and he would have loved that the car still smelled like lilacs.

His favorite books had been those of the scratch-and-sniff variety. Whenever she'd offered to read to him, he'd come running with a stack of books from his bookshelf and pile them on the coffee table—his short, stubby legs carrying him as fast as they could go. They'd snuggle together on the couch, him tucked firmly on her lap, resting against her chest, and they'd read through them together one-by-one. Straining towards the book she held in her hands, he'd lean forward, inhale deeply, smile, and say, "Mmm." Then he'd sniff again. Leila had always gotten a kick out of that.

At six years old and with Down syndrome, Luca had been more like a child half his age, but he could speak and understand well enough to communicate the basics, and then some.

Leila is boo-tee-full.

And you are my handsome little man.

I am your Luca.

You are my sweet Luca.

She'd loved him more than her own life. It was no wonder she felt half dead without him.

"Did you say *street*?" her mama asked, breaking into Leila's thoughts.

"What?" Samuel snapped.

Her mother opened a piece of paper taken from her purse and turned on one dome light. "This is Ridgewood *Street*? Not *Lane*? Our house is on Ridgewood *Lane*."

Samuel scoffed. "Well, mystery solved."

Carmen sighed. "I must have entered it wrong. I'm sorry."

"*Mierda*," her papa said under his breath. "How did we miss that?"

Samuel Molina was a devout Catholic who never swore in English, but somehow his moral compass was broken when it came to swearing in Spanish.

"*Lo siento*."

"*Está bien, cariña.* I will find it. I'm sure I told you wrong."

"No, it's my fault."

Carmen reached an arm across the space between them and stroked the back of Samuel's neck before refolding the piece of paper and tucking it into her purse. She turned off the light.

Leila's parents continued to talk, each trying to take the blame for being lost. They fell all over each other these days trying to be agreeable. Their exaggerated politeness towards one another was a little irritating, although Leila supposed she should be grateful. The way they coped with their grief was better than most. She'd heard of couples divorcing after losing a child, but her parents were closer than ever. And she'd never felt more distant from them both, which was ironic because she'd hadn't received so much attention from them since the time she'd been an only child, before Luca had come home from the hospital.

She turned her attention to Atticus, her yellow lab. He was her best friend these days. At thirty pounds, he was still a puppy, but if his paw size was anything to go by, he'd be at least three times this size full grown. Her parents had given him to her for Easter to cheer her up. And while he could never fill the Luca-sized hole in her heart, he'd met a need she hadn't even known she had.

❧

It didn't take long for the Molinas to get settled into their new home in the historic neighborhood of Ridgewood Lane. Their move-in date was June twenty-eighth, and by July fourth they were all settled in. Carmen had thrown herself into the work, unloading boxes and hanging pictures well into the evenings until everything was in its proper place. Leila helped, but with far less enthusiasm.

Her papa had those final days of June and all of July off, but by the first of August, Samuel began working full time as the head of custodial operations for his new employer, Nicolet State University. It was one of fifteen public universities in the state of Michigan and had nearly seven thousand students enrolled. These were the factoids Leila knew by virtue of her papa's profession. He'd spent the last six years as head custodian at Ferris State University's Grand Rapids campus, and while he didn't have a college degree himself, he had his finger on the pulse of the world of higher education in general.

School would begin soon enough for Leila, too, but she wasn't nearly ready. She'd found a new rhythm in her life, and it soothed her. Thanks to Atticus and his need for exercise, she'd been getting out and moving a lot herself, and she wasn't ready to have her new regimen replaced and disrupted by crowded hallways, slamming locker doors, and piercing school bells.

No, she wanted to continue to spend her days roaming the miles of sugar sand beaches and wooded trails that made up this outdoor wonderland. With Atticus by her side, she wasn't afraid to be alone in the woods, and so off she went for hours and hours each and every day. Carmen, though she tried to hide it, slept while the house was empty. She was putting on a good show. She made elaborate dinners every night; she ran all the errands and kept the house clean, but Leila knew her mama was depressed.

Her papa was too. When he wasn't working or feigning interest in what remained of his model trains and baseball cards—he could be found outside on the back patio smoking his cigars and staring off into the trees.

But with the exception of her periodic escapes into one of the many library books she kept in a basket next to her new reading nook, Leila couldn't sit still. She had discovered something here in this tiny little town. Moving her body, especially outdoors, did something to her she couldn't quite explain. It boosted her spirits and cleared her mind. It also resulted in the shedding of even more weight.

After Luca died, the pantry snacks had gone silent, stopping their incessant calling out to her at night. At first, she'd simply been too heartbroken to derive any pleasure from an Oreo cookie or any other treat. But later on, as time went by, she realized that sugar, her most loyal friend and constant companion since the eighth grade, had somehow lost its allure. She no longer needed or wanted its company, at least not the way she had before.

Now she had a new hobby, a new focus. She ate meals to feed her body, and as she ate, she imagined the vitamins, minerals, and proteins nourishing her, making her strong and healthy. Instead of asking for chips and cakes, she asked her mother to buy fruits and vegetables to snack on. It made her happy to do something good for herself. For her body.

Slowly, that body changed. Within the first two months of Luca's death, fifteen pounds had melted off, and she'd had to exchange her size fourteen clothing for size tens at Goodwill. But then another month brought an additional seven-pound loss. Leila's new clothes became roomy, and she had to hold her pants up with belts. But her weight wasn't the only thing that changed. Her skin gradually cleared of the acne that had inspired the awful nickname of "Pizza Face," and her hair took on a new and healthy shine. She let it grow until it reached the middle of her back.

Before school let out in Grand Rapids, Leila had begun to turn a few heads, not that she would even consider giving any of those boys a second look after years of being tormented by them. Still, it had been a little gratifying.

Now, after weeks of newly discovered exercise in Nicolet, she'd dropped another dress size, and Leila's transformation was complete. Being that she was a full-blooded Molina, she would always be curvy, but there was an athletic leanness to her now that she liked. By the time August rolled around, she was curious to see if her eyes were telling the truth, so she pulled out the scale from her parents' bathroom cabinet and weighed herself. She'd lost a total of thirty pounds, and yet she'd never been stronger.

Trail running invigorated her as nothing else ever had. Navigating her steps over the roots and rocks on the trail systems she ran with Atticus kept her thoughts occupied, and while she ran, she concentrated on the rhythm she beat out, allowing only that and the sights and smells to penetrate her mind.

Similarly, at the beach she paid attention to the little things—the texture of the warm sand beneath her bare feet and between her toes, the cold sting of Lake Superior on her skin and the way it felt to come up out of the water and into the warm breeze—refreshed, renewed, replete.

More and more, Leila felt God's presence, as well as the Blessed Mother's. She'd been wrong thinking they'd left her, abandoning her to her hollow grief. They'd been there all along. They'd stayed with her, walking beside her each day, and they'd given her an unexpected gift with this move because there was no doubt about it: Little by little, this place was mending her broken heart.

Leila was enjoying life again. As she threw sticks out into the water for Atticus, she took pleasure in his enthusiasm and happiness as he fetched, and she laughed when he'd chase his tail and fall to the ground after getting tangled up in his own legs. Even her parents chuckled at his antics, and there was something about those moments spent watching Atticus savor his life that reminded them to take pleasure in their own. Still, too often after a good laugh, they'd look at one another apologetically once they remembered Luca again. Once they remembered they were supposed to be sad.

They were afraid to move on, Leila realized. Each of them was scared to go forward in life without Luca, but they were ready to at the same time. Leila could see her own ambivalence reflected in her parents' eyes, but really, what choice did they have? They weren't buried in the ground next to Luca. They were alive in the world, and they needed to make the most of it.

"Where are you going today?" Carmen asked, as Leila laced up her sneakers one bright August morning, four weeks before the start of her senior year. Atticus danced about happily, his nails *tap, tap, tapping* at the hardwood floor beneath him. He was young, but he was smart, and he knew what Leila's shoes coming out of the closet meant.

"I'm not sure. Probably that trail I found yesterday. The one that follows the Whitefish River around the base of the ski hill."

"I'd like to go."

Leila glanced up in surprise, leaving her left shoe untied. "You would?"

Her mama gave her a single nod, and removed her yellow-and-white striped apron, setting it on the table. "*Mija*, I see a color in your cheeks that wasn't there before. You are so beautiful and alive and glowing with health." She reached out to touch Leila's face and treated her to a sad smile. "I need that too. I need color in my world again. I don't want to intrude, but may I come this once?"

Guilt washed over her. Of course Leila wouldn't deny her mother this, even though she felt a little protective of her solitude. "Of course, Mama. I didn't know you wanted to, or I would have asked you to come before."

"I didn't want to, before. I do now."

And it was there, on the trails of the North Woods and on the beaches of Lake Superior, that the Molina family allowed themselves to heal. Immediately, Samuel, hearing of their adventures, asked to join them. And so each night after dinner, they went out as a family. They didn't run, but they walked. And as they walked, they would let conversation ebb and flow where it wanted. Sometimes they even talked about Luca.

Chapter 11

"Jackson, get in here!" Philip Lang called from the den. His voice contained an unconcealed irritation that reached Jackson's ears from his lone spot on a bar stool at the kitchen counter. It was day two of the reheated spaghetti his mom had made for him before she'd left town to visit his sister, who was job hunting after recently graduating from Michigan State. She was helping Lizzie get set up in her new apartment in East Lansing and would be home tomorrow—not soon enough.

When Lizzie had first left for college her freshman year, it had been a pretty big adjustment for Jackson. They'd been close growing up, and with Lizzie under the roof, he'd felt he had someone in his corner. Someone who understood the pressure that went along with being Philip Lang's child. But Lizzie didn't call home that often anymore, and they'd lost touch. He figured it was one of those out of sight, out of mind situations, and he envied her that.

Not that long ago, Jackson was confident he'd get a scholarship to play hockey at Michigan State, or if not there, somewhere else.

Anywhere else.

Lately, he was beginning to wonder if it would happen at all. He'd hit a plateau in his game at the end of last season, and he was still stuck. He had a real fear that the magic was gone for good because the harder he tried, the worse it seemed to get. The more he worried about making mistakes, the more mistakes he made, and the more mistakes he made, the harder Philip rode him.

And now his father was calling him to the den with that tone. It was the only one he used with Jackson anymore.

Philip called his name a second time, and Jackson got moving. He hopped down from the stool and headed toward the den with a stomach full of dread and old spaghetti. He hated when it was just the two of them in the house together. With his mom home, he at least had a small buffer. Without her, he felt completely exposed.

When Jackson entered the room, Philip's back was to the doorway. He was seated in his high-back leather chair, and all that was visible of him was the top of his head. His father still had a full head of hair, something Jackson knew he was proud of. No receding hairline or male-patterned baldness for Philip Lang. He wore his thick, dark hair slicked back and spray-gelled into place. Jackson's friends all thought he looked like Al Pacino from *The Godfather*, and the way they feared him, Philip may as well have been Michael Corleone himself.

Jackson stopped at the threshold of the den and willed himself to relax. He rested his shoulder casually against the jamb of the door. "Yeah?"

Slowly, Philip turned. His eyes were hard and his mouth was set in a thin line. In his hand, he held a piece of paper. "Jackson, what the hell is this?"

Jackson's mind raced. What had he done now? It couldn't be a report card. It was the middle of summer. Besides, he'd pulled straight *B*s last year, though it had nearly killed him.

"I don't know."

His father sneered. "You. Don't. Know. Isn't that always how it goes with you? You don't know a damn thing, but you sure think you do."

Jackson stiffened. He'd heard something in his father's voice just then, a slight slurring quality that had Jackson frantically searching the room with his eyes. And then he spotted it peeking out behind the computer. It was hidden, but not quite.

A bottle of bourbon.

"Dad, you're drinking." The words were out of his mouth before he could run them through the filter he always had in place when talking to his father. It was a grave mistake, but there was no taking it back now.

Philip hopped to his feet in a flash so quick, Jackson took a step back and stumbled. His father's face had gone from red to purple. "You got something to say to me, Jackson?"

"You told Mom you quit." He hated it that his voice shook.

"I tell Mom a lot of things, and what she doesn't know won't hurt her. You understand?"

Jackson gritted his teeth. "Yeah."

Philip held his gaze, his opaque stare threatening in its intensity. "Good," he replied steadily. He took a step forward and then another.

It was all Jackson could do not to back up, but he maintained his ground. A small victory.

"We're not here to talk about me, Jackson. We're here to talk about you. And your spending."

Jackson looked at the piece of paper still clutched tightly in his father's hand. He could see now that it was a bill.

Philip shoved it in Jackson's face. "Why don't you start explaining to me how it is that you spent over four hundred dollars last month. Explain that."

Jackson thought frantically. Had he really spent that much? He took the credit card bill and scanned the transactions. He'd made purchases at gas stations, mostly, but there were some restaurants on there as well as some store purchases. He'd taken his mountain bike in for a tune up a few days ago, but he didn't see the charge on there, which was a relief. He'd also bought a new helmet, pack, and some riding gloves while he was there. His dad would flip when it all came through on the next month's credit card bill, because if Jackson remembered correctly, the grand total had come to one hundred sixty dollars and change.

"How much have you worked at the store this month, Jackson? One day? Two?"

"I've had practice."

"What you've had is a whole lot of time to sit around and spend *my* money. I can't get you to lift a finger around here. Hell, Brian Beninger down the road has done more work around here for me in one summer than you've done your whole pathetic life."

Jackson, having been compared to Brian far too many times in the past, bristled. His dad thought that kid was perfect: a hard worker and go-getter who knew what strong work ethic was. And Brian, though not much of a hockey player, had far more heart than Jackson ever would. Blah, blah, blah. Jackson was sick of it.

He couldn't help himself. "That kid's a freak."

"*That* kid has a proud father at home, which is a whole lot more than you can say. You're an embarrassment, Jackson. You strut around this town like you own it, like you're something special, but at the end of the day, do you know what they call you?"

Jackson refused to answer. He clenched his jaw shut and looked at a spot just over his dad's shoulder.

"Philip Lang's son, that's what. Because that's all you are. That's all you'll ever be. Without me, you're nothing."

He'd heard it all before, but today the restraints inside Jackson snapped, and he wouldn't be silent; damn the consequences. "You mean Philip Lang, the drunk asshole's son," he corrected. "That guy we all pretend to like but can't stand. The pathetic salesman who sells a few mattresses and Barcaloungers and thinks he's God's gift to this town."

Philip went rigid, his muscles contracting like a leopard ready to pounce, but that didn't stop Jackson. His need for self-preservation had disappeared, replaced instead by an indignant rage so strong, he shook with it.

"You think it's news to me you're not proud? You think I haven't known that my whole life? Here's a question: What else do you want? What could I possibly do that would make you proud, huh?" He ticked off on his fingers. "I'm on the honor roll. I'm captain of my team and on the first line. I do the workouts you give me *and* the ones my coaches give, plus ice time, and I wake up early every morning to get it all done. I worked at the store *nine* days this month. Maybe you could count if you weren't wasted already on the second night Mom's gone."

Jackson didn't see it coming, and he didn't have time to duck. His father dealt him a blow to the face so hard and so vicious, Jackson lost his equilibrium momentarily, staggering to the side and holding onto the bannister of the stairs leading to the second floor to steady himself.

Through the sparks that lit up his vision, he straightened and stared at the man he both loved and hated. Dragging in jagged breaths, Jackson watched a mix of emotions play across Philip's face: anger, regret, bewilderment. Just like last time.

"That's twice."

Philip, after momentary speechlessness, finally responded, "You're lucky that's all it's been."

Swallowing, Jackson tasted blood. He could feel the sting of a cut on the inside of his cheek.

Philip advanced on him and wagged a warning finger in his face. "Not a word of this, of any of this, to your mother, or you can kiss your credit card and your set of wheels goodbye. You got it?"

There was so much Jackson could have said, but any fight he'd had in him a moment ago had just been beaten out of him. "Yeah, I got it."

"Let's try for *yes, sir* and see how far that gets us?"

Refusing to register the sting of tears behind his eyes, Jackson gave in. He'd never win with Philip. Never.

"Yes, sir."

Chapter 12

"Hop out, boy," Leila said after lifting the hatchback of the red Dodge Magnum her parents had recently acquired. Samuel had gotten it from a professor who was going to have it hauled off to a junkyard, but with a bit of work, Samuel had it up and running again. Thanks to the old history professor who "wouldn't know a socket wrench from a pry bar," they were now a two-vehicle family.

"One last stretch of your legs for the day, okay?"

Atticus jumped out of the car and bolted down the path towards the Whitefish River trail. Leila smiled. Sometimes she wondered who was walking whom. Atticus always led the way, but he never got too far ahead before he'd stop and look back. Once he was assured she was coming along, he'd continue on, only to stop again after a short time. Leila liked to think he stayed close to protect her.

It was just the two of them this evening. Her parents had gone out to dinner with another couple. Carmen had met the woman at the support group she'd been attending at a local church. The woman and her husband, Joanne and Andrew Jenkins, were a wealthy older couple who had lost their teenage son eight years earlier.

Andrew owned and operated one of the local banks, but together they also owned several downtown storefronts they leased out to businesses. Apparently, Joanne had suggested that Carmen reopen a bookstore that had closed down in one of her storefronts. It still contained all the shelving, and according to Joanne, it wouldn't take much to have it up and running again. In a shocking development, Carmen was actually considering it.

Tonight was all about determining whether it was financially feasible. Leila had been invited, but she wasn't interested in being a third wheel. She could tell her mom was torn—fretting over leaving Leila behind while also struggling to contain her excitement over the possibilities the evening might bring.

Leila still didn't really know anyone in town—just church acquaintances. In a way, she felt she hardly knew her own mother. Carmen Molina wanted to open a bookstore? Where had that come from?

So here she was walking, yet again, on a trail with her dog. It was still good for her soul, but she considered it a positive sign she was desiring some interaction with other people.

She needed a friend. Lately, she craved one.

Here she had a clean slate. She wasn't *Pizza Face* any longer, and she wasn't that girl whose brother had died. Maybe that's why Mama had pushed so hard to come. They all needed a fresh start. School would begin in a week, and Leila wondered who she would meet. Would she be accepted? Would she like her teachers?

It was with these thoughts in mind that she traversed the narrow trail that paralleled the river, periodically stopping to throw a stick for Atticus, sometimes up the trail and sometimes down the embankment and into the river.

After about forty minutes, Leila reached a good turnaround point, a place where a wood-slatted bridge that resembled a dock crossed the water at a narrow point. The trail disappeared around a tight curve with heavy foliage on the other side and continued to follow the river on the opposite bank. She'd gone further on other hikes, so she knew what lie ahead, but today she thought she'd stop, take off her shoes and socks, and sit on the bridge with her feet dangling in the cool, rushing water. It tickled her toes, and she giggled. Atticus turned and looked at her curiously before having himself a long drink from the clear water.

Nothing was dirty in Nicolet, Leila had noticed. Every yard was mowed, every roadside clear of debris, and every body of water she'd seen, whether lake or river, was clear down to the very bottom. This relatively shallow river had a rocky bed, and while the bottom was populated with smaller rocks, a few big boulders stuck out here and there causing a lovely trickling sound as the water moved past them.

Once Atticus had quenched his thirst, he began fishing for rocks. It was something he'd just started doing, and Leila thought he could probably work at it for hours without growing bored. He would spot a rock, paw at it a few times, almost like he was trying to dig a hole, and then, with his paws wrapped around it, he would plunge his face down into the depths and pop up with it between his jaws. Then he would walk his prize up onto the shore, spluttering all the way, and drop it on the ground. After staring at it for a few seconds, he'd shake, look at it once or twice more to make sure it didn't run off on him, and then head back to the water for another one.

He was on his third rock when it happened.

A loud noise startled Leila from her reverie, followed immediately by the abrupt appearance of a mountain bike carrying a rider who cursed loudly before riding his bike off the bridge and into the river in order to avoid hitting her. Leila, mouth hanging open widely in shock, watched as the large male rider went clear over his handlebars and head-first into the water, narrowly missing a large bolder. His bike wasn't so lucky, and as it hit the boulder head-on, the air was filled with the sound of crunching metal.

"Oh, my gosh!" she cried as she scrambled into motion, jumping down off the bridge and into the river before she could think better of it. Her right foot landed awkwardly on a rock, and she cried out as a sharp pain shot up the side of her ankle. When her legs buckled underneath her, she landed on her butt—submerged up to her armpits. A whining Atticus, rock forgotten on the bank, bounded into the water with three quick barks before coming up beside her. He licked her face.

"What the hell!" The rider, a dripping wet boy who looked to be about her age, limped towards her. He was bleeding from a few gashes on his arms and one on his knee.

Leila let out an involuntary whimper as she grabbed her ankle with one hand and Atticus' collar with the other. Glaring, she turned her attention to the boy who would rather yell at her than help. "You took that turn way too fast!" she accused.

"That's because I wasn't expecting someone to be sitting *right in the middle* of the bike path!" He pointed towards the bike, whose bent frame rested against the boulder. "Look what you did to my bike!"

"Look what *I* did? You're the one who rode it off the bridge!"

"It was that or run you over. What kind of idiot sits down smack in the middle of a biking trail?"

"What kind of idiot takes a blind corner that fast?" Leila shot back. She turned her attention to her ankle, peering at it through the water. Whatever she'd done to it was not good. It was already starting to swell.

Atticus whined and looked back and forth between Leila and the boy. She let go of his collar, grabbed her throbbing ankle with both hands, and began to rock. Why did pain bring a need for movement? Tears escaped from her eyes despite her unspoken order that they remain put. Of course, now would be the time she could finally cry again. As much as she didn't want to cry in front of this jerk, she couldn't help it. The pain was excruciating.

He finally registered her injury, and Leila watched as his face went from angry to concerned. "What's wrong?"

"My ankle." She gave an involuntary moan. "I came down on it funny."

Through the knee-deep water, he limped the rest of the way over to her. "Is it broken?"

"Am I a doctor? I don't know, but it really hurts!"

He hushed her. "Let me see."

Atticus sniffed at the boys' hair as he crouched down to look at Leila's ankle. When he lifted it out of the water, she winced. It was so huge, it almost hurt more to look at it. The boy, taking stock of their situation, glanced back and forth between her and his bike and cursed again, this time more colorfully. "Look at it," he ordered. "The wheel's bent all to hell!"

So he cared more about his stupid bike than he did her. Nice. Real nice. "At least your bike can't feel pain."

He let out an annoyed sigh. "It's not about the bike. I wanted a new one anyway. But I can't put you on it, and you can't walk on this ankle. I'm gonna have to carry you out of here."

Guilt and embarrassment caused Leila to flush. "I don't need you to carry me out. I-I can get back on my own."

He stood. "Oh yeah?"

"Yeah."

He made a wide, sweeping gesture with his arms. "Fine. Have at it."

Begrudgingly, Leila took his proffered hand and stood, putting all her weight on her good leg to start. Tentatively, she tried to distribute some weight to the other leg, only to cry out once more and clutch his arms with both hands. She couldn't even stand on it, so she definitely wouldn't be walking on it.

He shot her a wry smile. "Like I said."

She wasn't as heavy as she used to be, but at one hundred thirty pounds, she wasn't a petite woman. That he might not be able to lift her filled her with mortification. "You honestly think you can carry me all the way back to the parking lot?"

"What I think is I'm your only hope out of here, so you'd better be nice to me."

He had a point, and Leila pinched her lips tightly together.

He grinned at her. "That's better. Come here. I'll carry you up."

Leila's heart thudded violently against her ribs. She didn't know what to do. She'd never been held or carried by a boy before. What if she was too heavy, and he threw out his back? Worse, what if she smelled bad?

But before she could come up with some other plan, any other plan, he'd lifted her easily into his arms and she'd wrapped one of her own arms around his neck for added support. She had a vision of herself as the English damsel in her dog-eared novel that awaited her at home, and he was the dangerous Scottish highlander who had plucked her from the safety of her uncle's house, carrying her in his strong arms across the barren moors to an abandoned castle where he would have his way with her.

Leila's face burned as she shook off the image. She'd been on a harlequin romance kick all summer. Too long, apparently. It was probably time to open a murder mystery again. Better yet, maybe she should turn to one of those self-help books her mama left lying around. Those would cool her off in a hurry. Because one thing was for certain: Leila was on fire, and not just from embarrassment.

Pressed against his chest as she was, the heat of the boy's body burned her like a brand through the wet barrier of their clothes. It was the most intimate experience of her life, and she had the ridiculous thought that she might actually combust as her heart kicked into even higher gear.

Under her hand, she could feel his own pulse racing at a pace that nearly matched her own, and the cords of his muscles tightened and strained as he navigated them both across the rocky riverbed and toward dry ground.

How odd it was to be this close—body to body, breath intermingled and blood pumping in unison—with someone whose name Leila didn't even know. And she didn't know if it made things better or worse that he was so unbeliev-ably good looking.

Better, she decided. Definitely better. Being pressed against and carried by an ugly guy would definitely be worse. She tried not to stare at his eyes, but she couldn't look away. They were a startling turquoise blue against his summer tan. And his hair looked like the type that used to be blond but had darkened with time. Although she didn't know what color to call it, on him it was pretty perfect.

Atticus trailed closely behind them until the boy paused and whistled. "Come on, Dog, get away from my feet before you trip me."

Atticus needed no other prompting. He raced ahead of them and up the bank.

Once on shore, the boy carefully deposited Leila on dry ground and told her to wait for him there, as if she could go anywhere. She used the time to cool down and settle her racing heart.

"I'll get your shoes off the bridge and check the bag on my bike. If my phone isn't ruined, I can try to call someone to come help us."

He had a cell phone? Even her father, a lover of any new gizmo and gadget, had yet to buy one, although that was probably because of the price tag. He made a decent living, but they were solidly middle class, despite the appearance of their new home.

Who was this guy who could already afford a cell phone and didn't care that his mountain bike was ruined? What was it he'd said? He wanted a new one anyway?

Leila watched him, trying desperately to ignore the awful throbbing of her ankle that had synchronized with her heartbeat. She could see the muscles of his back through his wet tee-shirt. His calf muscles were well-defined, too, and she tried not to be impressed. Muscles aside, chances were good, based on his language and his obvious materialism, that he was a jerk. Or a jock.

Or both.

Weren't they one and the same? A jockey jerk. He wouldn't be the first one she'd met. She was determined not to like him. Absolutely determined.

Okay, well, maybe not *absolutely*. Just inclined. She was *inclined* not to like him.

Or maybe she could just like some things about him and not others. That was reasonable. Responsible, even. She was a good Catholic girl, after all. She was supposed to love everyone.

First, he grabbed her shoes and socks. Then Leila watched as he crossed the bridge, still favoring his left leg, to the opposite bank and waded back down into the river. As he lifted the bike with his free hand, it was clear it wouldn't be rideable, not with the frame twisted and bent as it was. He must have been holding out some hope that it would still work because yet another curse word escaped his mouth.

Yeah, he might be insanely cute, but he was rude and crude, and Leila couldn't stand guys like that. Still, she couldn't look away.

He reached for a sopping wet bag attached to the seat post and unzipped it, retrieving what looked to be one of those black Motorola Razr phones she'd seen on commercials. It was the latest and greatest in technology, and judging from the next word out of his mouth, it was no longer functional.

He sent a long glare in her direction. Leila quickly looked away at Atticus, who sat beside her, his tail giving a periodic wag as he, too, watched the boy across the river.

"Well, that's just great!" he yelled. "No bike and no phone." He chucked the Motorolla into a tree trunk and then heaved the bike up onto the bank before turning and making his way toward them through the water.

As he limped back toward her, he muttered things to himself, and at one point she thought she heard him mumble something about how his dad was going to kill him. His expression was one of despair, and suddenly he looked pitiful. A good bruise was forming above his left knee, and he was pretty-well banged up everywhere, which she hadn't fully appreciated before. She was hurt, but he was hurt too.

Leila waited until he was close enough to hear her before she spoke. Her voice came out more softly than she'd intended, and he missed what she said.

"What?" he snapped.

"I said I'm sorry. I'm really s-s-sorry about everything. It's all my f-fault!" Leila choked on a sob as she looked up at him.

He pressed his lips together in a grim line before answering. "It's alright."

He didn't offer an apology of his own, but Leila didn't really care. She was too emotional and her ankle hurt too much and she was too worried about how she would make it back to the car to concern herself with petty things like apologies.

She pulled herself together. Tentatively, after a deep breath, she said, "You're all scraped and bruised and limping. It's a long way back. Are you sure you can carry me?"

"I'm gonna have to."

"We could wait for someone to come by," she suggested, but she could hear the doubt in her own voice. She'd never bumped into anyone on this trail until today, and she'd walked or run it every day for the last few weeks.

"We'd be here all night." He crouched down, helping her put her socks and shoes on, although they quickly discovered that neither the right sock nor shoe would fit. Her ankle was twice its normal size.

She grabbed the lone sock and shoe from him. "I'll just hold these."

He nodded once before effortlessly scooping her up in his arms again.

Atticus danced around playfully near their legs as if he thought they were about to play some kind of game. Maybe he thought the boy would heave her into the river for him to fetch out. Who knew? Atticus was sweet, but he was almost certainly brainless. "Atticus, no," Leila said sternly. "Go on."

He barked once before taking off ahead of them and up the rest of the bank and onto the trail.

The boy followed suit, grunting a few times as he worked to gain the proper footing to climb the bank. By the time they reached the trail, he needed to stop and rest.

This did not bode well.

Defensively, he said, "Normally I'd be fine, but I was already tired."

"I'm so sorry—" Leila said again.

"Stop saying that!" he snapped. Then he sighed, running an agitated hand through his thick hair. "It doesn't change anything, okay? So just stop apologizing."

A new heat coursed through her, this one angry. "Fine! I'll just stop talking period!"

He didn't respond to that, and they rested another few minutes in silence—Leila sitting on the forest floor, fuming and trying not to cry, and the boy standing over her, irritated and edgy until, wordlessly, he scooped her up and started out again.

They didn't speak. She didn't want to, and she wasn't sure he even could. His breath came out in shallow, labored pants as he bore them both along the trail towards the parking lot where her papa's car was parked.

After what couldn't have been more than ten minutes, he stopped again, this time depositing her on a large, downed maple tree before seating himself beside her on the log. Reluctantly, Atticus laid himself at their feet. He appeared as though he could go on for miles longer.

Leila looked at the boy from the corner of her eye. She couldn't stand another minute of silence. She thought she might scream in frustration. "What's your name?" she asked tonelessly, picking a blade of grass from the forest floor and pulling it into tiny pieces.

"Jackson."

He said nothing more, and he didn't ask for her name.

How rude! She'd tell him anyway. She ripped another piece of grass out of the ground. "I'm Leila, not that you care," she offered stiffly.

"You must be Mexican, huh?"

"*What?*" She glared at him indignantly. So much for the preliminaries. Had this kid been raised in a barn? "No, I'm not Mexican."

"It's just—I noticed your shirt," he explained. "And then, I just thought you looked Mexican maybe."

Leila glanced down. She was wearing her *ponte las pilas* shirt.

"That's Spanish, right?" he asked.

"I'm Puerto Rican!"

"Oh." He shrugged. "Same difference though, right?"

"What—same difference?" she blustered. "What do you mean, *same difference*? Mexico is another *country*."

He stared at her blankly.

Incredulous, and with brows raised, she tried again. "Puerto Rico is a commonwealth of the United States."

Still nothing.

"An island in the Caribbean? Ring any bells?"

He folded his arms across his chest and looked away. "Whatever."

Leila tucked a strand of hair behind her ear. "Unbelievable. I'm Hispanic, so to you, that automatically means I must be from Mexico. Do you have any idea how many Hispanic countries there are? I could be from anywhere. Guatamala, Ecuador, the United States, even."

"Whatever," he repeated, sounding bored, but the deepening stains on his cheeks revealed he wasn't quite so unaffected by her criticism as he tried to appear.

It helped cool some of Leila's anger. Not much, but some. People like him gave Americans a bad name, and it really bugged her. Either they didn't take their education seriously, or they were so narrow-minded that they had no clue about anything else going on beyond the borders of their own country. There was a great big world out there!

Once, in geography class, her teacher had asked a kid—one of the football stars—to come up to the front of the room and point to Africa on a map.

He couldn't find it.

Who could miss an entire continent? Leila would bet money this kid would. She didn't want to have to be carried and pressed up against him—skin to skin.

She hated it.

She really did.

Chapter 13

They started out again, this time with Leila behind him, riding piggyback, which was a lot easier for Jackson to manage. Why hadn't he thought of that from the beginning? It mortified him that he'd struggled so much to carry her. She was a little on the taller side for a girl, maybe five-foot-six, but she really wasn't all that heavy. It was just that he'd already had hockey practice that morning, dryland workouts that afternoon, and now a long bike ride. He was toast and his legs were jelly, but after what had happened last night, he didn't want to be home alone with his dad, so he'd been staying as busy as possible.

It didn't help that now his knee felt like a rusted-out hinge. He'd definitely done something to it. He'd felt a pop when he'd taken his foot off the pedal and caught it on a root just before he'd gone over the handlebars. Jackson experienced a wave of dread. If his dad didn't lose his shit over the broken bike and phone, he would over the knee. It was the last thing he needed today after the night they'd just had.

Jackson had never understood it. Any time he was injured and couldn't play hockey, his dad acted like Jackson must have done it on purpose or something. Like when he'd missed playoffs last year because he had pneumonia. The old man had been pissed at him. Hadn't talked to him for a week.

He couldn't shake the feeling that with every step he took, he was doing more damage. What if he'd torn something and needed surgery? He could end up missing most, if not all, of the season, and if that happened, Philip would probably disown him on the spot.

But what did it really matter? Jackson was beginning to understand that he would never measure up, no matter what he did. It was impossible. He'd been trying for eighteen years, and things were worse for him now than they'd ever been.

The girl, Leila, a name almost as beautiful as she was, squirmed against his back. Any other time, Jackson might have found that to be a turn-on. But she was hurt, he was hurt, and he felt like he was carrying the weight of the world on his shoulders. The ride hadn't helped, and now he was in an even bigger mess with his father than he'd been when he'd left.

Life was going to be unpleasant for a while.

At least it wasn't all bad. She was easy on the eyes, this Leila, with her plump mouth and liquid brown eyes. She reminded him of someone. That hot actress who had played in the movie *Wild, Wild West.* What was her name?

He couldn't remember, and it didn't matter. He still wanted an answer to the question he'd attempted to ask earlier. But instead of finding out if she was bilingual, he'd received a lesson in cultural geography. Admittedly, that topic wasn't his strong suit, and despite his continued embarrassment at having looked like a total idiot, he tried again, "Do you speak Spanish?"

He could almost hear the rolling of her eyes when she answered him. "Of *course* I speak Spanish."

Jackson gritted his teeth. He was trying here. The least she could do was throw him a bone. He worked to keep his voice light. "That's cool."

"What's so cool about it?" she shot back.

He counted to three. "That you can speak two languages."

He felt her body soften a little. She was still rigid, but not quite so much.

He ventured further. "Do your parents speak English?"

She let out an exaggerated sigh.

Well, did they? It was a perfectly valid question. He stayed silent. Waiting.

"My dad grew up stateside in Arizona. He didn't move to Puerto Rico until he was almost twenty, so yes, I bet he speaks better English than you do. So does my mom. She was born and raised in Puerto Rico, and everybody there speaks both Spanish and English, and they can all find Africa on a map too."

What the hell?

They were all smarter than he was then. That's what she was getting at. Fine. He wouldn't argue with her. He'd heard it enough times from his old man, so maybe he really was an imbecile. But hell if he would just keep taking the insults the rest of the people in his life hurled at him. He was done. He might not be able to do anything about the old man just yet, but he was good and done with this chick. He didn't care how pretty she was. Noticing a log a few feet ahead, he veered over to it and stopped. "Get off."

She didn't move. "What?"

"I said, get off. You want to be a brat, fine, but you can do it here in the woods all by yourself."

She protested once more, but he held firm. Once she'd hopped down, he stomped away a few yards and turned around to see her gingerly maneuver her way over to the log and sit. She looked up at him then with frightened eyes, but he refused to feel guilty.

"You can't leave me here." Her voice was pleading. It made him feel powerful.

"Oh yeah? And why's that?"

"Because I can't walk!"

"You should have thought of that before you got all high and mighty and ... and *insulting*!"

"You called me a Mexican!"

"So what? I wasn't insulting you. I made a wrong assumption, I guess. So fine, sue me. I was trying to make conversation, and—" He stopped and put up his hands. "You know what? I'm done. I don't need to explain it. I'm sorry I hurt your feelings. I had no idea being a Mexican was such a terrible thing."

"It's *not* a terrible thing. What's terrible is—"

"Spare me another lecture, *please*," he interrupted. "I get it. I'm stupid. I'm dumb. Everyone else is better. You're better, your parents are better, even Brian *frickin'* Beninger is better, and I'm so sick of it. I'm so sick of being beaten up and talked down to and ... ugh!"

He grabbed at his hair with both hands and took a couple of deep breaths. When he spoke again, his voice was a little calmer. A little less frantic. "There's never a break, okay? I never get a break. It's just constant, and it doesn't stop, and the pressure is—and I came out here today to try to get some peace, and instead, everything is worse. And now I have to go home and—I'm gonna break, okay? I can't do it. It's crushing me, and I'm just—what am I supposed to do?"

He hadn't been looking at Leila, but he looked at her now, and what he saw nearly broke him. Any hostility she'd felt earlier was gone. Instead, compassion had softened her features, and she stared at him with eyes full of understanding. But she couldn't possibly understand. Nobody did.

"Please, Jackson," she said, gently patting the spot beside her. "Come sit."

He wanted to, but he couldn't. He also couldn't leave her. He knew that.

"It's ... fine. Let's keep going." He crossed the space between them and gave her a hand. When she stood, she lifted her eyes to meet his. And then she did the strangest thing. She reached out her hand and stroked near his mouth with a feather-light touch. He held his breath.

"You have a bruise here," she whispered. "Did that happen today?"

He couldn't speak, so he shook his head instead. She was so close to him, he could see the tiny flecks of gold in her eyes.

"When?"

He swallowed. "Yesterday, but it was just ... an accident."

She held his gaze until he looked away.

"I'm sorry you had that accident," he heard her say, "and I'm sorry for what I said a few minutes ago, and for all the trouble I've caused."

He nodded again, feeling everything too deeply and not trusting himself to speak anymore. Instead, he turned and offered Leila his back. She hopped up, and they started out again without another word.

Jackson hadn't accessed the trails from this side of the ski hill in a long while, but if he remembered correctly, the parking lot was another thirty to forty minutes away. He really hoped his knee would hold up that long. The intensifying ache was making him feel a little nauseated.

Deliberately, he shifted his focus from the pain in his knee to the feel of the girl on his back. She was quiet behind him, but he could hear her breathing near his right ear. She'd dropped a little on his back, and she shifted her weight. He stopped to boost her back up again, and he couldn't help but notice the way her thighs felt in his hands. There was plenty to squeeze, which he liked, but she was firm. Fit. He was more than just a little attracted to her, even if they had gotten off on the wrong foot. Even if he had just embarrassed himself with that little rant.

"Do you need to stop a minute?" she asked, breaking the silence.

"No, I'm alright." Jackson walked for several more minutes, careful to keep his left knee as straight as possible. His rhythmic breathing sounded loud to his ears.

In, out, in, out. One, two, one, two, he counted, keeping pace until Leila's voice broke in again from behind him.

"What do your parents do?"

"We have some furniture stores," he said after a brief hesitation. "Yours?"

"My mom's not working right now, but she's looking into starting a business. Just something small. My dad's a custodian at the university. The *lead* custodian."

The pride in her voice was unmistakable. He liked that. He always felt the need to downplay what his parents did. He was uncomfortable with wealth, despite what a lot of people thought. He'd been called a spoiled rich kid more times than he could count. "Nice. Do you have brothers or sisters?"

When she didn't respond right away, Jackson realized it wouldn't be a yes or no answer, and he was sorry he'd asked. They'd been so close to recovering some semblance of normal conversation.

When she finally answered, his suspicions were confirmed. It was complicated.

"My brother died not that long ago," she said.

The pain in her voice cut straight to his heart, and he held her legs a little tighter. "I'm sorry."

"Thanks," she whispered, and her warm breath against the side of his neck gave him goose bumps all over. "I'm not over it."

He spoke tentatively, afraid of saying the wrong thing. "I don't think you can ever get over something like that, can you?"

"No," she said softly. "I don't think you can."

"What was his name?"

"Luca."

"Is that a ... Spanish name?" He felt her smile against the back of his neck. "It's Latin."

Okay, that sealed it. He really was an uncultured idiot. But Leila must not have thought so because she continued, "I think the meaning of the name has something to do with light, which makes sense. He lit up my life. All our lives."

"What happened to him?"

"He had Down syndrome, and he died of complications from pneumonia. He just couldn't fight it. He was so small ..." her voice drifted off.

Jackson was silent. His thoughts immediately jumped to Todd Hall, a kid with Down syndrome who used to attend his high school. Jackson and his friends spent freshman year poking fun of him and calling him *Retodd*. Thinking about it now made him feel sick, and he focused on putting one foot in front of the other.

"People stared and said mean things sometimes because he was different. They called him names or said stuff like he shouldn't have been born, but Luca had a beautiful life, and he made our lives beautiful too." She paused. "I'm sorry, it's hard to explain."

"You miss him," he acknowledged before stopping and setting her down on another fallen log. He needed to rest, yes, but mostly, he needed to look at her. He needed to see her face.

"I do." Leila adjusted herself on the log and stared at her feet. "I really do. You have no idea. He was perfect, and I still love him so much. People could be so cruel, and I would feel it here, you know?" she asked, patting the space over her heart. "Way deep inside. It still hurts. I think it might always."

Jackson looked into Leila's shining brown eyes and experienced a rush of shame. Just this morning, he'd hurt Brian Beninger's sister exactly the way other kids had hurt Leila. He was certain of it. Brian was out mowing his yard, as he often was. He had a *thing* for that yard. It was always immaculate, which was why his dad had hired Brian to take on their yard as well. Unable to help himself as he drove by with one of his teammates, Jackson hurled an insult at Brian through his open window. It was really just to let off some steam after everything his father had said and done the night before. Jackson figured since Brian wouldn't be able to hear him over the noise of the riding mower, there'd be no harm in it.

But he hadn't noticed Kay there in the driveway, not until after. Brian's older sister had been hidden from view behind one of the parked cars, and when she stepped out into the open, not more than fifty feet away, Jackson had seen the intense pain and fierce anger reflected on her face. It had left him with a feeling of such strong self-loathing, he could still feel it even now.

The thing was, Brian wasn't a bad guy. Jackson had always known that. But the kid was different, a little off somehow, and Jackson hadn't hesitated to exploit that. They'd played hockey together from the very beginning, and after every single game, Jackson watched as Brian received an *attaboy* from Mr. Beninger. Every single game, Brian got a pat on the back. And what did Jackson—easily the better player—get from his own dad? Irate criticism.

But sitting here now, with this soft, sweet girl with eyes so big and brown and full of goodness, he didn't want to be vicious anymore. He wanted to be different.

He wanted to like himself again.

He wanted Leila to look at him and see a good man in front of her. He wanted to put his arm around her and comfort her, protect her. And then he wanted to kiss her senseless.

He didn't do that last thing, but he did put an arm around her shoulders. "I'm really sorry about Luca."

"Thanks."

Neither one of them said anything more about Luca, and they didn't talk about Jackson's little meltdown either. They just sat, pressed together on the log, with the sun filtering down through the trees in soft, slanted beams. The early evening light dappled and danced on the forest floor. The birds chirped, and the leaves fluttered as the warm breeze floated by them, carrying with it the smell of sweet pine and summer.

Atticus gave a deep, contented sigh, and Jackson knew how the dog felt. He had a potentially wrecked knee, another mile to walk, and a furious father waiting for him at home, but right now, in that moment, he was at peace. And then something amazing happened. Leila rested her head on his shoulder.

Chapter 14

Leila could not eat the breakfast her mother had prepared for her. It was the first day of school, and she felt like she was about to be fed to the lions. She was going to limp into that building without knowing a single soul there—well, except for that boy Jackson. She hadn't seen him since he'd carried her out of the woods, but she'd thought of him nearly every moment since.

He'd shown a vulnerability that had completely disarmed her. Something had happened to him to make him feel heavily burdened to the point of breaking that day, and she couldn't stop wondering what it was. He'd mentioned a name—Brian somebody—and needing a break and being beaten up. She thought of his bruised cheek. Who had done that? He'd claimed an accident, but that didn't seem as likely considering what he'd said. She'd spent some time trying to guess, but she didn't like any of the possibilities.

It had taken some real effort on Jackson's part to get them out of the woods and back to the parking lot. By the time they made it to the car, he was heavily limping, but even so, Leila was pretty sure he was disappointed when their time together ended. She knew she was.

He'd driven her home in her father's car and then had his mother, newly back from a trip, pick him up from her house. Leila had hoped he would ask for her number, but he hadn't, and with her ankle sprained as it was, she hadn't been able to go back to the trail in hopes of bumping into him again. Doctor's orders were to ice often and take one week off her ankle to give it the rest it needed to heal. She'd spent two days on crutches, attempted to read six novels, and nearly lost her mind with impatience to see Jackson again.

Today, they would almost certainly cross paths, and she'd carefully selected her outfit with that in mind. She wore yellow shorts and a white button-up top with short sleeves. It was one of three new outfits her mama had splurged on and bought her brand new from the Maurices at the Nicolet Mall. Her go-to white strappy sandals showed off her freshly painted toenails, and she wore her dark hair long and straight.

Looking at herself in the bathroom mirror, Leila took a deep breath. She wasn't used to her new self yet, and it still sometimes felt like a stranger was looking back at her. Just last week, Joanne Jenkins—the lady her Mama was going to rent the store space from—told her she looked just like Salma Hayek. Leila looked the actress up later and had to admit that she could see a small resemblance. It thrilled her.

Still, she worried about what Jackson thought of her. She wasn't big, fat Pizza Face anymore, but what did she know about his tastes? For all she knew, he preferred the overwhelming number of blue-eyed blonde bombshells she'd been seeing since she'd moved to town.

There was a heavy Finnish influence in Nicolet. In fact, her papa had read that the Upper Peninsula had the greatest population of Finnish Americans than any other place in the entire country, and by a lot. It wasn't like there were loads of Latinas walking around the U.P. What if she wasn't his style?

While it was true that Jackson hadn't impressed her much in the beginning, by the end of their time together, she couldn't deny it. She was smitten, and her feelings had continued to grow in their intensity every day since. He was rich, spoiled, and possibly slightly under-educated, but the vulnerability she'd seen in him was endearing. Outwardly, he was probably the best-looking boy of her acquaintance. His eyes alone would have put him in that category. But she'd glimpsed what lay beneath all that, and she liked what she saw.

Of course, she'd told her mama all about him. Carmen had said something about crushes being magical, but this wasn't a crush. Leila had experienced crushes before. This was different. For one thing, this boy might actually be attainable now that she could walk without her thighs chafing together. The possibility that he might actually like her back sent waves of excitement rolling through her. And now, with the first day of school finally here, those waves had built into one giant tsunami.

Not having a car of her own, Leila rode to school with her father. Samuel treated her to a pep talk the whole way there. It wasn't until they pulled into the drop-off circle that he finally grew quiet, but only briefly. At the front of the circle, he put the car in park and turned to her.

"Leila, I pray to Saint Thomas Aquinas that you will pursue truth in your education, and also to Saint Rita to lead you to a true friend of the heart in this school. You will find each other, *mija*. Be patient, and it will come. I will pray all day, as often as I think of you. *Te quiero*." He leaned over and kissed Leila on the cheek.

"*Te quiero, papá*," she said around a small lump in her throat. Quickly, she got out of the car, and she didn't look back as she walked into the school.

She couldn't.

He'd watched for her all morning with no luck, and by the start of third period, Jackson wondered if maybe she wasn't there at all. But when he heard Peter Lindberg talking about the new hot girl who sat next to him in his second hour AP Physics class, Jackson knew he was talking about Leila.

"Trust me," Peter said to a group of their friends as Jackson slowly made his way towards them, "you've never seen anyone like her."

"Where's she from?" Jackson's best friend, Freddy Loma, asked.

"Who cares?" Peter shot back. "What matters is where she's going, and that's with me. Twenty bucks says I'll have her in the backseat of my truck by Saturday night."

Jackson set down his crutches and took the seat directly in front of his nemesis, taking a deep breath to knock back the sudden rage he felt before calmly inserting, "If you're talking about Leila, you can forget it."

Peter smirked. "What do you know about it?"

"I know I'm driving her home after school and taking her to Freddy's party on Friday."

Peter swore.

"Wait, is this *the* girl?" Freddy asked. "The one who wrecked your knee?"

"Yeah."

Peter swore again and sat back in disgust. Jackson smiled. He loved one-upping Peter.

"They met out in the woods a week ago," Freddy supplied. He nodded at Jackson's knee. "She sent Jackson head-first into the Whitefish River."

"Why don't I know anything about this?" Peter demanded.

"Cause I don't tell you my shit, that's why."

Peter scowled. "So, what? You going out with her now?"

He'd have to lie. *Going out* meant that she was his girlfriend, and she wasn't—yet. But she would be, and saying so would be the only way Peter would stay away from her. If Jackson said no, he'd consider her fair game. Peter was always competing with him for everything. So far, he had yet to come out on top, and Jackson planned to keep it that way. "Yep."

Peter eyed him up suspiciously. "So you met her in the woods, went over your handlebars, tore your MCL, and now you're dating her?"

"*Partially* tore, so don't get too cozy on first line, and yeah, I'm dating her, so back the hell off."

Peter put two defensive hands up in the air. "Relax, man. All I said was she's hot."

He'd said a whole lot more than that, but the bell rang, and Jackson let it go, turning to face the front of the room. As he turned, he saw Peter mouth something to their buddy, Drew—something Peter would pay for just as soon as Jackson could get back on skates.

When lunch passed with still no sign of Leila, Jackson grew agitated. Nicolet High was a big school—about fourteen hundred students attended—but it wasn't so big that a girl could go a whole day without being spotted at least once. Where was she?

It probably didn't help that Jackson was moving so slowly on his crutches. While he was grateful he'd only partially torn his MCL, which was about a four-week recovery, it still sucked to be stuck on crutches and missing practice. Peter had slid into his spot for the time being, and Jackson didn't like it.

Philip *really* didn't like it.

Finally, in his last class of the day, Jackson saw her. He crutched into psychology class, a class he'd signed up for in order to get an easy *A* since everyone knew the teacher was a total joke, and saw her sitting in the third row. A seat was empty behind her, and he propelled himself forward to reach it before someone else could.

Hearing the sound of the crutches, Leila turned her head, and her eyes widened as she took him in.

"Jackson!"

Those students who were already seated glanced at them curiously, but after a few seconds, they lost interest.

She turned the rest of her body around so that her long, tanned legs rested in the aisle. She really did have beautiful skin.

"I wondered if I'd see you today," he said, unable to suppress the wide smile that took over his face. They had a class together, which meant he was guaranteed to see her every day. The world had just become a much brighter place.

"What's wrong?" she asked, her face still registering horror at his condition.

He shrugged. "My knee."

"Is that from when we—when you ... ?"

"When you sent me crashing into a rock? Yeah," he confirmed, still grinning.

She turned the color of beets and buried her face in her hands. "I'm so sorry."

"I only partially tore something." He gestured at her sandaled feet. "How's the ankle?"

She looked sheepish when she answered. "It's fine now."

"In three or four weeks, I'll be fine too." He switched gears. "Where have you been all day?"

"Have ... have you been looking for me?"

"Since this morning."

"Oh." She pressed her lips together to keep from smiling, but she couldn't hold it, and it was like that, with the two of them grinning at each other, that Mr. Carlson started class.

While he was droning on about the syllabus, Jackson studied the back of Leila's head. She had the most beautiful, shiny hair. It was so long it reached the middle of her back. He wanted to touch it. He wanted to bury his face in it. He leaned forward to see if he could catch a whiff of her shampoo. He could. She smelled like coconut, just as she had in the woods. He took a deep, slow breath.

Sensing him, Leila turned and raised her eyebrows.

He grinned and whispered, "Do you have a ride home?"

She gave a small shake of her head before whispering back, "Bus."

"Can I drive you home?"

She flashed him another smile before nodding once and firmly directing her attention to the front of the room.

Jackson, warm with pleasure, leaned back in his seat, stretched his legs out into the aisle, and closed his eyes. Leila might not know it yet, but she wouldn't have to pay any attention in this class, and she'd still pass with an *A*. Mr. Carlson was the biggest slacker on staff. He was also boring as hell. But with Leila in the class with him, Jackson knew he'd be anything but bored.

Their lockers were not only on different floors, they were on opposite sides of the building. No wonder Jackson hadn't seen her in the halls. Leila was tucked away in the bowels of the high school near the pool and with all the freshmen. It must have been the only available locker.

They headed there together to grab her backpack and the rest of her things. Jackson hadn't needed to stop by his locker. He hadn't been there all day. One benefit of being on crutches was they let him wear his backpack around to classes.

"You got shafted having your locker way over here," he commented as she worked her combination. She'd confessed to having eaten her lunch in this dimly lit hallway, back pressed against her locker. It would be the first and only time she'd have to do that.

Leila concentrated, spinning the dial right, left, and right again before popping it open. "I know. It was stressful today. I was late to almost every class. They're all on the other side of the building. I barely have time to get back here, especially with my ankle still sprained."

He'd noticed a small limp. "Does it still hurt?"

"Only a little." She flashed him a guilty smile. "I can't believe you carried me out when you were the one who was hurt the most. Wasn't that so painful for you?"

Of course it had been, but he shook his head.

She gave him an assessing glance. "You're tougher than I am."

"I hope so. I am a hockey player," he said, sounding arrogant to his own ears and not caring. "I'm used to pain."

She rolled her eyes, but the corners of her mouth turned up in amusement before she closed her locker and lifted her backpack straps over one shoulder first, and then the other.

"How was your day otherwise?" he asked as they set out to walking all the way back to the other side of the school where his car was parked.

"It was pretty good."

They walked several steps in silence.

"Did you meet anyone?"

"Not really. I mean, people were nice, but I didn't really have time to get to know anyone."

"What about Peter Lindberg?"

Her face registered recognition. "Ah, yes. Peter Lindberg. A real player. I did meet him." She stopped and turned to him. "How did you know?"

Jackson smiled sardonically. "He mentioned it."

"Did he tell you he asked for my number?"

"Did you give it to him?"

She shook her head. "I told him I just moved here and don't know it yet."

He laughed. "Good one."

She grew more animated. "You know who I did meet today? A guy I actually bumped into a few times out on the South Trails."

Jackson felt his stomach clench. "Who?"

"The advisor of the running club."

He relaxed. "Mr. Lucas?"

"Yeah. He's my trigonometry teacher."

"You're in trigonometry?" This girl must be some kind of genius.

"He recognized me and asked me if I was interested in running with them," she said, ignoring the question. "They go out on the trails twice a week, rain or shine."

She was obviously very excited about this. Jackson couldn't relate. He hated running. He ran to condition for something he loved, not for the love of running itself. He didn't say that, of course. He shot her a smile. She was practically jumping up and down with excitement. "That's cool, but what about your ankle?"

"The doctor said I should be able to run on it again next week. I have a brace I can wear and stuff."

"Cool," he said again.

They talked about their classes and teachers as they made their slow journey out to the parking lot. It turned out that Leila was in all Advanced Placement classes, with the exceptions of trigonometry and psychology. Five AP classes. This girl was absolutely out of his league.

Jackson didn't care. He had to have her.

There was something about her that went beyond her looks. She was different than the other girls. He wasn't sure what it was, but he liked it, and he wanted more time with her. Glancing at his watch, he saw he had an hour before he was due at physical therapy.

"Want to grab some ice cream down at the harbor?" he asked. "They're still open another couple of weeks."

She hesitated. "I don't know. Mama's expecting me at home."

"Want to call her?" He reached into his back pocket and offered her his phone.

Her face brightened. "You fixed it!"

"No, it's new."

Leila's jaw dropped, but she didn't say anything, which was a relief. In a minute, she was going to see what kind of car he drove, and then what would she say? Jackson was used to people commenting on his family's money. It bugged him, but what could he do about it except pretend not to care? Embrace it, even. But it mattered to him what she thought.

Thankfully, Leila said nothing when they reached the car, but he could see her thoughts play out on her face as she looked it over. This girl would suck at poker. For a second, Jackson wished he were more like Freddy. His buddy saved up for years to buy his ten-year-old Honda Accord. It was rusted out and had a dented door, but it worked, and nobody had handed it to him.

With burning cheeks, he opened the door and got in.

Leila tried not to react. Jackson didn't drive a *car*. He drove a brand new HUMMER H2. It was red and wonderful and *expensive*. Leila happened to know this because it was her papa's dream car. He'd wanted one for years, and ever since the creation of the internet, he'd torture himself by watching video after video of Hummers driving over rocky terrain, through deep muck, and even over other cars. She didn't understand her papa's fascination, but she figured Jackson would.

She schooled her features. She would *not* let on how absolutely appalled she was that a teenage boy owned a car that a hard-working grown man would never be able to afford. What were his parents *thinking*?

Instead of remarking upon it, something she was certain everyone else did, Leila opened the door and slid into the front seat, as if she rode in a Hummer every day of the week. While she waited for Jackson to get himself situated and divested of his crutches, she glanced around. It was neat as a pin in here. At least Jackson took care of his things. He might be spoiled rotten, but he wasn't careless with his stuff.

Sure, he'd broken both his phone and his bike, but that had actually been more her fault than his. But the fact that he already had a brand new phone spoke volumes about his family's position. She tried not to be jealous. What she had in life was enough. Two parents who loved her, a dog, a house, food, clothes. What more did she really need?

He offered her his phone a second time. "Did you want to call your mom? Tell her you're getting some ice cream?"

Leila took it from him this time, staring at it for a second before flipping it open. She'd only seen these on TV. The silver keypad shone and was lit up by a blue back light. It truly was a piece of art, and she tried not to want one for herself.

She looked up at him before dialing. "Jackson, I don't have any money with me."

"That's alright," he said easily. "I have plenty."

She bit down on her lip and watched him. "I can see that you do."

"I'm kinda used to flaunting it," he admitted.

"It won't impress me," she warned.

He studied her. "I know. I like that about you." He turned the key, and the engine roared to life. "It doesn't impress me either, but I still want to take you for ice cream if you want to go."

"Why?" she asked.

He smiled a slow, devastatingly sexy smile. "Because I waited a whole week to see you again, and all I got was forty-seven minutes of staring at the back of your head."

She burst out laughing, but a delicious heat washed over her down to her toes. "You're impossible."

He winked at her and put the car in reverse. "Call your mom."

Chapter 15

It was Friday night, and Leila sat on the downstairs window seat looking out over the front yard and driveway. Jackson wasn't due for another ten minutes, but she was a bundle of nerves and wondered if he might be early. He'd driven her home every day after school for the entire week, but tonight he was taking her on an actual date. They were going to a movie and then over to his friend Freddy's house. He was having a party.

Leila was just getting to know Freddy and his girlfriend. She'd eaten lunch with them and Jackson the rest of the week, which was definitely better than sitting alone at her locker with only her peanut butter and jelly sandwich for company. They'd both been really nice to her, and she liked them fine, but she didn't want to go to this party.

Freddy's parents were out of town, and his older brother was "babysitting." Apparently, job duty number one for his brother was to buy Freddy a keg. Job duty number two was to let him throw a gigantic party.

Leila had expressed her reluctance to go, which she knew had surprised Jackson. She wanted to meet people, but she'd never been to a party like this one, and she was nervous.

In the end, she said she'd go but that she didn't want to drink. Jackson accepted that and told her he wouldn't drink if she didn't, and if she didn't like it at the party, they'd leave. She felt a little better.

Still, she had butterflies. What if he didn't like her after tonight? What if he thought she was boring?

"Promise you won't embarrass me!" Leila yelled toward the stairs. Her parents were up in their bedroom getting ready for a date themselves once they finished seeing her off. They'd already promised once, but a girl could never be too careful. Especially with parents like hers.

And don't make a big deal of his car, she'd warned her papa earlier.

I won't even look directly at it, lest it blind me, Samuel had solemnly vowed.

More and more, she was seeing glimpses of her parents' old selves. They laughed again, and her father sometimes told his horrid jokes at the dinner table, just like he used to. Carmen was moving forward with the bookstore, and she had an energy about her now that Leila wasn't sure she'd ever seen before. Carmen had already decided on a name. Luca's Books.

Leila loved it.

"Of course we won't embarrass you, *mija*," Carmen's voice floated down from the top of the steps. It sounded a little odd. "Your papa and I will be on our very best behavior. Right, Samuel?"

Leila turned. The stairs had creaked, and her mama's voice was closer now. Sure enough, she appeared on the landing with Samuel directly behind her.

Leila's jaw dropped.

Carmen wore the brightest, reddest lipstick Leila had ever seen, and as she descended the four remaining steps, Leila could see she'd applied her blush in two bold stripes across her cheeks. With bright blue eyeshadow to top it all off, her mama's face looked remarkably similar to that of a clown.

Leila jumped to her feet, nearly stepping on Atticus. "Mama, what—"

After catching a full glimpse of her father, she was left momentarily speechless. Samuel Molina wore his pants pulled up to his ribs, and tucked into them was a well-worn, white tank top that he usually wore under his shirts. Standing next to each other, they looked like a pair of sideshow circus performers. Atticus, perhaps catching the playful vibe in the room, jumped to attention and ran for his ball.

Papa said something Leila didn't quite catch. All she could think was that Jackson could *not* see her parents like this.

She took a quick glance out the window to make sure he hadn't arrived yet before stomping over to them and pointing back at the steps. "Go back upstairs right now. You can't come down here like this."

Atticus dropped the ball at her feet and stared at it with his tail wagging.

"What, you don't like my pants?" Samuel asked innocently. He laughed, and as her mama joined him, Leila could see red lipstick thickly smeared over her top front teeth.

"He'll be here any minute!" she cried, waving frantically at the door. "He can't see you like this!"

Atticus wined, and Leila kicked his ball towards the kitchen. He took off after it.

"Like what?" her mother asked, trying to keep a straight face and failing miserably. "This is how we always look when your boyfriends come over."

Leila felt the blood drain from her face. This wasn't funny. "What boyfriends, Mama? He's the only one I've ever had, and if you don't get back upstairs right now, he'll take one look at you and run away forever."

"Well then, we will have done our jobs, right *Carmencita?*" Samuel asked his wife with a wide grin.

Carmen, seeing her daughter had been pushed to the edge, relented, and she put a hand on her husband's shoulder. "Alright, alright, *mija.* We were just having a little fun."

Leila reached behind her and grabbed a tissue from the credenza. She held it out. Carmen took it from her and smiled sheepishly before wiping first at her lips and then at her teeth. "We promise to behave ourselves when he gets here, *cariña.*"

Atticus came back and dropped the ball at Leila's feet. Samuel dropped his pants back down to his natural waist. "I'll go grab my suspenders and put on a shirt, my Leila. Not to worry. And I'll only show this boy my gun collection once as I remind him of your curfew."

Leila cradled her head in her hands before opening her arms to receive Carmen's hug. She'd laugh at this later, but right now, she was too mortified. What if Jackson had seen them looking like that? As far as she could tell, he was the most popular boy in school. The last thing she needed was for him to go running for the hills and shouting to everyone along the way that she and her parents were freaks.

She didn't want that to happen here. As often as she'd told herself back in Grand Rapids that it didn't matter what other people thought, it *did* matter. She did care, and if she was going to attract attention in Nicolet, she wanted it to be for all the right reasons. She wanted a grand romance—the kind she read about in the books she checked out from the library.

Okay, maybe not *exactly* like the kind in those books, but maybe the PG version of it. And she wanted friendship. Her father had prayed for one, but so far ...

Leila reminded herself that it had only been one week, but she still hadn't made any friends. No *girl*friends, anyway. And worse than having no friends at all, she was pretty sure she already had an enemy, a girl named Amelia that

Leila had literally never spoken a word to, but who stared daggers at her from across the lunch room all the same.

At least she had Jackson, for now. He called her every night after practice, just to talk, and she found it surprisingly easy to spend two hours on the phone with him without even realizing it. Like clockwork, the phone rang at eight-thirty, and like clockwork, her insides performed a series of cartwheels before she picked up the cordless phone and took it to her bedroom for privacy.

Tonight, her parents had demanded to meet the boy who tied up their phone line every evening and dropped off their daughter every day in a vehicle that cost almost three times more than Samuel's annual salary. Jackson would come to the door today, and Leila needed it to go well. She wanted her parents to like him, and she wanted the feeling to be mutual.

Leila watched their retreat up the stairs, and once she was satisfied that the joke was well and truly over, she patted the dog on his head and returned to her perch at the window where she picked at her nails.

By the time Jackson arrived, her parents were all put back to rights, and true to their word, they behaved themselves. Jackson was completely at ease, greeting Atticus and shaking the hands of both her parents. They made some small talk for several minutes before her parents remembered to thank him for carrying her out of the woods. After they inquired after his knee and told him they'd be praying to Saint Raphael for healing, Leila signaled it was time to go by opening the door.

Samuel followed them out, and unable to help himself, he commented on the Hummer in the driveway. "Nice set of wheels there."

"Thanks," came Jackson's sheepish response.

"You know, a lot of people don't know that the Willys Jeep was a military vehicle too. Some people say the Wrangler is far superior to the Hummer off-road, but you can't beat that fully independent suspension even though the articulation's not so good, don't you think?" Samuel's eyes danced with amusement, and Leila suppressed a groan. He knew Jackson would have no idea what he was talking about.

"Er, yeah, I think you're right about that."

Samuel grinned before turning serious. "Have her home by eleven, Jackson, and not a second later."

Jackson balanced on his crutches as he offered Samuel his hand once more. "Yes, sir. I will."

Chapter 16

Jackson had gotten them movie tickets to an action thriller called The *Bourne Supremacy*. Leila had a hard time following the plot from the very beginning since all she could focus on was the excruciating awareness of Jackson sitting so close to her in the dark. When he put his arm around her about an hour into the film, she gave up trying to follow the movie altogether. The thrill she felt at his touch was far better than any car chase through the streets of Moscow could ever be. Who needed Matt Damon on screen when they could have Jackson Lang in the flesh?

By ten o'clock, when they arrived at the party, Leila couldn't help but wish the movie portion of their evening could have lasted all night. Freddy's house was loud, hot, and packed, and she didn't really know anyone. In Spanish, she would have said she felt like a toad from another well, but in English she'd have to settle for being a fish out of water. Regardless of the idiom, she was uncomfortable, plain and simple.

A handful of kids were dancing in the living room, and a few boys she recognized were doing keg stands in the kitchen. Leila hadn't even known a person could drink beer—or anything else—upside down. They took turns while a crowd of people cheered them on as if it were some kind of athletic event.

Leila had always wondered what these parties were really like, and now she could confirm she hadn't been missing out on much. She felt like a disapproving old biddy. She'd already seen one girl throwing up through the open door of the small bathroom near the kitchen, and another kid was passed out on the couch in the living room.

Jackson tucked one of his crutches away in a broom closet and hobbled along as they continued to make the rounds. He introduced her to most of the people he greeted, and Leila immediately forgot their names. Sometimes she couldn't even hear them, the music was turned up so loud. She did a lot of smiling and nodding.

After making it from one end of the house to the other, Jackson turned to her. "Let's go upstairs," he shouted over the music. His timing was perfect because, as he'd been talking to a guy named Max, Leila had caught the attention of that girl from school—Amelia.

There was no doubt about it. Amelia didn't like her. She took turns staring at Leila through tiny, angry slits and speaking to her friends, who seemed duty-bound to hate Leila with their eyes too.

But instead of feeling that old familiar churning deep in her stomach like she always had in the past when confronted with the meanness of her peers, this time Leila could mostly brush it off. Maybe Luca's death had taught her something: While people could still hurt her feelings, they could no longer crush her spirit. She wanted friends, but she didn't need popularity. The important things in life, she already had.

Leila turned away from the group of girls and toward Jackson. He smiled at her, waiting for a response, and she gave him a quick nod. Slowly, he limped his way up the stairs before leading her to a bedroom with hockey posters hanging on the walls. He closed the door behind them, shrouding them in shadow.

When he didn't turn on the light, Leila's heart raced. Had she just made a colossal mistake? She was in a dark bedroom in a strange house with a boy she really hadn't known all that long, and even though she could still hear the music and feel the bass reverberating through the floor, it was suddenly far too quiet, even with her pulse thudding loudly in her ears.

Jackson must have seen the panic on her face because he rushed to explain himself. "I thought we could sit out on the roof and talk."

Leila let out a huge breath she hadn't known she'd been holding. He only wanted to talk. He wanted to sit and talk to her on the ... roof. She glanced out the window behind him. "Wait, what?"

He grinned. "I do it all the time. Me and Freddy have been friends since the sixth grade. I can't tell you how many times we've sat out on the roof right here. We'll just crawl out through the window."

"Is it ... safe?"

He laughed. "Of course it's safe. I wouldn't take you anywhere that wasn't safe, Leila, I promise."

"Okay," she responded skeptically. "But what about your knee?"

"I've got the brace on, but I'll still be careful."

He took her by the hand and led her to the window. He went first, leading with his good leg, and then helped her out.

Once outside, Leila breathed another sigh of relief. It *was* safe. The roof had very little slope where they were. They sat off to the left of Freddy's window and leaned against the siding of the house. It was a small little enclave that seemed to have been created just for them.

"You're not having fun," Jackson noted.

She turned her head and looked at him. "Now I am. I guess I'm kind of a quieter person."

"I like that about you. You make me feel ... calm."

"I do?" She flushed with pleasure from the compliment.

He searched for words. "I'm not a very restful person, I guess you could say."

"So, what, you're restless then?"

"Restless, wound up, high-strung, I don't know. I have more penalty box time than anyone else on the team. I even keep a second water bottle in there," he admitted with a laugh.

She grinned and bumped him with her shoulder. "So you're a fighter, not a lover?"

He stared at her for several seconds before looking away. "Yeah. Something like that."

Leila looked off into the distance, too, and filled her lungs with the crisp night air.

Without looking at her, Jackson reached for her hand and held it. It was warm and strong and an outward sign of the invisible connection she'd felt with him since their time on the trail. So far, he was everything she'd thought he was: entitled, popular, and strong, but also gentle, kind, and surprisingly sensitive.

After sneaking a quick glance at him, she saw his eyes were closed. Maybe Jackson was high-strung, but for the moment, at least, he looked restful. While she hated to disrupt the moment, she wanted to ask him more about his family. She'd met his father that evening, just briefly, when Jackson had stopped to grab a sweatshirt after the movie, and she hadn't known what to make of him. Jackson rarely talked about him, and she was curious.

"It was nice meeting your dad," she began tentatively.

He snorted and looked at her. "No it wasn't. He was awful."

"He wasn't ... *awful*," she lied. "He's just ..." She searched for a word.

"A jerk?"

She gasped. She couldn't imagine calling her own father that.

He gave her hand a small squeeze. "Sorry. But he is."

She didn't argue. "What's your mom like?"

"My mom's great. You didn't really get to meet her that day when she picked me up from your house, but you'll really like her. My sister, too."

Joy coursed through her. He wanted her to get to know his mom and meet his sister? That had to mean something. "Where were they tonight?"

"They're on a cruise."

"Just the two of them?"

"Yeah, it was a last-minute thing. My mom was just down in Lansing with Lizzie—she got home the day I carried you out of the woods—but then Lizzie called with an SOS. Her boyfriend dumped her, and she was feeling a little low, so my mom booked them a quick cruise to the Bahamas."

"Oh." Leila didn't know what else to say. She tried to imagine what it would be like to just book a cruise on a whim like that. No planning. No saving ahead of time. But then, the Langs were enormously wealthy, which she'd suspected from the get-go but had confirmed tonight when they'd stopped at Jackson's place. "Your house is really pretty," she said.

The look he shot her was one of puzzlement, and Leila realized she'd jumped topics.

He scratched at a shingle with his nail. "It's okay."

She bit down on her lip. Describing the Lang house as *okay*, or even *pretty*, didn't begin to do it justice. It was a beautiful brick mansion with big windows and pillars, and it was right on Lake Superior.

Jackson didn't know how he came off to others, she decided. He'd been given so much, and either he didn't like it, or he didn't value it. Either way, he had no idea what it would be like to live the way she did, not that her family was poor or anything, but they definitely didn't take cruises. Her parents operated on a very careful budget and knew how to stretch a dollar.

"Your extra garage is bigger than my entire house," she couldn't stop herself from saying.

He grinned. "Hey, you live in the Longyear neighborhood. It's *historic*," he added, making air quotes, "so you're not exactly slumming it yourself."

Looks could be deceiving, but Leila decided to leave it alone. "What's in that garage, anyway?"

He shrugged. "The old man's toys."

"Like?"

He shrugged again. "A boat, couple of jet skis, a tractor, some other stuff."

She laughed. "Is that all?"

"I liked your parents," he said, abruptly changing the subject. "Your dad would be scary if he wasn't so nice. They were both really nice."

Leila smiled softly. Samuel Molina was built like a lion but had the temperament of a lamb. "Yeah, they're pretty great. They've been through a lot."

His thumb caressed her hand. They'd covered the topic extensively already. "You all have." After a few beats of silence, he changed the subject again. "What's Puerto Rico like?"

She laughed. "Hot."

"What do you miss most about it?"

"My cousin, Elena. We moved stateside when I was ten, but up until that point we were like sisters."

"But you still visit, right?"

"I spent a few summers there after we moved, but now we don't get there as often. I wish we could visit more, but ... you know, flights and everything. We talk on the phone a lot though."

He nodded and continued his questioning. "What did you like best about it, other than the family part?"

She thought about that for a moment. "The colors," she decided. "Everything is so bright and colorful there. The ocean, the lush foliage ... gosh, I love the trees. Obviously, the palms are iconic, but I really love the mangroves and flamboyan trees. The flamboyans grow these amazing fire-red blossoms all through the spring and summer. They're gorgeous. Even the houses are colorful in Puerto Rico."

"Hey, our houses are colorful," he pointed out, gesturing toward the siding of the house they sat against.

She leaned forward and looked behind her. "This is grey."

"Still a color," he said straight-faced.

She laughed. "True, but over there, houses are yellow and teal and orange and pink. I think that's one reason my mother's always liked old Victorian homes. They're full of color."

"The Longyear neighborhood is full of Victorians. They're all really nice."

Leila knew what he was getting at. The Longyear neighborhood was upper class and old money. The Molinas were neither.

She could have told Jackson that the house had been a special gift from Samuel to Carmen. That he'd sacrificed some of his most prized possessions to get it for her, to make her dream a reality. That to afford it, he'd sold off several valuables that had been very meaningful to him, valuables that had been handed down to him from his father.

But she didn't tell him any of that.

What her papa had done for her mama was too special for words. Leila still couldn't believe he'd done it, but then Samuel loved her mama in a way not every husband did. Jackson's father came to mind again. She had only just met him, but he seemed like an unhappy man. What kind of father was he? The kind to leave a bruise on his son's cheek?

Leila shivered. She could only hope Jackson had a much nicer mother.

While she wondered about Jackson's parents, he wondered about hers. "You and your parents seem to get along. You all seem really close."

"We've always been tight."

Jackson must have sensed that she'd been about to say more because he encouraged her to go on with a small nod.

Leila stretched her legs out in front of her and crossed them at the ankles. "It's just ... I've heard that when a child dies, it can break a family apart, so I'm glad that hasn't happened to us, but we'll never be the same. Everything is just different now."

He let go of her hand and put his arm around her shoulder, pulling her closer. She leaned into him. He was warm and solid and strong, and if she'd been a kitten, she would have purred.

"What was it like for you?" Jackson asked gently. "With your brother."

Leila knew what he was asking, and she didn't pretend not to. She didn't blame him at all for being curious. People got weird when confronted with disabilities. Usually they were in one of two camps: the gawkers or the avoiders. She was intimately acquainted with both. They'd either stare rudely at Luca or pretend not to see him at all. A simple curiosity and desire to know more was kind of refreshing.

"It was happy and sad," she admitted. "I would have done anything for him. He was the coolest little kid around, and so sweet, so beautiful." She swallowed. "Somehow, I would simultaneously think of Luca as being perfect just as he was and at the same time wish for him to be ... whole, so he could do all the things all the other boys would get to do. I would give thanks for him every day, but then sometimes I felt mad at God too. Everything was harder for Luca. Walking, talking ... just *everything* was so much harder for him. And, I don't know, I feel like a part of me died with him. I feel like a part of my parents died with him too. He was the best part of all of us, and I guess that's why we're different now."

Jackson remained silent. He watched her.

"I loved him so much," she said, her voice breaking. He held her tighter. "People could be so cruel, even without meaning to be. At the funeral somebody from our church told my mama it was probably best that he'd died young."

Leila felt him stiffen against her. His voice was incredulous. "Somebody actually said that?"

"Not in those words, but that was what she meant. And that lady couldn't have been more wrong. Luca had so much life to live. And he wasn't a burden to us. I mean, it was hard, and he had a lot of needs, but we never felt that way. For all of us, he was our favorite. He was such a beautiful child—"

She was repeating herself. Leila closed her mouth and then her eyes, and for a moment, she could see him. She could feel her little brother on her lap; smell the Burt's Bees baby shampoo in his hair.

She took a deep, steadying breath. "He would have had a happy life. It's not fair. None of it."

They were both quiet. The air was still all around them.

"I'm sorry, Leila," Jackson finally whispered, and then he gently kissed her hair.

Something warm unfurled inside of her, like a pastry plumping in the oven. It was the sweetest, most perfect thing he could have done, and Leila snuggled in even closer. She caught his scent, piney soap mixed with teenage boy, and as she breathed him in and shared his warmth, she felt a fullness settle over her. She wanted to hold on to it forever.

That night, when Jackson dropped Leila off at her house five minutes before eleven, he crutched beside her to the dimly lit front porch despite her protests that he didn't need to. Once on the porch, he rested his crutches against the front door, told her what a great time he'd had, and pulled her in for a kiss.

She flinched when his lips touched hers. She literally flinched. The same girl who had been as soft and pliant as a freshly boiled mouth guard twenty minutes ago, was so full of tension, he could feel it radiating off her.

Jackson straightened his arms to hold Leila out in front of him, and as he studied her, he saw the truth in her bewildered eyes. He could have kicked himself.

Smooth, Jackson. Real smooth.

"Leila, I didn't—"

"Kiss me again," she whispered.

"But I didn't—" he tried again. "I mean, have you ... Is this your first kiss?"

She looked down at her feet and nodded silently, blushing all the way to the tops of her ears.

Stupidly, he'd assumed she'd be like all the other girls he'd ever said goodnight to after a date, when so far she hadn't been like *any* of them. Of course Leila wouldn't take kissing lightly. For everyone else, it was just one of the bases to run through on the way to home plate, but Leila had been enchantingly unique in every way, and it followed that she'd be different in this one too.

Still, it was a bit of a shock. How could someone who looked the way she did still be untouched like that? It made no sense to him. She was nothing short of stunning. Every boy in school wanted to make a move.

But she wanted *him*, and she wanted him to kiss her again.

It filled him with pride, and honestly, a bit of relief too. Because if Leila hadn't allowed anyone else to kiss her, it was because she had high standards, and she hadn't found anyone worthy of her—until now. And that meant that Jackson couldn't possibly be as bad as his father made him out to be.

If he were as bad as Philip said he was, there was no way someone like Leila would have anything to do with him. If Jackson was as bad as Philip always said he was, there was no way a man like Samuel would let him within a foot of his only daughter.

The realization couldn't erase years of damage, years of lies Jackson had been sold and always bought, but it was a start, and when Leila whispered again, "Kiss me," he didn't need to be told a third time.

Gently, Jackson cradled Leila's face in his hands, and realizing her second kiss would need a lot more finesse than the first, he lowered his lips softly to meet hers. It was a light, lingering kiss, and it was all he could do not to smile in victory when she sighed sweetly against his mouth.

He was debating when or even if he should deepen the kiss when Atticus barked from the other side of the door and the sconces on either side of it flickered on and off. He and Leila sprang apart, and Jackson knew—with grave disappointment—that the night had come to an end.

He was going in for one final hug goodnight when Samuel's muffled voice sounded from inside the house.

His words were puzzling. "Hey, Jackson! Knock, knock."

Jackson's eyes grew wide as he looked at Leila."What?" he mouthed.

She covered her mouth with one hand, but her brown eyes danced in amusement.

Seeing that she would be no help at all, Jackson played along. "Uh, who's there?"

"Halibut."

Leila stifled a groan.

Jackson grinned. "Halibut who?"

"Halibut you stop kissing my daughter and get her inside before my watch says 11:01."

Chapter 17

Jackson liked being at Leila's house, but he couldn't get over there nearly as much as he wanted to. His life was so crammed full of things to do and places to be. If he wasn't at school, he was either on the ice or at the store, but every spare minute he did have, the Molina house was where he wanted to be.

Obviously, Leila was the biggest draw. He was crazy about her, and Freddy said he was whipped. Jackson didn't care. He didn't even try to deny it. He didn't *want* to deny it because being with Leila felt good. There was a *rightness* to it, a soothing of his soul when he was with her—in her space and with her family—that he'd never found with anyone or anything else. It was real and true, and although he hadn't told her yet, he knew he loved her.

Even though it was a first for him, he didn't doubt the sentiment. He might just be a dumb kid, and no doubt there were people out there who thought teenage love didn't exist at all. But it wasn't just lust—although to Jackson's delight, Leila had become quite the enthusiastic kisser. And it was a whole lot more than a mere liking, which he definitely did too. She was like a best friend and a girlfriend, all wrapped up in one.

He could listen to her talk for hours and not grow tired of hearing her voice, and making her laugh gave him so much more of a thrill than scoring a goal ever had.

He loved her.

And he loved her with an intensity that almost hurt. It was an excruciating pleasure-pain, and there was nothing he wouldn't do for her. Nothing he wouldn't sacrifice. She could ask him to give up hockey, and he would. She could ask him to give up friends, and he'd do that, too, although she'd never ask that of him. She was kind. Pure. Good.

And she'd broken his heart the day she confessed to him that she hadn't always been pretty. He hadn't believed her. Someone like Leila could never be ugly, not in a million years, and he'd told her so. Instead of taking his word for it, she'd insisted on showing him proof. With hands that shook, she'd retrieved several photo albums. She said she needed to know if it would change how he felt about her. It hadn't. But what it had done was make him even more fiercely protective of her than he already was.

"You'll always be beautiful to me," he'd said.

"But what if I got fat again?"

He heard the fear in her voice and held her close. "Even then."

"You'd break up with me," she insisted.

"Never."

That he meant it gave Jackson a new feeling of pride in himself. He must finally be growing up. Never again would he stoop so low as to ridicule another person for no good reason. In the past, nothing and nobody had been off limits. Looking back, in middle school he'd been an absolute tyrant. He had a lot to atone for, and he'd start by being the best friend and boyfriend Leila could ever have.

But it wasn't just Leila that drew Jackson to the Victorian every free moment. He loved spending time with her parents too. Walking into her home, even before he kicked off his shoes, he felt the weight of the world fall away. He could breathe at the Molina house. They had family dinners nearly every night, and they even talked while they ate.

And they always, always prayed first. It was a curious tradition, but they were a devoutly Catholic family, and Jackson didn't mind. He bowed his head, closed his eyes, listened to them give thanks and ask for stuff, and then he watched them make the sign of the cross after saying *Amen*. Often he wondered if anyone was really listening, but he never asked them.

Carmen was kind and gentle, and he liked her a lot, but it was Samuel who Jackson felt closest to. They'd had a lot of talks already. Sometimes they were surface and sometimes they were deep. Either way, Samuel shot straight with him, and Jackson liked that about him. He respected Leila's father for it, even though on one notable occasion, he wouldn't have minded if Samuel had been a little less candid.

At the beginning of October, four weeks after Jackson had taken Leila out that first night, Samuel seized upon an opportunity to speak with him alone.

Carmen and Leila had gone out for ice cream to make hot fudge sundaes, and before the car was out of the driveway, Samuel made his move.

He grabbed himself a cigar out of a drawer in the kitchen, poured Jackson a Coke over ice, and led him out to the back patio where he'd sat him down and dictated to him that under no uncertain terms would he be taking Leila's virginity.

Jackson hadn't seen it coming, and if embarrassment could stop a heart, his would have arrested right there on the spot. And while he could understand Samuel's need to protect his daughter, Jackson hoped to never ever have to discuss sex with Samuel Molina ever again, so long as he lived.

It couldn't have been easy for the guy. In fact, Jackson wasn't sure whose face had been redder in that moment, his or Samuel's, but the man loved his daughter and was more than willing to do the hard things—including making Jackson squirm in his chair like a worm on a hook until he was given a promise. And a promise is what Samuel had gotten.

What else could Jackson have done but given his word? He'd keep it too. It would kill him, but he'd keep it. To do otherwise would be to let down the only man who'd ever given a damn about him, and if Samuel believed sex outside of marriage was a mortal sin that would hurt Leila, Jackson would just have to find a little self-control.

Or a lot.

Jackson found Leila's father fascinating. Samuel's father had been a writer who specialized in translating books from Spanish to English, and vice versa. That did a lot to explain how Samuel, a janitor, had a better vocabulary than any English teacher Jackson had ever encountered.

His mother had been an artist. Mostly, she painted watercolors, and many of her paintings adorned the walls of the Molina home. Jackson's favorite was the Southwestern landscape that hung in the dining room above the sideboard. Samuel claimed his parents, orderly and focused in their work, hadn't known what to do with a small child who wreaked such innocent havoc in their home in a single-minded pursuit of figuring out how everything worked. Door handles, clocks, cabinet hinges, even the VCR—nothing was off limits.

"How many times did my father turn a door handle only to have it fall off in his hand?" Samuel asked once. Jackson had laughed at the image of a young Samuel taking apart his house piece by piece.

"I have no siblings, Jackson," Samuel continued. "That tells you everything you need to know about what it was like for my poor parents. Before I was even a year old, Javier and Ana Molina knew they were out of their depth. Catholic or not, they were done." He mimed snipping with scissors and laughed that deep-throated laugh of his.

One unseasonably cold day in late October, Jackson and Samuel had been in the living room discussing baseball in front of the old brick fireplace. It was a topic about which Samuel was passionate and Jackson knew next to nothing.

Ten minutes into the conversation, Samuel popped up out of his easy chair and demanded Jackson accompany him upstairs. Jackson was reluctant to leave the warmth of the fire, but he got up anyway, and as they passed through the kitchen where Leila and Carmen were busy making caramel corn, he reached out and gave Leila's ponytail a gentle tug. Smiling, she batted his hand away, and he continued following behind Samuel, who turned at the last minute before leaving the kitchen to let Carmen know they were heading upstairs to the attic.

"To the attic, huh?" she'd said in surprise, pausing in the act of transferring the coated popcorn into a baking dish. She exchanged a look with Leila, whose smile grew, before saying, "Impressive, Jackson. Samuel has invited you to his lair."

Jackson felt ridiculously pleased.

The sweet smells wafted up to the second floor and even followed them to the third. Like the rest of the house, the attic floors were made of old, wide plank. Whereas downstairs they were stained and buffed to a perfect shine, up here they were unfinished and uneven, probably from the large fluctuations in temperature. A window fan rested below the solitary window on the far wall—no longer needed now that the cool weather had set in.

The floor creaked and groaned as they made their way across the expansive space towards a small wooden desk that sat to the left of the window. Beside it was a cloth sofa with a rip in the armrest, its floral pattern pilled and worn from the passage of time. Jackson guessed it might be older than he was.

Impressive as that was to a boy unaccustomed to anything but the latest and greatest in the world of furniture, what really caught Jackson's attention was the vast length of cluttered countertop on the opposite wall. Underneath were eight to ten wooden cabinets, and above were rows and rows of open shelving. Model trains stretched across them, all lined up in one direction as if they were about to begin a stagger-start race.

Cluttered on the counter's surface were more trains, but also all the makings of a small model town. It was helter-skelter, with trees, homes, buildings, logging trucks, oil towers, and other bits and pieces covering every square inch of the counter. Jackson felt like a giant looking down on a small community that had just been leveled by a tornado.

"What is all this?" Jackson asked. Fascinated, he walked over to the display, leaving Samuel at the desk.

"My train collection, or what's left of it," Samuel responded distractedly as he ran his hand underneath the lip of the desk. He found what he was looking for. "Ah, here it is."

Producing a small key, he waved it at Jackson. "If ever anything should go missing, I'll know who to question." The older man winked and shuffled towards him. "Excuse me now, son, I need to get into that cabinet there by your feet."

Jackson stepped aside as Samuel crouched down and inserted the key. A moment later, he came back up holding a medium-sized wooden box.

"Whatcha got there?" Jackson asked, moving closer.

Samuel gestured for Jackson to follow him, and together they went to the couch, where Samuel set it down on the cushion between them and lifted the latch. "I'll show you."

He rummaged through a pile of baseball cards, all housed in hard, protective plastic. There had to be at least fifty cards in there, Jackson realized.

After several seconds of shuffling, Samuel stopped, coming up with a card. "Ah. Here it is."

As with the game itself, Jackson knew little about baseball cards, but he recognized the picture of Mickey Mantle on one that looked brand new. "Nice," he said, impressed.

Samuel shook his head. "Nice? *Mijo*, this is the best card I have. A 1952 Bowman Mickey Mantle."

Jackson did his best to look more properly impressed. "*Really* nice," he expounded lamely.

Samuel chuckled. "You *really* need to stop saying that. Look," he said, moving closer, "this is in PSA seven condition." His smile broadened as he took in Jackson's blank expression. He chuckled again in disbelief. "You don't know what that means."

The statement hung in the air, and Jackson felt his neck and face prickle with heat as he shook his head. This was the kind of stuff he'd know if his dad gave even the smallest of damns about him. Didn't the good dads out there do this kind of thing with their sons? Watch baseball games and collect rookie cards? Samuel's dad obviously had.

The only sport Philip watched with Jackson was game film from his hockey games, which wasn't great bonding. Actually, it was the opposite. It was two hours of torture where his dad critiqued every little nuance of Jackson's play, rewinding and replaying every mistake, and somehow finding fault even with scored goals.

Seeing Jackson's distress, Samuel sobered quickly and gave him a small, awkward pat on the knee, card still in hand. "I tease. I only tease, Jackson. Nobody is born knowing these things. They must be taught, you see? If my father hadn't taught me, I wouldn't know either, but if you'd like, I'll teach you. For now, I'll save you the lecture and tell you the only thing I cared about when I was your age." He handed Jackson the card and paused for dramatic effect. "That little card you hold is worth 5,500 dollars today."

Floored, Jackson studied it closely before looking at Samuel through wide eyes.

Samuel nodded proudly.

"How did you get this, your dad?" Jackson glanced at the remaining cards in the box before adding, "And are they all worth this much?"

Answering his questions in order, Samuel said, "Yes, my father was a collector, and no, the rest aren't worth so much. This card is my best now."

With a furrowed brow, Jackson asked, "What do you mean, it's your best *now?*"

"I sold my three best cards. I had another Mickey Mantle and Willie Mays. Both 1962 Topps." He paused again for effect. "And I had an Eddie Mathews 1952 Topps. That one got me twenty-five grand."

Open mouthed, Jackson shook his head. "Why did you sell them?"

Samuel laughed. "For the same reason you're spending your Saturday night here in the attic with an old *hombre* like me." He chuckled again and rested a hand on Jackson's shoulder before he stood. "I sold them for the love of a girl, Jackson." He grinned and shook his head. "For the love of a girl."

Later that night, Jackson and Leila were alone on the couch in the living room watching a movie in front of the dwindling fire. Atticus lay directly in front of low, languid flames. The tired pup was asleep and soaking up the remaining warmth while Jackson was busy trying to cool himself down. He was ready to combust with lust for a girl whose virtue he'd promised not to compromise. It had been seven weeks since that first kiss. Seven weeks, and they were still solidly on first base. There would be no steal to second, he knew that much. At least not for a while.

Hmm. Maybe he did know a thing or two about baseball.

Last spring, he'd crossed home plate with Amelia Channing in seven *minutes*, and in seven *weeks*, he was still trying to figure out a way to introduce Leila to French kissing that wouldn't scare her or get him banished from her house if Samuel found out. Maybe tonight was the night.

Jackson heard Samuel cough in the kitchen, and Carmen yelled down to him that he needed to use his inhaler. She said she'd bring it to him and they could play a quick game of scrabble before bed. Those two sure loved their Scrabble, the most boring game on Earth. Either that, or setting up the game in the kitchen was a way to monitor what was going on in the living room beside it.

Jackson wasn't allowed in Leila's bedroom, so for the last seven weeks at the Molina house, it had been a quick kiss in the living room or not at all. Well, except for a couple of memorable evenings earlier in the fall when they'd parked his car at the overlook of McCreaty's Cove.

It might be time for another visit. He didn't care if it was too cold now. He'd bring blankets.

Settling more deeply into the couch cushions, Jackson resigned himself to the knowledge that there would be no lessons in French tonight. Instead—if it was anything like the last time—he and Leila would hear Samuel insist that *Qat* was an actual word, and if Carmen would only look it up, she'd find it defined as some type of shrub. She'd tell him to dream on and put down a real word already or forfeit his turn. He'd bring out a dictionary, flip to the Q section, and plop the book down in front of his wife with a smug smile, and that would be that.

Jackson grinned. Yes, he was disappointed, but it was enough just to be in their midst, his arm around Leila as he feigned interest in this ridiculous movie they'd rented where a pink-clad Reese Witherspoon chased some pretty boy to Harvard Law School with a stupid Chihuahua riding along in her purse. Leila had already seen it and told him he'd love it. Next time, they were watching *Die Hard*.

Partaking in the daily happenings of the Molina family was one of Jackson's favorite things to do. He could sit and listen to them for hours. What was incredible was that they seemed to feel the same way about him. They thought he was funny. They laughed at his jokes, and they loved hearing his stories. Whenever he came over in the evening, they wanted to know how his day was—what the best part had been—and he could tell them. And he could do it without worrying he'd trip over some invisible landmine and suddenly find himself in trouble, which was really kind of freeing.

Everywhere else, Jackson was always trying too hard, striving for some elusive thing he felt he needed but couldn't name. He did it at home, he did it at school, and he did it on the ice. Even with Freddy, he wasn't able to be fully himself. Here, he felt seen. Understood. Appreciated, even.

Jackson loved his mom, and he knew she tried, but she walked on the same egg shells at home that he did. Sometimes he wondered if that's why she jumped at the chance to lead every committee in existence in their small town. Why, at the tiniest suggestion Lizzie might need her, off she'd go for a visit.

She was rarely at home, but she still complained sometimes that she didn't see him enough. It was as if she expected him to be sitting there waiting for her when she could finally break away from all her commitments and spend some time with him. As guilty as Jackson felt admitting it, he'd rather be here with the Molinas than at his place any day. Obviously, he'd rather sit around their dinner table than alone at his kitchen counter, but even if his family suddenly became the *gather-for-dinner* type, he still would prefer the Molinas' dining room to his own.

And then there was Leila. He'd rather have sweet, innocent Leila, who drove his teenage body crazy, than any of the girls at school who offered him theirs. In the past, he'd been more than happy to take whatever they gave, casting them aside when he was done with them like a used dryer sheet. It turned his stomach. It never used to.

But one trip over his handle bars and everything had changed.

He'd changed.

/ Chapter 18

NOW

Despite his protests, the doctors kept Jackson overnight for observation. It wasn't necessary. Once he'd warmed up, been given fluids, and eaten a little something, he felt mostly back to normal. Sure, his muscles ached, and he was tired, but that was to be expected after such a long swim, never mind the cold water.

But he wouldn't close his eyes. He wouldn't let himself. Not yet. Visiting hours had long passed, but Jackson still watched the door because he knew she'd come. He just didn't know when, and he refused to sleep until she did.

Leila might hate him now for reasons he didn't understand, but she'd loved him once, and he'd almost died today. She'd saved his pathetic life, and there was no way she wasn't thinking about him right now. No way she wouldn't need to see him. It had been a long time, but he knew enough about Leila to know she wouldn't be able to stay away.

His mother had been first to the hospital, meeting him in the emergency room. Her face was white as bleached flour until she was given repeated assurances he'd be okay. Lizzie and Matt hadn't been far behind Virginia, and as Lizzie cried and fawned all over him, Matt fretted beside her, urging her to stay calm for the sake of the babies.

Philip had been the last to come, but then, to be fair, he'd been the last to know. He arrived after they had taken Jackson up to his third-floor hospital room. He'd come alone, and his face was grim, either due to concern over Jackson or concern over his precious boat, which was most certainly at the bottom of Lake Superior now.

Philip hadn't said much, and neither had he. To his father's credit, he didn't say a word about the boat, inquiring only after Jackson's health. It was awkward and brief, and Jackson was just glad Lizzie and his mom hadn't also been in the room to complicate the whole scene even further.

Jackson had considered bringing up that last interaction they'd had—the one his mother would probably always refer to as "the incident"—but he hadn't, and neither had Philip. No good would have come from it anyway. The truth was, their relationship was too far gone now to attempt any sort of recovery, and while it was true that forgiveness could wipe a slate clean, painful memories weren't so easily erased.

Jackson would never, no matter how hard he tried, be able to forget the years of verbal lashings and the handful of physical ones he'd received from a father who was incapable of loving him.

It was a hard truth to accept, but Jackson had promised himself one thing as he made his way towards shore, one swim stroke at a time: If he survived, he was going to do whatever he could to move on. He'd been crippled long enough by his need to earn the love and approval of a man who was never going to give it.

Survival had not been a foregone conclusion, not at all. Easily, he could have died. And at one point, Jackson thought he *would* die, but then something *miraculous*—it was the only word he could find to explain it—had happened to him out there. Something he wasn't ready to dig into just yet. Looking down at his fingers, he wiggled them to reassure himself, yet again, that he really was still alive; that he had actually made it.

It was then that Leila arrived.

Something, some kind of sixth sense, alerted Jackson to the fact that she was standing in the doorway, and he looked up. Those coco-brown eyes stared back at him, and her lips pinched together in a grave, straight line.

Jackson didn't speak, and neither did she. He, because every word he thought to say stuck in his throat like a wad of unchewed bread, and she, most likely because she couldn't stand the sight of him. A rush of emotion bubbled up from a place deep down inside him. He still couldn't believe the girl from all those years ago, the one who had claimed to love him more than anyone else in the world, could have abandoned him without a word.

Her voice interrupted the silence between them, but she didn't venture further into the room. "You're awake."

There was still a traffic jam in Jackson's throat, so he bought himself some time by looking through the bedding for the controller to prop himself up to a seated position.

After watching him fumble around for several seconds, Leila sighed heavily and moved to his bedside. Bending, she lifted it from the floor where it had fallen. "Here."

"Thanks," he managed. He studied her as he pressed the button to raise the head of the bed. She wore a white lab coat over blue scrubs, and a badge hung from her front pocket. He cleared his throat. "You're working?"

"Just leaving. I got called in earlier to help for a few hours."

Jackson tried not to look pleased that she'd seen fit to string so many words together in the longest communication they'd had since college. No, that wasn't exactly true. She'd talked to him a lot in the water. He didn't remember what she'd said, but he remembered her voice. He'd clung to it like the lifeline it was.

"Pull up a chair," he suggested, trying to sound casual and failing.

"I'm not staying. I only wanted to check on you quick before heading home."

She thought he'd be asleep, Jackson realized. She'd thought to just peek in on him "quick" and then go on her merry way.

She'd thought wrong.

"Sit down, Leila." His voice was harder than he'd intended, and when it appeared she would refuse him again, he spoke more gently. "Leila, please."

Jackson watched the evidence of an internal battle play out on her face. She'd never been able to conceal much. Every thought she had was reflected outwardly for all to see, and right now she was struggling against two warring needs: her need to remain distant and angry, and a strong desire to make certain he was okay. Her caring nature won out, and she pulled up a chair. It was a small victory, but he wouldn't celebrate it. Not yet.

"I suppose you want to know what happened," he began.

She pressed her hands together in her lap and spoke in a monotone. "Your boat sank. Paul already told me."

"Paul?"

"Paul Young, your ER doctor."

"The boat was my dad's."

She snorted. "I'll bet that went over well."

Jackson smiled. Her understatement gave him hope. It was like a joke. If she could joke, then maybe they could talk. *Really* talk. He grabbed the fabric of his hospital gown and said, "I think the gown saved me. He couldn't yell with me looking like this."

She didn't have anything to say to that.

Okay, so she wasn't ready to joke. "Listen, Leila. Thank you. I don't know what would have happened if you—"

"Let's not do this," she interrupted.

"What do you mean, *this*?"

"The whole, *you saved my life* bit."

Earnestly, he leaned forward.

She looked away.

"It's not a *bit*, Leila. You did save my life, and we both know it."

"Fine." She met his eyes. "But I don't need your thanks, and I don't want it."

Jackson sank back into the bed and shook his head in disbelief. "Unbelievable. You won't even let me thank you?"

She sat stubbornly quiet.

"Leila, please."

She jumped up. "Please? Do me a favor, Jackson, and don't ask me for anything."

He spoke slowly, and his anger built with each word he said. "Leila, for thirteen years I've had to wonder what the hell happened that would turn you into such a cold-hearted bitch."

Her mouth fell open. "Don't you *dare* call me that!" she hissed.

He should stop now before he permanently ruined any chance of reconciliation—no matter how slim—but who was he kidding? There would be no reconciliation, and Jackson felt the crush of disappointment in his chest at the realization.

Leila had held onto her anger for thirteen long years, freezing him out of her life with no explanation and no opportunity for him to find out why. The injustice of it all was too much, and whether she'd saved his life or not, she was finally going to listen to him.

"For months, Leila, *months*, I tried to find out what happened, what I did wrong." He used his fingers to tick off a list of everything he'd attempted to get a response from her. "You ignored all my calls and visits to your dorm, you didn't return my emails or letters ..."

Even now, thinking about it made him angry, and Jackson took a deep breath to calm down before continuing.

"I made that trip to Ann Arbor, over four hundred miles each way, I'll remind you, and I did it *twice*, and you couldn't be bothered to even *talk* to me." He shook his head. "I asked that man-hating college roommate of yours for just five minutes of your time, and you know what she told me through the intercom? She said I didn't deserve five seconds."

"Caitlyn wasn't a man-hater," Leila defended. She seated herself again in the chair.

Jackson rolled his eyes. Leila's roommate had founded a campus club called SAP: Standing Against the Patriarchy. Those first few weeks of college, he and Leila had laughed at some of Caitlyn's more outrageous statements, such as her opinion that all cities were patriarchal because skyscrapers were "phallic" in their construction. Apparently, where most of the world viewed a high rise as an architectural marvel, Caitlyn saw something else entirely.

She was a nutcase, and there was no way she hadn't filled Leila's ears with all kinds of nonsense about him, influencing her to cut him off without so much as a "see you later." She'd been the definition of a man-hater, and once Leila had turned on him, Caitlyn had protected her with a single-minded determination that rivaled that of the Secret Service.

"And then there were your parents," Jackson went on. "They wouldn't tell me anything either. About all your dad would say was that he needed to respect your wishes and was sorry it hadn't worked out."

The last time he'd gone to the Molina house, Jackson had nearly cried. Samuel's eyes had been kind, but it was clear where his loyalty lay. He wouldn't give Jackson any information, but to take some of the sting out, he'd wrapped Jackson in one of those bear hugs he'd come to crave.

Afterward, as Jackson turned and stepped off the Molina's porch, he knew he was stepping out of their lives for good. He'd lost Leila and the only man who'd ever loved him. Twice, Samuel had said the words, and each time, he'd pulled Jackson in for one of his signature hugs, giving him one giant thwack on the back to keep it manly.

I love you, son. You're a good kid. Remember that.

It made Jackson want to cry like a baby, even now.

Especially now.

"Leila, what did I do that was so terrible?" he implored. "It was just *poof* and you were gone. It was like you never existed. Like *we'd* never existed."

Leila closed her eyes, and he imagined her counting to five. When she spoke, it was slow and deliberate. "Jackson, you didn't need me or my dad—or my roommate—to tell you what you already knew."

Jackson was about ready to throw something. "What I already knew? Leila, I knew *nothing*. I still don't!"

Leila was quickly losing her cool too. He could see it on her face, and when she next spoke, he could hear it in the sharp edge of her voice that gradually grew louder until she was shouting. "You *betrayed* me, Jackson, and no, you didn't deserve five seconds of my time because that's the choice you made!"

Jackson hushed her and looked toward the doorway, expecting to see someone come to check on them, but when no one did, he continued in a low voice, "What do you mean, *betrayed*? I never betrayed you."

Leila pressed a hand to her temple and rubbed before slowly rising from the chair. "I shouldn't have come. You're a liar. You were a liar then, and you're a liar now."

With that, she turned on her heel and quit the room, leaving Jackson in his hospital bed wondering what in the world had just happened and how she could think he would ever betray her.

Over the next month, Leila kept busy. It was hard work to help her mother move while simultaneously moving herself. The Victorian was a revolving door of arriving and departing boxes, all labeled so nothing would get mixed up.

The condo Carmen had chosen for herself was everything the Victorian wasn't. It was small, with an open floor plan and modern design. It was hard for Leila to picture her mother living there because, while it was light and airy inside, it lacked the whimsical charm of the house Carmen had held so dear. There were no nooks and crannies, no intricate detailing in the woodwork, and no creaks and groans as it shared its history, but it was attractive and efficient and Carmen seemed pleased with it, which was all that really mattered.

Her unit was on the ground floor with two sliding glass doors that opened to a small patio that she was already planning to decorate with pretty planters and white wicker chairs when spring came. For now, the pavers would sit empty through the winter, which had come early this year. The frost on the windowpane spoke more of Christmas than it did of Thanksgiving, the holiday they would celebrate tomorrow.

"Mama," Leila hollered, backing into Carmen's unit from the dimly lit hallway. She adjusted the large box she held. "Where do you want these framed pictures?"

"Right there on the counter is fine, *mija*," Carmen answered from the master bedroom. "I'll need to go through them."

"What about these DVDs?" Elena asked from behind Leila. She carried Carmen's entire movie collection in a large box. "I mean, does anyone even watch DVDs anymore?"

"Mama does." Leila set down her box and pointed. "You can just put them there under the TV. She can sort through them later. So long as we have *It's a Wonderful Life* ready to go for this weekend, she can take her time going through everything."

Elena lowered the box to the floor and reached into it, pulling out a case. "Will *Milo and Otis* make the cut, do you think?" She'd meant it as a joke, but Leila gave the question serious consideration.

She smiled softly as she remembered those cozy evenings with family, popcorn, and soda. Luca had loved that movie. He would always squeeze his eyes tightly shut when Milo careened over the waterfall in his small box, but then he would cheer euphorically when he opened them to see the orange tabby cat safely floating in the tranquil river at the bottom.

"I doubt it," she concluded. "That was a real favorite for a while."

Moving forced a person to make a lot of decisions about a lot of things. Did they throw items away they'd had forever—like the Molina family's full Disney collection, which hadn't been watched in decades—or hang onto it just in case they had a whim to watch *Bambi* again?

Leila had gone through her own belongings with a heavy hand, but so far, Carmen hadn't parted with much, and she'd now added new furniture for the condo to her long list of belongings.

"Most of this furniture won't match my new decor," Carmen had said one day early in the moving process as she'd surveyed the old house. "It was meant for this place, so if you want it, you should keep it."

Leila still felt a little guilty—furnishing the Victorian herself would have cost thousands, so she was saving a great deal of money—but she had to admit, it made solid sense. Over the years, her mama had taken great care to fill the Victorian with furniture worthy of it. Most of those pieces would be all wrong in the modern space of the condo.

Leila wanted it all. She wanted the antique credenza, the English roll-arm sofa, the refinished pedestal dining table, and all the rest. It belonged there. It was a part of the house's story. Part of their family's story.

But it felt a little strange to be in her mother's new home and not recognize much from the old one. The new micro-fiber sofa matched the new slate-colored easy chair, which complemented the new mango wood and iron coffee table. Even the area rug underneath the new furniture was new. Instead of the soft floral rugs like the ones at home, this one had bold colors and geometric patterns that were found also in the throw pillows adorning the couch. Leila never would have imagined her whimsical, old-fashioned mother would have chosen such contemporary decor. It was jarring.

It was a bit of a relief, then, when Leila noticed the old shadow boxes to the right of the gas fireplace. Displayed on them were the same Llado figurines that had rested on the fireplace mantel at the house, and Leila breathed a relaxed sigh. A bit of home was here in this place too.

Elena shifted her attention to another box on the floor—a longer, skinnier one. "What's in here?" she asked.

"The Christmas tree. We'll put it up tomorrow after dinner."

Elena looked skeptical. "On Thanksgiving Day?"

"It's tradition. We decorate it and then watch *It's a Wonderful Life*."

Leila's cousin placed a hand on her hip over the top of the high-waisted mom jeans she wore, which did anything but make her look like a mom. Elena could wear a garbage bag and still look amazing. It wasn't quite fair. "But it's not Christmas yet," she argued. "You can't rush Christmas, or it's not as especial."

Leila smiled. Elena still sometimes said words that started with *s* the way most native Spanish speakers did, with the soft *e* at the beginning—*e*special, *e*space, *e*school.

Shrugging, Leila remarked, "It's never stopped being special for us."

She could remember a time when they'd only gotten real trees for Christmas, but Carmen had always loved to draw out the holiday as long as possible, and after two Christmases in a row with a brown tree, she'd made the difficult decision to invest in a fake one. It wasn't the fullest-looking fake tree around, but with as many decorations as they liked to put on it, an observer could never tell how sparse it was by the time it was all loaded up.

Carmen came into the main room from the back. "Well, that's done. My clothes are all put away, and I'm beat. Let's call it a day."

"Yes, bring out the wine," Elena declared. "*El vino, vino, vino!*"

"What wine? I don't have any." Carmen plopped herself down in the easy chair.

"Yes you do," Elena countered. "I put a bottle of Moscato in the fridge an hour ago." She was already in the kitchen and opening cupboards. "Now, where did we put those glasses?"

Leila pointed to the cabinet to the right of the stove. "In there."

Elena made work of pouring them all a generous glass of the sweet dessert wine, and as she recorked the bottle, she slyly addressed Carmen. "Well, *Tía*, I met a *very* cute older gentleman today."

Leila observed the rosy flush that inexplicably appeared on her mother's cheeks. She turned her head to address her cousin. "Who?"

"Mr. Jarvi, the neighbor of your *mamá*," Elena went on with a wide grin. "Have you met him, *Tía*?" She grabbed two of the glasses and brought them over to the coffee table before heading back to the kitchen for the third.

Carmen shot Leila a quick glance and cleared her throat. "I have, yes."

"Jarvi?" Leila didn't recognize the name. "What's his first name?"

"John," Carmen answered quickly. "He helped me with some boxes yesterday."

"That was nice of him." Leila studied her, not liking the feeling in the pit of her stomach.

"Mm-hmm," her mama responded into her wineglass as she took an uncharacteristic gulp of wine.

Elena carried her own glass into the living room and sat down beside Leila on the couch. "He's very handsome, *Tía*, for an older gentleman."

"Elena, what are you doing?" Leila snapped.

"What?" Elena asked innocently. "I'm just pointing out the obvious."

"Well, don't." The last thing her mama needed was some predatory man living next door. She was still a grieving widow.

Wasn't she?

Leila took another look at her mother, who was avoiding eye contact with her. She was going to have to meet this John Jarvi, she decided. And sooner rather than later.

Carmen changed the subject. "Tell me about your work, Elena. How is it going? Have you met some interesting people?"

"Interesting people" was Carmen Molina's code for men.

Elena launched into the details of her work life, which had drastically improved now that she was on friendly terms with Erin. Everything was roses at work, except for having "the student from hell" in her fourth hour and the fact that she'd backed her car into the superintendent's suburban just yesterday.

"Of all the cars in that lot to hit, it had to be his," Elena lamented before tipping back her glass and swallowing a generous sip.

Leila hadn't heard this story. She hadn't even noticed any damage to Elena's car. Guiltily, she realized she'd been pretty self-involved lately. When she wasn't working, she was moving boxes, and when she wasn't moving boxes—and even when she was—she couldn't keep Jackson out of her mind.

"Oh, dear!" Carmen fretted. "This was yesterday?"

Elena nodded. "After school."

"Is there damage?"

"Not to his vehicle, except for a little scraped off paint, but my car's bumper cracked and fell off."

Leila frowned. "You're driving around without a bumper?" She'd have to lend Elena some money. Teaching was such a noble profession, but it paid diddly squat. Her cousin drove a beater as it was, which was a crying shame.

"Gabe helped me tape it back on until I can afford to get it fixed."

Carmen shot Leila a pointed glance, and Leila could tell her mother was thinking the same thing she was. "You call him 'Gabe'?"

Elena set down her wine. "Yeah, why not?"

But Carmen was old school, and she shook her head disapprovingly. "You can't call him 'Gabe,' Elena. It's not respectful."

Unconcerned, Elena kicked off her shoes and tucked her feet up underneath her. "Everyone else does."

"Don't they all call him 'Gabe the Babe'?" Leila asked. She'd heard Erin and the girls talk about him before. Gabriel Wright was new to town and the youngest superintendent in the district's history. Erin had a love-hate relationship with him and talked about him a lot. Apparently, he was a demanding boss. Leila had never seen him, but she'd heard him described as looking like a Calvin Klein underwear model.

"The women do," Elena answered easily.

Carmen looked scandalized. "Do you?"

"No, *Tía.*"

"Don't you roll your eyes at me, Elena Torres. I know you well. A rescue by a good-looking man? You must now have him in your sights."

"He *rescued* me with a ring of duct tape, *Tía.* Not exactly the tool of a hero. Plus, he has a daughter, and I don't date dads."

Carmen nodded, pleased with Elena's answer. "Good."

But Leila knew Elena well too. Well enough to recognize that her words didn't quite match her body language, which was suddenly very fidgety. Leila suspected that this wouldn't be the last she heard from her cousin about Gabriel Wright.

"Now, let's finish planning for tomorrow's dinner." Carmen grabbed a small notepad and pen off the coffee table. "Who's making the cranberry sauce?"

Thanksgiving dinner had long since been cleaned up at the Maki house, and Jackson sat with Lizzie, Matt, and Virginia in the living room with the game on. Lizzie was stretched out on a recliner, Matt and Jackson sat on opposite sides of the couch, and Virginia was at the dining room table directly behind them working on an impossible-looking puzzle. For the last hour, they'd been enjoying a languorous evening together where conversation ebbed and flowed wherever it wanted. But Jackson didn't feel quite as settled as he looked.

There'd been plenty of shop talk about where things stood with their business venture, which excited him. The legal partnership was in place, they'd named the store *Superior Sporting Goods*, and renovations of their building were already underway. It wouldn't open until late summer, with the grand opening tentatively scheduled for the last Friday in August.

Jackson couldn't wait. He hadn't told Sean or anyone else at the university that he'd be leaving, but he would have to do it soon.

Maybe after the holidays.

He and Lizzie had invited their mother to come on board, but she'd declined. She'd help here and there when they needed it, she promised, but she enjoyed her job at the bookstore too much to leave it. "Besides," she pointed out, "you don't really need me. You'll make a great team, and I'm so very proud of all three of you."

Jackson was proud of his mother, too, and although he hadn't come right out and said it, he thought she knew. Despite all the turmoil, she'd handled herself with such grace these last several weeks.

The divorce was nearly final, and her lawyers had more than come through for her. They wouldn't be allowing Philip to cut her out of anything, and she would receive a hefty sum from the sale of the furniture stores. The house was on the market, and the proceeds of the sale would be split evenly between herself and her soon-to-be ex husband. She was actively looking for a new place, something smaller and closer to downtown, where she could walk to Luca's in the summer.

Virginia didn't need to continue working, but she wanted to. She liked being in the store; greeting half the town as well as the tourists made her feel like she was in the thick of it all. A part of something bigger. It was different than the furniture store, she'd said. More laid back. More fun.

In Carmen Molina, his mother had found a good friend. Jackson never asked, but he wondered if they talked about him and Leila sometimes. If they didn't, it must sit between them like a giant Asian elephant.

Once the excitement of his near-drowning experience had worn off, he hadn't heard Leila's name spoken by anyone. Not his mom, not his sister, and certainly not Carmen when he stopped by the store to visit, even though he got the sense she wanted to. She was warmer to him now than she'd been since his falling out with Leila. She'd hadn't been mean before, just distantly friendly.

Lizzie and Virginia were enormously grateful to Leila, and Jackson knew for a fact that they'd met with her to thank her in person, but he didn't have any details. He'd been dying to ask, but he couldn't bring himself to.

Instead, he threw himself into his work, for both the team and the store, and spent any time he had left over distracting himself with one beautiful blonde after another. So much for turning over a new leaf.

But all he did was think about her. Thoughts of Leila came to mind, unbidden and unwanted, all day long. He'd thought it would get easier, but as time wore on, it only got worse. Every night when he went to bed, and every morning when he woke up, she was there in his mind.

With each passing day, Jackson grew more and more agitated. Leila said he'd betrayed her. How could he have done such a thing without even knowing it? You couldn't *accidentally* betray someone, could you? He had been nothing but loyal to Leila all through high school, and even after she'd left for college, not even his eyes had strayed.

Okay, well, maybe they'd noticed a pretty face a time or two, but surely that didn't constitute a betrayal, and even if it did, she couldn't have known about it. All through high school, girls had thrown themselves at him, and that hadn't stopped when he'd gotten to college, but while he was with Leila, he always shot them down. Always.

Nicolet was a small town and gossip was a way of life here, so it was possible that someone from home had shared a made-up story with her through social media or something. But the problem with that scenario was that Leila would have been on the phone with him immediately, giving him a chance to refute the claims. She wouldn't have just frozen him out. The girl he'd loved would never have done that.

Jackson recalled the last visit he'd made to see her down at the University of Michigan. Nothing had been amiss. They'd had a great weekend, and the only negative to the entire trip had been Leila's insistence that she was gaining the dreaded *freshman fifteen*. Jackson hadn't really noticed, but she was worried enough about it to have mentioned it several times, and he remembered being a little annoyed by it.

Leila had always been paranoid that the fat girl she'd left behind would suddenly reemerge out of nowhere, and he'd dump her like a pair of old hockey gloves. Maybe that should have been his first clue as to how little she thought of him.

He'd been angry with her that night at the hospital, and while the intensity of that emotion had dissipated, Jackson still felt frustrated and bewildered by it all. The more he tried to guess at what had happened, the more those feelings grew. Whatever her reasons, he knew he had deserved a whole lot better than what she'd done to him back then. He'd deserved those five seconds and more.

He deserved better than what he'd gotten his whole life from his old man too. No part of his childhood had been easy, but his last year of high school and his brief stint in college had been particularly brutal periods of time. He'd taken several painful beatings for no good reason. It had taken too long, and it had cost him a father, but he'd finally fought back. Now he could move forward.

It was clear to Jackson that he needed closure with Leila too. He needed to demand an answer. He refused to receive any more punishment from her without knowing the reason for it. But the idea of seeing her again, talking to her—

"What are you thinking about over there, little brother?" Lizzie's voice interrupted.

He nearly jumped. "Hmm?"

His sister observed him with an amused smile from across the room. Reclined as she was, with her feet kicked up and hands resting on her protruding belly, she looked like the human version of a beached manatee. A very pretty manatee, but a manatee nonetheless.

"You were daydreaming."

Matt took his eyes off the television and shot Jackson a glance before addressing his wife. "He's just watching the game."

"Quick Jackson, who's playing?" Lizzie tested.

"Um," Jackson answered, buying some time as he studied the screen. He could identify teams in a matter of seconds. "Vikings versus Patriots."

Lizzie's smile grew. "You weren't watching."

He lifted his hands in surrender. "You got me."

"What were you thinking about?"

"Leila."

That got everyone's attention. All eyes were on him. Matt hit the mute button, Lizzie attempted to sit up and failed on her first and second tries before giving up, and Virginia scooted her chair out from the table and came into the living room to seat herself in the glider beside him.

He should never have opened his mouth. "This is a little scary," he joked.

"Tell us," Lizzie demanded.

Jackson raised his hands again. "There's nothing to tell, but you asked, and that's what I was thinking about."

"The rescue?" his mother asked reverently.

He hadn't stopped thinking about *The Rescue* since it had happened, so it made sense it would be on his mother's mind too. It had been the first thing Matt had given thanks for when they'd sat down to eat. Everyone knew how differently things could have turned out. How lucky he'd been.

But deep down, Jackson knew it had been more than luck. It had been some sort of divine intervention. He never should have survived. That he had, and that out of all the people in Nicolet, it was Leila who was there that day, it had to mean something. He made it to shore for a reason, and he couldn't shake the feeling that he was being given a very clear, very deliberate, second chance. So far, he was kind of blowing it, at least where his love life was concerned.

"She accused me of betraying her," he blurted. "When she came to see me in the hospital."

His sister cranked the lever on the side of her chair, and in a blink, the foot rest disappeared as the chair careened her forward. Reflexively, Matt's hand shot out to keep her from rocking right out of the chair and onto the floor.

Well, that was one way to do it.

"Why would she think that?" Virginia asked at the same time that Lizzie screeched an incredulous, "*What?*"

"I have no idea."

"Did you cheat on her?" Matt asked, eyebrows raised.

Lizzie shot her husband a disgusted glare. "Of course he didn't cheat on her. Leila was the love of his life."

"Then why is it I'd never even heard of her until last month?" Matt looked sincerely skeptical.

Lizzie rolled her eyes. "Because it's painful for him to talk about her."

"Then why did you just bring her up?"

"I didn't! I just asked what he was thinking."

"Yesterday you told me he was always thinking about her, and that's why he's been so distracted."

Lizzie sighed. "Fine, you got me."

Jackson couldn't suppress a laugh. Those two, as in love as they undoubtedly were, really knew how to push each other's buttons.

Virginia, ignoring Matt and Lizzie's banter, regarded Jackson thoughtfully. "I could ask Carmen."

It was a tempting offer, but he shook his head. "I need to speak to Leila myself."

"She'll be at the store tomorrow," Virginia supplied. "She and her cousin are coming in to help with Black Friday."

"You think I should come to the store?"

His mother shrugged. "Why not?"

Jackson thought it over.

Tomorrow. Yes, he could do that. He'd finally have an answer. He'd demand an answer. She wouldn't be able to leave in a huff, at least not easily, and she wouldn't want to cause a scene.

Jackson considered where the most private place for this conversation would be. At a table in the cafe portion of the store? One of the reading nooks?

"She'll be doing most of her work in the back room. It's nice and private," his mom offered, reading his mind.

"Perfect." Suddenly, *tomorrow* seemed simultaneously too soon and too far away.

Chapter 19

THEN

It had been a big day, and as Leila pulled the covers up to her chin and let her head sink into her pillow, she smiled indulgently despite the nervous flutters in her stomach. Worried or not, sometimes climbing into bed at the end of the day was absolute heaven. If only Jackson would call her back, she could sleep easy.

Today was the first day of Christmas break, and Leila had started it off with an hour's worth of chores around the house. Both her parents had gone in early for work and had left her a list of tasks to complete before she joined Carmen at the bookstore for her shift.

Leila loved the bookstore at Christmas. The shop was all decked out for the season, and for six hours, Leila experienced a steady rhythm of customers in and out, the bells on the door chiming like clockwork every few minutes. The bells, the Christmas music, and the smell of the peppermint candy canes in a dish near the register all gave Leila a warm and giddy rush of anticipation for the holidays.

It would be their first Christmas without Luca, and while they were sad sometimes, they were doing okay. More and more, the memories of Luca brought joy instead of pain. During Thanksgiving dinner, there had been more laughter than tears as they reminisced.

They remembered last year's Thanksgiving when Luca had picked all the mushrooms and celery out of the stuffing and hid them in his cloth napkin.

Leila's mama had covered her face as she thought back. "It all fell out in a mashed wad into the washing machine when I went to do the laundry two days later."

They recalled how Luca had pulled down Santa's beard at Tilly's Toy Store when he was four, exposing Tom Tilly as a fraud to the rest of the children waiting in line, and they couldn't stop laughing when Samuel reminded them that Luca refused to make Christmas cookies for Santa that year.

Leila's brother used to love sifting through the ornaments and picking his favorites to hang. He sometimes had a hard time with his fine motor skills, so often they had to help him get them hung where he wanted, but seeing the whole process through Luca's eyes made an ordinary task of tree decorating feel magical.

For Leila, it was a relief to find that the magic persisted despite Luca not being there. It would be her first Christmas with a boyfriend, and everything felt extra special. Neither one of them had said it yet, but she knew she and Jackson loved each other. Why they held back, she couldn't quite say. Leila had known her feelings a long time, but the longer she went without acknowledging them to Jackson, the harder it became to speak the words. She'd tell him soon. It was Christmastime, and love was in the air.

After finishing her shift at the store, she'd kissed her mother goodbye and left to pick up Abby Greene, Freddy's girlfriend. Together, they watched the boys play in their last hockey game before the new year.

Jackson had played well. He assisted two goals but scored none of his own. Leila spotted Philip in the crowd toward the end of the game and could see his displeasure. She and Abby had only stuck around briefly afterward to congratulate the boys before leaving. In a short amount of time, Leila had learned when to give Jackson and Philip their space.

Unfortunately, Jackson hadn't answered any of her calls since she'd been home. Virginia was out of town again, and Leila was struggling not to worry about him being alone with Philip.

It was hard for Leila to watch Jackson twist himself into knots trying to accomplish the unaccomplishable. Nothing he could ever do would make Philip happy. He's said so himself, but those were just words. Leila could see he still tried. He still desperately wanted to make his dad proud. But it was futile.

So, even though she was cozy in her bed, she couldn't quite relax. After tossing and turning for a good hour, she finally got up and tiptoed down the short hallway and out into the living room, Atticus following dutifully behind her. Leila reached into her book basket and got comfortable in the window seat while Atticus looked on with a yawn.

She flipped on the small sconce just above her head that her papa had wired up for her to use as a reading lamp. Its soft glow reflected off the dog's shiny coat, while the twinkling lights of the Christmas tree were mirrored in the darkened windows of her reading nook.

Atticus gave a soft wine.

"It's okay, boy. Lie down."

With a grunt, the dog obeyed, and Leila opened the novel. She'd found it at the store the day before and bought it after reading the back cover. It was a Christmas love story that took place in the mountains of Colorado. The hero had just rescued the heroine from her frozen, half-buried car and taken her to his warm cabin. Things were just getting juicy when she heard a faint but unmistakable knock.

Atticus lifted his head, and his ears twitched. Leila closed her book and listened.

Above the loud thudding of her heart in her ears, she heard it again. Atticus gave a low, abbreviated bark and followed her to the front door, where she peered out onto the porch. Nobody was there.

The knocking sounded again, a little louder and more persistent this time. Atticus let out a full, deep-throated bark.

"Atticus, no!" Leila scolded him in a whisper before they both scurried toward the noise—down the short hall and toward her bedroom.

She ran on her tiptoes back into her room, flipped on the light, and moved the curtains away from the window.

Jackson's face greeted her from the other side. He wore a white tee-shirt and a pair of jeans, and even in the dark she could see he was sporting a shiner around his left eye, which was swollen almost all the way shut.

Leila moved quickly, opening the window and helping Jackson climb into her room. "Oh, Jackson, you're freezing! What happened to you?" She reached out to touch the small gash above his eye, but thought better of it and pulled back her hand.

Instead of answering, he reached for her and drew her close to him in a crushing embrace. His whole body shook in her arms, and against her neck, his breath was hot and ragged. Leila held him, whispering assurances in his ear and telling him everything would be okay in a tremulous voice, even though she wasn't sure it would be. She'd seen him after the game, and his face had been fine then. This wasn't a hockey injury.

His father had done this.

❧

Jackson knew he must be crushing her, but he couldn't help it. He molded himself to Leila as tightly as if she were a solid rock in the midst of a rushing river. If he let go, he'd be swept away forever. In that moment, he felt as though his life depended on her, and he breathed in her coconut scent in ragged gasps.

He needed to get control, but he didn't know how. Even as he fought them, he felt tears dampen his eyes, and he squeezed them shut. The tears fell anyway, heating his skin on their way down his cold, wind-whipped cheeks.

He'd done it again. The old man had struck him again, twice. A right hook to the eye followed by a punch to the gut. Jackson had thrown up right there in the kitchen.

Good, let Philip clean up the ten-piece chicken nugget and large fry Jackson had washed down with a vanilla milkshake on their way home from the rink. At least that would serve as some sort of punishment.

Jackson had taken it from his dad the entire way home while he silently chewed his dinner. Philip tore him apart, piece by piece, play by play. It was nothing out of the ordinary, but when they'd been home twenty minutes and Philip still hadn't run out of steam, Jackson lost his cool. He'd been so worked up, he couldn't even remember his exact words, but basically he'd told his dad to get a life. A stupid move on his part.

In a low voice, so as not to wake up her parents, Jackson shared the story with Leila. He told her everything, back to the very beginning. They sat down on the edge of the bed, holding hands as Atticus snoozed at their feet, and by the time he was done, he felt much calmer. That's always how it was for him with her. He could tell her the hard things, and once he did, he felt a weight lifted.

But when he looked at her with his one good eye, he took in those brown irises, luminous with misery, and her bottom lip that quivered with emotion, and he wondered if the burden he'd unloaded on her was too much.

It was his turn to soothe her. "*Hush,*" he said. "I'm fine."

She shook her head vehemently, unable to speak.

"Listen, I really am. I'm used to this. It'll all blow over in a few days."

He watched as her face crumbled and she broke into a loud, deep sob. Her voice was shrill, slightly hysterical, when she said, "You're *used* to this? Jackson, that's even w-w-worse. You deserve so much better than that."

He hushed her again, but this time because she'd become alarmingly loud and he was afraid she'd wake her parents.

She didn't listen. She went on, growing louder with each word she spoke. "I can't stand it! Look at your eye, Jackson. He hit you hard, and f-for what? You didn't do anything wrong! What is *wrong* with him?"

He pulled her close, giving small shushes as she sobbed, but it was futile, and he knew it. Sure enough, a light switched on, faintly illuminating the short hallway that led to her room, and Jackson listened to two sets of footsteps descend the stairs. Atticus jumped up and ran off to greet them.

"Leila?" Samuel called. "Leila, are you alright?"

Jackson hopped off the bed. It was bad enough he was in her room, which was forbidden territory during the light of day, let alone at one in the morning. He didn't want to add to his troubles by being found on Leila's bed on top of everything else.

"Jackson!" Samuel said in surprise as he passed through the doorway with Carmen right behind him. "What is all this?" He gestured back and forth between them, surely taking in Jackson's black eye, Leila's tear-streaked face, and the open window of her bedroom.

Carmen didn't hesitate. She ducked under Samuel's raised arm that pointed at the window and clucked her tongue. "Oh, Jackson, your eye! Come to the kitchen," she ordered, taking him by the hand.

Samuel stopped them. "Wait. We will certainly tend to the eye, but first I want to know what happened to you, and I want to give you a chance to explain to me why you are here in my daughter's room at this hour of the night."

He spoke calmly, but Samuel's voice was no-nonsense, and Jackson knew the man wouldn't rest until he had the full story. Briefly, Jackson considered lying. He didn't like sharing his dirty laundry with others, and he felt a need to protect his family. He could have easily explained away the black eye as a hockey injury and his presence in Leila's room as just everyday bad teenage boy behavior. But this was Samuel, and Jackson couldn't lie to him. He told him the truth.

"This is not the first time?" Samuel asked when Jackson had finished his condensed version of the story.

"No."

Wordlessly, Carmen turned to the window, closing and locking it with slow, deliberate movements. When she turned back, Jackson noticed her eyes were shiny.

"Oh, Jackson," she murmured. Gently, tenderly, she embraced him. "You came to the right place, *cariño*. Let us help you." A few seconds later, she released him and turned to her husband. "Samuel?"

Samuel sat down on the corner of Leila's bed and ran a hand through his sleep-tousled hair before nodding at Carmen and turning to his daughter. "*Mija*, please go to the kitchen with your mama and brew some *manzanilla* while she gets the first aid kit down. We'll be there shortly."

Reluctantly, Leila followed her mother out of the room, but as she left, she shot Jackson a look of such pure tenderness, Jackson thought he might cry again.

"Sit down, son," Samuel said, patting a spot beside him.

Jackson did as he was told.

"You're eighteen, is that right?"

Jackson nodded.

Samuel scratched at his head. "Child Protective Services wouldn't do much in that case. I'd love to challenge your old man to a duel, but it's not the eighteen hundreds, and I'm not British. About the best I could do in today's world would be to punch his lights out. Shall I head over there?"

Jackson gave a small shake of his head and treated Samuel to an abbreviated smile, careful not to crinkle the skin around his eyes.

Samuel sighed. "No, I think we both know that wouldn't accomplish much, except maybe a night or two in jail for me."

Jackson looked at the floor. "I didn't fight back," he admitted ambivalently.

Resting his hand on the nape of Jackson's neck, Samuel gave a gentle squeeze. "You should never have been in that position in the first place. To have to decide whether to defend yourself against your own father ..." He shook his head. "That's a terrible thing."

The older man's words made Jackson feel a little better. He really was in a lose-lose situation either way, whether he fought back or not. After a few seconds of quiet, Jackson lifted his head and glanced at Samuel. He was stroking at the whiskers of his chin, and a deep furrow creased his brow. Jackson watched him, waiting, until the older man finally seemed to settle on something in his mind.

"You know Jackson, I can call the police. You could press charges."

Jackson's mouth went dry, and he licked his lips. The police? Could he do that? Yes, he decided. To Philip, he could, but the scandal that would result from taking that sort of action would embarrass the whole family. His mother too. "I can't."

"It might be your best bet. I would encourage you to consider it."

"Maybe next time," Jackson said, speaking once more to the floor.

With a gentle touch, Samuel lifted Jackson's chin and turned the boy's head so he could look him square in the eye. "*Mijo*, I don't want there to be a next time."

Jackson lowered his eyes and shrugged.

Samuel sighed in defeat, letting go and putting his arm around Jackson's shoulders. "Alright then. This is what I *can* do. You are welcome here. You come anytime you need. We have a guest room upstairs next to our room, and I sleep as lightly as Atticus does, so I know there won't be any funny business. That room is yours. It's got your name on it, and it's there for you if you need it, no questions asked. But"—he raised one tall finger in the air—"you announce yourself and you come through the front door. No more windows."

Jackson attempted another smile. "Yes, sir."

"No, no. Don't you *sir* me. There's no need for that. You're not in trouble with me or Carmen, son. You have a place here, in our home, Jackson, and if you need us, you come. Understood?"

"Understood." Jackson swallowed past the ache in his throat. "Thank you."

Samuel nodded and gave Jackson's hair a quick tousle with his giant hand. "Now, let's get that eye seen to and have a cup of tea. We'll add some honey tonight."

Jackson had never had a cup of tea in his life, but he sipped it dutifully in the Molinas' kitchen at their small pub table. Between sips, he let Carmen tend to his eye with some homemade ointments she claimed would work wonders over night. Once a bandage was secured over the cut, they gave him a bag of frozen peas, and as soon as he touched it to his face, his phone rang in his pocket.

All eyes were on him as he pulled it out and checked the number. "It's my dad," he said unnecessarily.

Samuel, seated across from him, reached out his hand. His face was grim. "May I?"

Jackson debated. There was no way Samuel would pretend everything was a-okay fine. It wouldn't be a call where pleasantries were exchanged between the two men, and that might mean there'd be hell to pay with Philip later, but then again, what did he have to lose? There'd be hell to pay anyway since he'd run off with his dad's BMW in the middle of the night. Jackson had just grabbed the first set of keys he could find and high-tailed it out of there.

One thing might work to his advantage, though. Samuel could be an imposing man. Even his *voice* was imposing, deep and full-bodied. Jackson suspected Leila's father could make a formidable adversary if necessary, and he was suddenly inordinately grateful to have Leila's burly dad on his side. Jackson passed him the phone and met Leila's wide eyes. He imagined he looked just as anxious.

Samuel moved from the kitchen to the dining room on the other side of the wall, but they could still hear him when he answered Jackson's phone, his voice even and polite.

"Hello Mr. Lang, this is Samuel Molina ... Yes, he is ... Oh, I'm afraid I can't do that. He'll be staying here with us the rest of the night ... No, Mr. Lang, that won't be happening ... Well, you can certainly try, but I wouldn't advise it."

Seconds ticked by in silence, and Jackson went crazy trying to imagine what his father was saying on the other end of the line.

Finally, Samuel spoke again, his tone and cadence easy and relaxed. "That's some real liquid courage you've got there, Mr. Lang, but you should know a police car will be here in the driveway to greet you, and ... Oh, really? I wonder what they'll say about the mess you made of your boy's face, and I wonder what they'll think of you driving drunk to force him back home against his will."

Jackson didn't know how Samuel maintained such a level of calm. There was no way Philip was being anything but awful on the other end of the line, especially if he'd been drinking, but Leila's father was completely unfazed by it, refusing to take the bait. It must be driving his own father into a fit of rage.

"Mama—" Leila began in a whisper.

Carmen hushed her.

"... Oh, you can bet on that, Mr. Lang," Samuel continued, "and you can bet on another thing too. If you *ever* lay a hand on your son again, you might as well voluntarily stop breathing ... Why? Because you'll never engage in that particular activity again once I'm done with you, that's why ... Hmm, I see. Well, I'm perfectly willing to take that chance. Good night, Mr. Lang. I'll be praying to St. Peter to help you tame that awful temper of yours."

Jackson and Leila looked at each other with mouths agape.

Carmen's lips twitched at the corners. "Samuel always prays for his ene-mies," she said, collecting their empty cups.

A half hour and a fresh bag of frozen peas later, Samuel and Carmen each hugged Jackson goodnight before heading upstairs.

"You have five minutes," Samuel warned, "and not a minute more. Come on Atticus." He gave a low whistle. "Give these two lovebirds some privacy."

Jackson listened to the creaking of the steps and the tapping of the dog's nails on the hardwood as all three made their way up the stairs. He and Leila stood in the living room, silent and suddenly awkward with one another as the mantel clock ticked away the seconds and the Christmas tree lights sparkled with joy over the coming birth of the Molinas' Saviour.

"Want to sit?" Leila asked, wringing her hands nervously.

Jackson nodded, and they moved to the couch. He set a hand towel Carmen had given him down on the coffee table. She hadn't wanted him to put the peas directly against his skin, but the ice cold felt so good over his throbbing eye, he couldn't help it.

Leila looked at him uncertainly. Something had shifted between them. There was a tension he didn't like. What if she saw him differently now? What if she saw him as weak? He wouldn't be able to bear it if she did.

"Leila—" he began tentatively.

"I hate your dad, Jackson," she blurted. "I'm sorry, but it's true. I hate what he did to you, and I wish you didn't ever have to go back. Where is your mom? I don't know why she's always gone, but she can't leave you alone with him anymore. It's not right."

"She'll be home tomorrow," he told her. "Everything will be better tomorrow."

"What will she say about your eye?"

He shrugged. "She'll fawn all over me the way your mom did."

"Does it hurt?" Leila moved his hand away so she could see it again, and she winced when it came into view.

This was his chance to show her he was tough. He set the peas down on the towel. "Nah, it's not that bad."

"Not that bad? Jackson, it looks awful! I'd be a crying mess right now. I kind of am anyway, and it's not even my eye. How can you be so ... so *calm* about all this?"

He shrugged again, inwardly pleased that she did look about to cry. He didn't really want her to be sad, but it was kind of nice knowing she cared so much.

"What will you tell her?"

"My mom? I'll tell her I took a stick to the eye. It happens all the time."

"I want to kiss it," she said fervently. "I want to kiss it and make it better. Jackson, I don't want any more bad things to happen to you because ... because I love you. I really, really love you, and I don't—" Her voice broke, and she squeezed her eyes shut to hold back the tears, but one escaped anyway.

A joyous sunburst opened inside of Jackson, and he moved closer, wiping the solitary tear away with his thumb.

Leila loved him.

Just like that, it didn't matter that his father didn't. It didn't matter that his mom was never home or that Lizzie rarely called. It didn't matter if his hockey rut was permanent or temporary, or that after three full years, nobody at his high school really knew him at all.

She did. Leila knew him, and she loved him.

She opened her eyes and whispered it again as another tear slid down her cheek.

Tenderly, he wiped at that one too. "I've loved you from that first day, and I'll never stop, I swear."

A slow smile curved her lips, and then she was laughing and crying and burying her face in his neck as she hugged him close. He felt the warm wetness of her tears on his skin and marveled at the intensity of a love so strong, he knew neither one of them would ever be the same again. This moment with Leila would be etched in the front of his mind forever.

Seated as they were, angled on the sofa, Jackson couldn't get close enough to her, so he stood them both up, cupping Leila's arms in his hands. She looked adorably confused and wet-cheeked as he brought her to her feet, but when he touched a thumb to her mouth and gently brushed it over her lips, they parted automatically in anticipation.

It was his turn to smile. She wanted to be kissed. It was written all over her face that she craved it just the way he did.

She was so beautiful to him, beautiful down to the depths of her soul. No part of her could ever disappoint him. Nothing she could ever do would change the way he felt about her. Slowly, he dipped his head towards her, experiencing the tickle of her warm breath as it floated against his own lips.

And then he was kissing her, loving her mouth with his, and showing her with every fiercely tender touch of their lips just how much. He couldn't give nearly enough of himself to her, and he couldn't get enough from her either. She was all softness and warmth, and for one crazed moment, he was pierced by a longing so fierce, he thought he might die from the need of her.

He forced himself to pull away. It was a small consolation when she protested, and he rested his forehead against hers as he tried to pull himself together.

He wasn't nearly good enough for her—he knew that—but he'd never stop trying to be. She made him want to work every day to be worthy of her. Leila deserved the very best of him, and he wouldn't let her down.

When she whispered that she loved him a third time, Jackson felt like a king. Anything was possible. No dream was too big. No mountain too high. No shadow too dark. With Leila by his side, he could do anything.

Four months later, Leila stared at a letter that had come in the mail. She'd read it through twice. Not only had she gotten into the University of Michigan, she'd been awarded enough scholarship money to make the tuition affordable for them. She'd hunted down every scholarship imaginable, spending weeks of her time writing essays and filling out applications. Obviously, it had paid off because, if she and her parents had calculated all the scholarships correctly, she'd only have to pay six thousand dollars each semester, and that included room and board. It was unbelievable, really.

All year the plan had been to go to Nicolet State, mostly because tuition was completely covered by virtue of her father's employment there. She'd live at home and get a free education. What could be better than that?

Well, it turned out that the University of Michigan, although not exactly free, just might be better than that.

At the very last minute, Leila's parents had encouraged her to apply, just to see what would happen and to keep her options open. Leila knew they hadn't expected this—a prestigious, highly coveted U of M education for a few thousand dollars? It was insane!

It was also a no-brainer. Of course she had to go. So why was she hesitating?

It was complicated. For one thing, the head and the heart didn't always want the same things, and her heart wanted to be near Jackson always and forever. That was the obvious reason, and the pull to stay in Nicolet with him was strong.

But another pull existed, and it was equally powerful. Whether or not it made sense, Leila felt she owed it to Luca to give a hundred percent all the time. She couldn't squander a single opportunity because his disability and eventual death had stripped him of all of his. She needed to live *bigger* because she was living for them both. Even when he'd been alive, she'd felt this way. Now that he was gone, she put even more pressure on herself. She'd taken six

Advanced Placement classes this year, for goodness' sake. *Six*! She couldn't say no to something like this.

She absolutely could not. But how could she leave Jackson?

A move like this one, to a place over six hours away by car, that could be the kiss of death for their relationship. What if they broke up?

Leila couldn't even think of it. The contents of her stomach revolted at even a hint that they might be separated. She needed him, and he needed her.

Poor Jackson! He'd been counting on a scholarship to play hockey somewhere else, specifically Michigan State in Lansing where his sister had attended. But no scholarships had been offered, not from Michigan State nor anyplace else, including Nicolet State, where his father had pulled all the strings he could think of. To his chagrin, the most Philip had been able to manage was the chance for Jackson to be a walk-on player to the team. Meaning, they'd let him try out, and if he was good enough, he'd play with no scholarship money that first year. After that, depending on how he did, they'd talk.

Jackson's confidence had taken a real hit, and so had whatever remained of his relationship with Philip. In Philip's eyes, if Jackson had only tried harder, he would have had offers. It wasn't about the scholarship money, obviously. The Langs had money to spare. For Philip, it was all about the status. The bragging rights. The ability to beat his chest and say, "My boy got a full ride to play for Nicolet State University."

The only thing that was keeping Jackson from sinking too low was the knowledge that there was a silver lining to his plan to go to Nicolet State and attempt to walk onto the team: They'd be together, he and Leila. They'd do the college thing side by side. He didn't know she'd applied anywhere else. He didn't know she was going to leave him behind.

Leila clutched her stomach and tried not to gag.

Chapter 20

NOW

It was Black Friday, the official start of the Christmas shopping season. Jackson had never understood why people got into it so much. Shopping on the best of days was a type of excruciating torture for him. Hitting the stores on a day when the entire town had the same idea? Everyone jostling everyone else just to be the first in line and through the doors, and all for something stupid like a new flatscreen?

No thanks. No deal was that good.

Today would be the first time Jackson ventured out and into a retail store the day after Thanksgiving, but he had a good reason for breaking with tradition, and it had nothing to do with scoring a deal.

Instead, if he was lucky, he'd score an explanation, and if he was really, really lucky, he might just win the grandest of all prizes: a reconciliation with Leila.

He admitted it. He wanted her back. She'd hurt him, yes, but Lizzie was right: She was still the love of his life. The truth was, the hope for a second chance with Leila had been hanging out in the deep recesses of his mind since she'd first frozen him out, and it had never gone away.

He wanted a return to what they'd had together once, and the very real possibility that it might not happen made his heart ache painfully inside his chest.

Jackson dragged his feet for most of the morning, coming up with excuses to delay the trip across town to Luca's Book Cafe. He was definitely going to go, but he needed to get his head on straight first.

So, he dilly-dallied in the kitchen for a time, emptying the dishwasher and scrubbing out the fridge and microwave, the result of which would have made his mother proud. He vacuumed the living room and even moved the furniture to get the dust bunnies out from underneath the couch and loveseat. He stripped his bed and had almost fully remade it when he stopped in the action of stuffing a pillow into a pillowcase.

He was officially stalling now, and he didn't like it. It made him feel weak. Whatever Leila might throw at him, he could take it. It was past time to man up, be tough.

So what if she rejected him? She'd already done that, and he'd survived. He ignored the rumpus of butterflies in his stomach, stirring up his morning coffee in a way that made him wonder why he bothered with the stuff.

A look outside his bedroom window told him he'd need to wear more than just the jeans and lightweight wool sweater he currently had on. The wind was kicking up, and the low, thick clouds had that slate grey hue that told of coming snow with far more accuracy than any meteorologist. Jackson grabbed his coat and threw on his Merrell boots for good measure.

By the time he parallel parked his Blazer in an open spot in front of Trader Truffles across the street from Luca's Book Cafe, it was five minutes to noon. He thanked his lucky stars that he'd located a spot so easily on such a busy day, and as he turned off the engine, he found himself fervently hoping his luck would hold.

A light dusting of snow covered the roads and sidewalks, and as Jackson opened his car door to the chill of the outside, he turned up the collar of his coat and braced himself for the cold bluster of the wind. A quick glance behind him told him it was snowing out over Lake Superior. By late afternoon, Nicolet would have three inches of accumulation from this system, and by midnight they'd have half a foot.

Jackson didn't mind the snow. Especially this time of year. The Christmas season without snow wouldn't feel like Christmas to him at all.

Before crossing the road, he looked around him, up and down Main Street, and saw that most of the storefront windows were decorated on the inside, and the downtown's exterior was also fully decked out for the holidays. Christmas wreathes had already replaced the fall harvest decor that just yesterday had hung on the lampposts that lined the street, and the small trees dotting the cobbled sidewalk were now strung with white twinkle lights. Overnight, the downtown had transformed into a winter wonderland, complete with a light dusting of soft, white snow.

As he took it all in, Jackson felt himself grow warm from the inside out. There was something really special about this time of the year that even he, a man who far too often had been accused of shallow emotions, could sense. One look at a few wreaths, and he'd already caught the holiday spirit, and he wanted someone beside him to share it with.

He wanted Leila.

A car stopped for him, and after waving his thanks, Jackson crossed the street. Carmen's storefront was decorated beautifully, just as it was every year. The two large display windows on either side of the door were framed with lit garland, complete with dangling silver and gold ornaments. Arranged on the inside was an impressive collection of Santas, including a Santa kneeling beside a manger holding a sleeping baby Jesus. There was also a display of a dozen outward-facing Christmas books.

Jackson stopped briefly to take it all in and give himself one last moment to prepare himself for whatever would meet him on the other side of the bookshop's door. *The Polar Express* and O. Henry's *The Gift of the Magi* were propped up in the snowy scene along with *A Christmas Carol* by Charles Dickens. Around the display, a train set Jackson recognized from Samuel's collection chugged along, and the sight of that alone tugged at his heartstrings. Thoughts of Samuel aside, Christmastime always made him feel like this: a kind of contentment mixed with a longing he couldn't quite name, except this year he could.

For the love of a girl, he heard the echo of Samuel's voice say.

It was time to go inside and see about that girl. Jackson took a deep breath and pushed through the door.

As he stepped into the shop, he was greeted with smells of freshly brewed coffee, new books, and—although he was no spice connoisseur—what he thought might be a hint of nutmeg and cinnamon. Burl Ives played quietly in the background, and in the children's section, little kids seated in the laps of their parents listened with rapt attention to a reading from *The Polar Express* by a girl with a lilting southern accent. Wearing a Santa hat, she sat in a chair in front of a large balsam fir that was decorated in reds and golds.

The area behind the register was empty, and a man who looked vaguely familiar stood at the counter, waiting. As Jackson passed, they exchanged the curiously friendly smiles of two people who recognized one another but couldn't figure out how.

A quick scan of the room told him Leila wasn't in the store. Either she was out on some errand, or she was in the back. The girl reading to the kids and the two identical twins working behind the coffee bar were the only visible staff.

Jackson figured that wouldn't be the case for long, not with the store as busy as it was, so he walked to an empty armchair in the travel section and sat down to wait. He settled in, resting his ankle on his knee. Outwardly, he knew he looked nice and calm—just a guy relaxing in a bookshop after too much turkey the day before—but on the inside, he was wound more tightly than a guitar string.

A book rested on the table beside his chair, and he glanced at it. It was a hardcover copy of *To Kill a Mockingbird*. "No way," he breathed, picking it up and studying the cover. This was some irony fit for an Alanis Morissette song.

Jackson flipped through the pages and was brought back in time to a conversation between himself and Leila shortly after high school graduation. They'd gone out for pizza to celebrate Leila's acceptance to the University of Michigan. Jackson remembered how proud he'd been of her that day.

And yes, distraught, too, but only because he knew how much he'd miss her.

He hadn't felt the least bit worried that the distance would prove fatal for a relationship he considered more solid than the iron ore mined around Nicolet. Obviously, he'd been mistaken about that. But that day at 906 Pizza, Jackson had been blissfully unaware of what was to come, and while they waited for their food, he happily engaged in a game Leila liked to play where they mapped out their future. They chose their careers, named their imaginary children and pets, picked out their future house—which for Leila was always her parents' house.

If he remembered correctly, on that particular day, she'd named their daughter *Reya* and their son *Langston*. He remembered those names vividly because he'd vetoed them both. Everyone would call their daughter "diar*reya*," he'd said, and their son could *not* have the name Langston Lang. They'd laughed long and hard at that.

"And we'll have a couple of dogs," Leila had continued.

Jackson questioned that too. His limited experience with Atticus was enough to tell him one dog was plenty.

"Two," she'd insisted. And they had to be yellow labs, and they had to be called Jem and Scout. Their family could never be complete without them.

When he'd asked where she'd come up with the names, she'd told him they were two characters—a brother and a sister—from her favorite book, *To Kill a Mockingbird*. She made him promise to read it, and he'd bought it the very next day.

Carmen Molina's voice pulled Jackson back to the present. "You're in luck," she announced, addressing the gentleman at the register.

Jackson set down *To Kill a Mockingbird* and watched the man smile. "Wonderful," he said.

Book in hand, Carmen entered the space behind the counter and passed it over to him. He flipped through some pages and nodded, obviously pleased.

"It took a lot longer than it should have to come," she apologized, "but it's the holidays. I'm just glad you won't leave here empty-handed this time."

The man told her not to worry about it. "Besides," he added, "I like having an excuse to come in here and chat with you and Virginia. Your smiles do a man's heart good."

Jackson watched Carmen blush a pretty pink. She was still a beautiful woman after all these years, he noted, and she wore her long, silver hair well.

"It's always nice to see you, Robert."

Robert. Now Jackson could place the man. It was Robert Taylor, the mayor. He'd seen him around before but had never been introduced. All he knew about the mayor was that he was the ex husband to the woman who now hung on his father's arm. Would that make Jackson and Robert some kind of ex relatives?

Of course not. There wasn't a word for what they were. Maybe he should invent one.

"How are those puppies doing?" Carmen asked.

"Doing good," Robert replied. "All ten. Five are already spoken for. Are you interested in one for yourself?"

She lifted her hands and laughed. "Oh, no. Been there, done that. Leila used to run our dog for hours, and he still had enough energy left over to chew up my baseboards. He even ripped open one of our mattresses and pulled out all the stuffing. That was a fun mess to clean up."

Robert laughed along with her.

Atticus.

Jackson hadn't thought about Atticus for a long time, and now already today he'd come to mind twice. He'd been a great dog, destructive tendencies aside.

After a little more small talk, the mayor left the store, and Jackson got up to greet Carmen, who was taking a moment to smooth out some bills in the till.

Seeing him approach, she looked up and smiled warmly. "Hello there, Jackson. Are you here for your mother, dear? She's in the back."

"No. But I can go say hi to her. I'm actually looking for Leila."

Her hands stilled. "Oh?"

"Is she here?"

"No, but she'll be back. She and Elena are grabbing some lunch for all of us. Would you like to stay and wait for her?"

"If that's okay."

Carmen smiled. "It's more than okay, dear." She looked at him a long moment before shaking her head. "Finally."

He was taken aback. What did she mean, *finally?*

Reading his mind, Carmen shook her head again. "I just mean you are both now ready to talk. And to listen. Both of you at the same time."

He studied his feet before meeting her eyes again, which were warm and filled with compassion. She'd always had such kind eyes and such a tender heart. "I hope you're right about that."

"I know my Leila, and she is ready. Now, what will come of this talk?" She lifted her shoulders in a shrug. "Lord knows. But he's the one who brought you together all those years ago on the river, and then again last month in such a powerful way. There must be some reason." She held up her hands. "I don't know what that reason is, mind you, but there *is* a reason. And so when Leila gets here, you take the back room for privacy, hmm? And take your time. Our lunch will keep."

There was so much Jackson wanted to say. In the end, he settled for two words. "Thank you."

She nodded. "Go let your mother know you're here. She's back there now, working on an order."

Just as Jackson entered the back room and spotted his mother, Leila burst through the exterior door, bags in hand, trailed by a wintry breeze and a beautiful woman Jackson recognized from pictures long ago—Leila's cousin from Puerto Rico.

Elena, he remembered.

She recognized him, too, it appeared, because her eyes immediately widened, and her red, lipsticked lips stretched into a broad grin. "Hel-lo there," she greeted, looking him over as cold seeped in through the open door behind her.

Leila stopped in her tracks, and Elena, closing the door gently, reached for the food bags in her cousin's hands. She gave Leila a small nudge and murmured something to her in Spanish. Leila frowned and shook her head.

Did that mean Elena was on his side? Maybe.

Jackson treated her to a tentative smile, which she returned in full.

"I recognize you from Leila's old pictures. I am Elena."

His mother jumped up from her desk and introduced him properly.

"Nice to meet you." He shook Elena's hand.

"Let's give them some privacy, Elena," Virginia prompted.

Leila wasn't having it. "We don't need privacy. Please, both of you stay."

"Oh, you need privacy alright." Elena winked at Jackson and let Virginia lead the way out.

As his mother pulled the door closed behind them, she gave him a smile of encouragement.

He and Leila stood for several seconds too long, awkwardly frozen in place.

"What are you doing here?" Leila finally asked.

Jackson couldn't think of how to finesse his way into this discussion, and he didn't know how long they'd have anyway. Curiously, all the butterflies he'd had earlier were gone, leaving behind a determination and resolve to speak the raw and unfiltered truth, straight from the heart. He took one step forward, closer to her. "I'm not sleeping well," he began, "and I can't focus on anything when I'm awake."

She raised her eyebrows. "I'm not your doctor."

"Maybe not, but you're the only one who can cure me."

"That's a terrible line."

"It's not a line." He took another step closer, determined to break through the wall she'd erected between them. Even with her face set in hard lines, she was beautiful. A beautiful stranger. It was a face he'd known so well once. Those lips used to curve into a smile whenever he looked at her. Now they pulled down at the corners. She didn't want his eyes on her now, and that knowledge was crushing.

"Leila, I have never gotten over losing you." When she didn't react to that, he went on. "I need to know what happened. Please. You loved me once—or at least it seemed like you did. Maybe I was mistaken."

The lightly flung arrow hit its mark. He could see it in her face, and it was gratifying. That wall wasn't so impenetrable after all.

"Stop it, Jackson."

"I can't stop, don't you see? If I could, I'd just walk away like you did and never look back. But I've tried, okay? And I can't. I'm asking you to spell it out for me, out of respect for what we used to have. Tell me what happened."

Some of the tension left her, and she sighed. "Jackson, we already did this at the hospital. We're reliving the same conversation."

He nodded. "And getting nowhere. So let's finally lay it all out there. You mentioned betrayal at the hospital, and I want to know why."

She expelled another breath, this time in exasperation. "You *know* why! That's why this is so infuriating!"

"I need to know," he repeated.

Leila chewed her lip as she considered him. "You're really going to make me tell you what you did?"

"Yes, because I don't *know*. That's what I keep telling you."

She threw up her hands and stepped around him. "Fine," she said as she sat down.

His heart missed a beat. Finally! They were going to talk. Really talk. She was sitting down and everything. It didn't matter that she was annoyed. It was progress.

Jackson rounded his mother's desk and dragged her chair to the other side. Leila waited for him to be seated before she spoke.

"As stupid as it is to tell you something you already know, here goes."

She took a deep breath.

"I came home, Jackson. To surprise you. It was a Friday toward the end of October, and it was a last-minute decision when one of my afternoon classes got canceled. I tried to get here to watch the last period of your game—I think you were playing Minnesota Duluth—but I missed it.

"You'd already left, but I found out from some people that the whole team was going to this afterparty in an apartment across from that little sub shop on Third Street, so I went home quick to drop off my stuff and say hi to my parents. I thought about calling you, but I really wanted to surprise you in person, so ..."

Jackson felt his heart sink. He remembered that night, or rather, he *didn't* remember it. It was the night that had caused him to swear off alcohol forever.

"It was a huge party, really loud and crowded," she continued, "but I found you in an upstairs living room. You were sitting on a couch when I came in."

Jackson's mouth felt excessively dry, and he licked his lips. "I didn't see you."

She rolled her eyes. "I know you didn't. You were a little busy with Amelia Channing. She was straddling your lap and kissing your face off."

Jackson's mouth hung open. He did *not* remember that. Granted, it was a long time ago, but he didn't recall Amelia even being at that party. That said, he didn't remember much about that night in general.

Half-heartedly, he'd joined his teammates at the apartment everyone called "The Hockey House" to celebrate their win against Duluth. It was the third and final game he'd seen ice time in. His coaches, impressed with his performance in practice, had allowed him to suit up and play. Unfortunately, his success during the week in practice didn't carry over to the weekend games, and his coaches were left frustrated and scratching their heads. He was an inconsistent and undependable member of the team, and even though Jackson knew what the problem was—or *who* the problem was—he had no idea how to fix it.

That game was the very last time his father had ever watched him skate. At the end of that first semester of college, Jackson quit school, quit the team, and joined the WHL in western Canada where he'd licked his wounds and played for a measly twenty grand a year for five years.

He shouldn't have quit the team and school, he knew that now, but he'd been young and stupid and Leila's rejection on top of everything else was more than he could handle. And so he'd walked away, leaving his hometown and everyone there behind.

"Don't you have anything to say?" Leila asked incredulously.

"I'm sorry," Jackson said. "I don't remember that about me and Amelia, and I guess I'm just—I'm trying to process it or find some inkling of a memory of it."

Tough chance of that happening. Normally at those afterparties he sipped on the same beer or two all night, having long since decided that the Lang family already had one drunk too many, but that night he'd really done himself in.

He'd gone to that party, found a place upstairs away from the crowd, and drowned himself in a bottle of whiskey.

He'd gotten to the party at ten o'clock, and he must have fallen asleep or passed out, because the next thing he knew it was four in the morning and he'd thrown up all over himself.

If Leila had shown up there and seen what she said she'd seen, she had witnessed Amelia kissing a nearly comatose man.

"I'm sorry, Leila," he repeated. "I don't—What you saw, I don't think it was what it looked like."

"What do you mean? It was exactly what it looked like!" she shot back. "You cheated on me with Amelia." She leaned forward. "*Amelia Channing*, Jackson, of all people. How could you? And now you get to claim this, this selective amnesia. How convenient for you."

Jackson rubbed the back of his neck. There was no excuse he could give that would sound good to his own ears, let alone Leila's. She'd hated it when he would have even the occasional drink in high school and college. He'd tried to reassure her, but she'd been adamant that nothing good could come of it, and he should have listened to her.

He'd always known how she felt about parties like the one he'd gone to that night, but he'd been trying to bond with the guys off the ice, and partying was what they did. It was definitely a lot more fun than hanging out in his dorm room alone, which is what he would have been doing if he hadn't gone along with them.

Unfortunately, he couldn't excuse his alleged behavior with Amelia by telling Leila he had been too drunk to know what he was doing, and that he didn't even remember it. It was the truth, but as far as excuses went, it was a lousy one. He only had himself to blame for having put himself in that kind of position in the first place. Amnesia would have been far preferable to the truth that he had simply been black-out drunk that night.

"I'm sorry you came home to surprise me and had to see that," he finally responded. "I can't imagine how you must have felt, and I'm really sorry. It wasn't intentional, and I don't have any memory of it happening, which I hope you can believe."

As he filled her in on the details of the story, starting with the tantrum his father had thrown after the game and ending with the bottle of whiskey, Jackson watched her hard-set features soften some—not quite to a place of forgiveness, but to something less than anger at least. When he'd finished, she was quiet as she mulled it all over. He gave her some time.

It looked like she was about to ask a question, but at the last minute, she changed her mind and said, "Whatever, it's all in the past anyway."

He leaned forward and searched her eyes. "Is it?" he asked softly.

She looked away. "What are you asking me?"

"I'm asking if that's really what you want, for everything to stay in the past. Nothing for the present. Nothing for the future."

Leila shook her head and stared at some distant point behind him. "I don't know what you mean."

"I think you do."

She met his eyes fully. "I can't do this right now."

"Why not?"

She gestured at the door. "Because I'm-I'm working. I have things to do here today."

"Your mom's fine with us doing this now. And I don't know about you, but I need to finish this today, one way or the other. I can't walk away from here until I know."

She scoffed. "Until you know *what*, Jackson?"

He took a deep breath. This was it. "If you still have feelings for me the way I do for you," he said quietly.

She stared at him, first in shock, and then with such an obvious and aching yearning that for a second he felt hope. But then that stubborn set of her jaw returned, and his hopes were dashed into tiny bits.

"No. I'm sorry. I don't have those kinds of feelings for you anymore, Jackson."

He searched her face. Her mouth and jaw were hard, but her eyes told a different story. They reflected a depth of longing that matched his own.

"Liar," he whispered, reaching for her.

"What are you doing?" she protested as he pulled her to her feet.

"This," he answered harshly before claiming her mouth with his.

Leila had no time to react. No time to engage her defenses. It was as if they'd pressed rewind and they were kids again. Two teenagers in love, united, fused together with their mouths and bound by their souls.

Jackson's lips were full and oh-so soft, just as she remembered, but the kiss itself was anything but. It was crushing and violent, designed to show her the intensity of the feelings he still had for her, and while her head told her to pull away, Leila's heart wanted more, and she let herself go.

Sensing her acquiescence, Jackson made a noise in the back of his throat and gathered her firmly to himself, pressing their bodies together and molding her shape against his own. Every inch of her skin prickled, desperate for his touch. His hands splayed across her back, settling briefly on her hips before moving to tangle themselves in her hair. The kiss deepened even further. Full of need, it took on a life of its own. Leila wanted to drown in it. She wanted more. She wanted ...

Abruptly, she pulled back and pushed him away. "Stop, Jackson."

Jackson stepped back, his chest heaving as he pressed the back of his hand to his mouth. His eyes searched hers as he allowed his breathing to slow. "Tell me again you don't have feelings for me," he finally said. "Tell me, and that'll be it. I'll close the door on us for good and finally move the hell on with my life.

I've been stuck. All these years, Leila, I've been stuck on you. From that very first day in the woods when you sent me head first in love with you."

He shook his head and gave a harsh laugh. "I love you, Leila. I always have. I've been limping along for years. Never letting myself feel anything real for anyone else. Picking women more shallow than a mud puddle to make sure I *couldn't* feel anything real. But I can't do it anymore. I can't live like that anymore."

Leila felt dizzy. She needed to sit, but all she wanted to do was run far away to some remote place where she could sit in solitude and sort through her thoughts one by one, because at the moment, she was more confused by her own warring desires than she'd ever been before.

She wanted to laugh; she wanted to cry. She wanted to be held in Jackson's arms forever; she never wanted to see him again.

Jackson continued on, filling the silence. "I finally have good things happening for me. I'm free of Philip for the first time in my life, and you have no idea how strange and how amazing that is. Leila, I have so much to tell you. It's like the sun is finally popping out after months of rain. I want to stand in the sunshine with you. I want the life we talked about." He chuckled, "I'll even let you name our son Langston if you really want to."

Leila didn't smile. She couldn't. What he was saying, what she was feeling ... it didn't make sense. She wanted it to, but it didn't. Something was wrong with both of them. Normal people did not carry a torch for their high school sweetheart into their thirties like this. It just didn't happen. "Listen, Jackson," she began, her voice soft. "It was a long time ago. We had a very sweet romance, made some mistakes, and then it ended. I forgive what happened. We can let it go now, both of us. Nobody meets the love of their life at seventeen years old."

Jackson was vehement in his response. "You're wrong. It happens sometimes. You can meet the love of your life as a dumb teenager. I did."

She shook her head, but she could feel some of her resistance crumbling. Would it be so bad to try again? They had some baggage to unpack, but things had been good once. There was no reason it couldn't be again. Why, then, was she hesitating? Why were alarm bells sounding in her head?

"What we had, it's still right here in front of us," Jackson persuaded. "Right within reach. But you need to be honest with me and with yourself. Yes, I messed up that night, but not in the way you thought. I drank myself into a stupor, and I know I'm responsible for what happened after, and I'm sorry for it. You have no idea how sorry.

"But I don't drink anymore. I haven't had a drink since that night, and I won't ever again. I don't even want it. All I want is you. I want us to be together."

The walls were closing in on her, and all over something that felt a lot like ... fear. It was a fear she couldn't even name. All Leila knew was she needed Jackson to leave. She needed a moment—or several moments—to get a grip on herself and on her thoughts.

The warning bells grew louder. He made it sound like it would be so easy, but it wouldn't be. Too much had happened to go back to the way things were, just like that. They were different people now. They'd been living completely separate lives. Leila's voice was thick and her eyes burned when she next spoke. "It's a small town, Jackson, and you've developed quite a reputation for yourself with the ladies."

He winced. "I haven't been a monk," he admitted softly. "I've done a lot of things I'm not proud of. But that's the beauty of fresh starts. I got a second chance that day in the water, Leila. There's a reason you were the one who saved me. Of all the people who could have been there, it was you. We can have a second chance, too, if we want it."

Leila's chin quivered when she whispered. "This is crazy, Jackson. I'm a thirty-year-old woman. We were just kids then. Nobody feels real love when they're kids."

"Stop that. Don't diminish what we had. I don't care how old we were. It was the real thing."

She shook her head. "I can't—I can't explain why, I'm just—"

"You're scared," he finished for her.

She looked into his turquoise eyes and saw the satisfaction there. He knew he'd found the truth.

"You're just scared," he repeated in a whisper.

The alarms reached a fever pitch, and Leila pressed her hands to her temples. "I just need ..."

"What? What do you need?"

"Time, I think. And space. Please, please Jackson. Just go."

"Leila—"

"Please. I need you to leave," she repeated.

A tiny pulse jumped at the corner of his jaw. "If that's what you really want."

She gave what she hoped was a decisive nod. "It is."

Chapter 21

It wasn't what Leila wanted at all, and for the entirety of Black Friday, she watched the door to see if Jackson would come back.

He didn't.

Leila's disappointment and inner turmoil were obvious to everyone. They all tip-toed around her and gave her jobs that involved working alone in the back room with all the boxes of new inventory. Even Nadia was aware something was amiss because as soon as the young girl finished her four o'clock reading of *'Twas the Night before Christmas*, she approached Leila.

They didn't know one another all that well, but Leila had been out to her sister's house on the Steele River Basin several times now, and Nadia had been there each time. The girl knew how to brew up a perfect batch of sweet tea, that was for sure.

She crouched down beside Leila and the box she was emptying. Leila paused in her task of unloading books and looked at the young girl.

"Are you alright?" Nadia asked in her deep, southern drawl.

"I'm fine, why?"

"Oh, I don't know. Maybe 'cause I spotted this good lookin' guy slink in here while I was readin' to the young'uns, and he was nervous as a long-tail cat in a room full of rockin' chairs. Next thing I know, y'all are in the back room for a hot minute until he comes out lookin' white as a sheet, and now we're all walkin' on eggshells around you."

Leila raised her eyebrows. That was one way of describing it.

"I'll say this," Nadia continued, "don't you dare let that one go."

Leila worked hard not to roll her eyes. "You don't even know him."

"I know he's Miss Virginia's son, and that woman is pure gold. Any boy of hers would be too."

"That's *slightly* oversimplified, Nadia."

"Maybe. All I know is life's too short to play cat and mouse over somethin' you know you need, but you're too scared to go after." And with that, she was gone.

For the next two weeks, Leila heard Nadia's words replay over and over again in her head; Jackson's too. She didn't want to be scared, so she'd driven past Jackson's house more than once, toying each time with the idea of pulling into his driveway. She never did.

With each passing day, whatever anger she had leftover about what had happened all those years ago dissipated little by little until none of it remained. It was replaced with a feeling of deep regret over how she'd handled things back then. Thinking back to that moment when she'd stepped through the doorway and seen him sitting there with Amelia on his lap, Jackson's explanation made sense.

The scene had been burned into her brain, and she could see it clearly even now—maybe with even more clarity than before since the image was no longer clouded with heavy emotion. At the time, Leila had been too upset to analyze the smaller details, such as why Jackson's hands had been down at his sides and not holding Amelia. Why his eyes had been closed when he'd always been an eyes-open kisser. Why, at Leila's audible gasp, only Amelia had turned to look at her.

Jackson and Nadia were right. She was afraid, and the time she'd taken to sort through it all had helped her identify why. The reason was simple: She didn't know if she could recover from a breakup with Jackson a second time. She'd almost rather not take the plunge and be left to wonder if they could have found their happily ever after than dive in head first, have things go south, and know for sure that they never would. The first time their love story crashed and burned had been hard enough. A second time would be unbearable.

But being without him these last few weeks almost felt like a breakup. She imagined him having already moved on without her, and it was enough to make her weep. She'd tried prayer, she'd tried working extra shifts, she'd tried increasing her weekly running mileage. Nothing was working. She felt an emptiness, and it gnawed at her insides, affecting her sleep, affecting her work, it was even affecting her Christmas spirit. She didn't have any.

Leila could have saved herself a lot of grief had she known what Jackson was up to. That he was planning a big surprise, and that he hadn't moved on at all. But she didn't, and she was left to allow her imagination to run wild in the worst possible way.

∽◦∾

"I need some advice," Elena announced one evening as she breezed into Leila's room and flopped down on her bed, cell phone in hand.

Leila set aside the book she'd been trying to read for the last two weeks. So far, she couldn't get into it. Maybe she should just start over from the beginning. "What is it? Did one of your students ask you to prom again?"

Elena pulled a face. She'd never outlive what had happened to her at her first teaching job. She'd been twenty-two, and one of her eighteen-year-old students had asked her to prom over Snapchat.

"No. It's about Marc Ghetty."

"Marc Ghetty," Leila repeated. "How do I know that name?"

"He owns Kingston Cliffs."

"Ah, that's right. I knew that."

Kingston Cliffs was famous, and not just in Nicolet. It was one of the largest log cabins in the world, at almost twenty thousand square feet, if Leila remembered correctly. She'd never seen it in person, but she'd seen pictures of it on the internet, and as beautiful as the cabin itself was, the property it rested on was even more magnificent. Right on Lake Superior, it had a mile of frontage along the rocky shore.

Marc Ghetty was a real estate investor from Columbus, Ohio and enormously wealthy, but he kept a pretty low profile in their area. Occasionally, he'd be spotted out golfing or at a restaurant in town, but he spent most of his time either back in Columbus, where his company headquarters were located, or out on Kingston Cliffs entertaining politicians and other elites.

Leila couldn't imagine what Elena would have to do with Marc Ghetty. "What about him?"

"Well, he, ah, sort of asked me out."

Leila sat up. "*Marc Ghetty* asked you out?"

Grinning, Elena nodded.

"The silver fox wants to date you?"

Elena giggled. "Is that what he's called?"

"According to an article I read."

"Well, it is fitting." She tapped and swiped at the screen on her phone several times. "I'll show you a picture of him that was taken just yesterday."

She handed the phone to Leila, who studied it for a full minute. She had never learned to whistle, but if there was ever a moment to produce the sound, now was the time. The silver-haired man, seated in a golf cart with another guy, was striking with his tanned, chiseled features and perfect, white-toothed smile. He oozed wealth. "Wow."

Elena settled her head against the pillow and sighed dreamily. "I know."

Leila wanted to test something because until now, she'd been almost positive Elena had her sights set elsewhere. "He makes Gabriel Wright look downright homely."

Elena lifted her head, her expression pinched. "That's not true. Why would you say that?"

Leila shrugged. "I don't know."

"Well I do know, and Gabe holds his own next to Marc just fine."

Leila held up a hand. "Alright, my mistake," she said easily, but she tucked away Elena's defensive response to examine another time.

She treated her cousin to a teasing smile and joked, "The babe versus the fox."

Elena laughed and rested her head back on the pillow. "That's the first smile I've seen on your face in days and days. I was afraid you might have forgotten how it's done."

Ignoring her, Leila handed back the phone and asked, "How did you meet Marc Ghetty, anyway?"

Elena was happy to fill her in. As the story went, last week she'd been waiting in the Central Administration office for a meeting she had with the district's director of personnel in order to finalize her Michigan teacher certification. The silver fox, a supporter of Nicolet schools and a frequent donor to various programs, had been there, too, awaiting a meeting with the superintendent, Gabriel Wright himself.

He and Elena talked a bit, and the next thing her cousin knew, Marc was following her on Instagram. They flirted over phone messages for a few days, and now they were going to dinner as soon as he returned from a business trip to Chicago.

"Is he hoity-toity at all?"

"Mmm ..." Elena considered the question. "He talks about money, but I kind of like it. He says he's going to get me a Louis Vuitton purse before he flies home."

Leila tried not to cringe. "That's ... something. How old is he again?"

Elena groaned. "Don't spoil my fun. I'm excited about this."

"I'm not trying to spoil anything, I'm just asking a simple question."

"I know what you're getting at, and he's forty-six, okay?"

Forty-six. That made him twenty-one years older than her cousin, and that was a pretty big age difference. He was a whole drinking-aged person older than Elena. "Does he have any kids?" Leila couldn't remember if the article had mentioned any.

Elena laughed. "Of course not."

At least Marc wasn't quite old enough to be Elena's father. Still, the term *Sugar Daddy* came to mind.

"You said you needed advice?"

Elena adjusted the pillow behind her. "Maybe not so much advice as just telling someone about him, and then admitting the truth about how I feel."

"And how's that?"

Elena reached for her hand and held it. "I like Marc, and I'm excited, that he asked me out, but I know he's way out of my league."

Leila snorted. "Why, because he's rich?"

"And powerful," Elena supplied. "He's rich, and he's powerful, and who am I? I'm just a Puerto Rican school teacher with duct tape on her bumper."

Leila's brows drew together over her brown eyes. "What does being Puerto Rican have to do with anything?"

"I don't know. Nothing, I guess, but there's a huge difference between me and him, Leila. You know that better than anyone. I mean, you saw how I grew up. You see how I live now." She grew unusually quiet, grabbing a lock of hair and twirling it as she stared at the ceiling. "I don't want to look like a fool."

Leila squeezed her hand. "You could never look like a fool, and you need to remember it's just money. Dollars and cents you can't take with you when you go anyway. You are absolutely, one hundred percent in this guy's league in every way that matters. If you like him, go for it. Don't let a little fear hold you back."

Elena studied her. "I could say the same to you, you know."

Leila shifted, scooching down and laying her head beside her cousin's. "Well, don't. I don't want to talk about it."

"I know. You need time to see if you can handle the risk, blah, blah, blah. I'll say this: You're drowning yourself in a glass of water."

Leila rolled her eyes. "That works okay, but you're supposed to say I'm making a mountain out of a molehill."

"However you say it, it's infuriating, *prima mía*, that you have lost your bravery, but I still love you."

Leila turned to her cousin. She might not always like hearing Elena's blunt take on things, but at least she had someone willing to give it to her straight. It was more than some people had. "I love you too."

Chapter 22

Two weeks before Christmas, Leila and Elena put up their tree—a fresh Douglas fir they'd picked out together at the local nursery. They'd strung the lights but waited on the ornaments until Carmen could come by and be a part of the tree decorating. By seven, Carmen had arrived with her signature caramel corn and her favorite Christmas album—Dolly Parton and Kenny Rogers' *Once Upon a Christmas*.

Elena chattered on happily, sometimes in Spanish and sometimes in English, filling Carmen in on the latest Marc Ghetty news. They'd gone out on two dates, and according to Leila's cousin, last night at dinner, he'd tipped the waitress two hundred dollars for bringing them their meal of burgers and fries. Either he was the most generous person in the world or the biggest show-off. Leila was having a hard time caring enough to guess which one it was. She'd only met him once, but being so miserable in love herself, she'd been inclined to dislike him, which probably wasn't really fair.

"Two hundred dollars, *Tía*. Can you believe it?" Elena was saying. "The entire bill didn't even reach forty dollars, and he tipped her *two* hundred." She smiled happily as she lifted an ornament out of the red plastic tote. "You should have seen her face. That girl was so happy, she must have thanked him a million times at least ..."

Elena continued to talk as she dug through the ornaments the Molinas had accumulated over the years, picking out her favorites and placing them in the *going-on-the-tree* pile. Here and there she would pause in her storytelling to ask Leila what she thought of the ones she wasn't sure about.

Leila sat under a plaid flannel blanket in the old wooden rocking chair her mother had used to rock Luca to sleep. Halfheartedly, she cast her votes on the ornaments, one after the other. As the piles grew, and as Dolly sang about her belief in Santa Claus, Elena finally reached her annoyance threshold.

"That's it, Leila," she said, standing and stepping carefully around the ornament heaps. She crossed the living room and stood, glowering down at her. "That's it. I absolutely refuse to watch you mope around anymore. Get up and go to that man's house, and I don't mean just drive by like some gutless creeper like you've been doing. I mean park your car, get out, and knock on his door like a grown-up."

Leila, startled by the sudden outburst, rocked forward in her chair. "I'm not moping," she insisted. "I'm relaxing."

Elena stomped over to the banister of the stairs where Leila's purse hung and carried it back to her. "No, you're not. You're moping, and you've been wearing that poochy mouth of yours for so long, I can't even stand to look at you anymore. It'll get stuck that way if you're not careful, and you'll get nasty frown lines and have to live out your last days an ugly, poochy-mouthed mess of a woman who used to be pretty once. Now go." She tossed the purse into Leila's flannel-covered lap.

Leila grabbed it and looked to her mother for support, but Carmen quickly looked away and busied herself with picking the cashew clusters out of her bowl of caramel corn.

"Mama?"

Carmen ignored her.

"Mama!"

Carmen gave up the pretense of being occupied and set her bowl down on the floral area rug they'd picked out together when they first moved to town. She looked Leila directly in the eyes. "Leila, you know I love you, but after everything you've told us, I don't understand what you're doing at all. I don't understand *you* at all."

"You don't understand me? You're my mother!"

"And as your mother, I used to say I knew you even better than you knew yourself. But I can't make sense of this. You are miserable, *mija*, and one quick drive across town will cure you of your miserableness forever. You love that boy."

Leila protested, but Carmen shut her down.

"No, you listen to me. Your papa and I mourned over your breakup. *Mourned*, Leila, and I'm not exaggerating. But you were our daughter, and of course we were loyal to you. He came to this house nearly every day for weeks, asking us for information. He cried in your papa's arms, Leila. And to know now that if we had just told him, we could have cleared all of this up"—she snapped her fingers—"just like that. And to know that you let him go after everything he said at the store, after God placed him in your path once more and allowed you to *save his life, Leila* ..." She shook her head. "No, I don't understand."

Leila sat a moment in silence, staring at the tree. Even though no ornaments hung on it yet, the white twinkle lights had already made it festive, and Leila remembered back to the Christmas Jackson had told her he loved her for the first time in front of a similar tree. It had been pure magic.

Holding her purse with both hands, she stood, and the flannel blanket fell to the floor in a heap. "You're right." She looked back and forth between them, her heart pounding. "Both of you."

Elena sighed heavily. "Finally! Does this mean you're going?"

"I'm going," Leila said decisively, though she wasn't at all sure this was the best way to go about things. Showing up unannounced on a snowy December night might not be the best idea, but she had to act now. Right now, before she lost her nerve.

She missed the gleeful hug between her cousin and her mother as she fled the house and drove across town to the west side and to Jackson's small bungalow.

As luck would have it, the house was dark, except for the lit Christmas tree in the front window.

Nobody was home.

After all that, after working up her courage and white-knuckling the entirety of her ten-minute drive, and Jackson wasn't even there.

Leila put the car in park. Now what? Did she wait, or would that be weird? She didn't have time to decide. Headlights from behind her lit up the interior of her car, and she turned to see Jackson pulling up behind her in the Blazer she'd seen parked in this driveway countless times. Her pulse raced as the lights turned off, and she watched Jackson get out and close his door.

She rolled her window down as he approached. He didn't look at all surprised to see her in the driver's seat, she noted.

"Hey," he greeted with a wide grin.

"Hey," she repeated.

Even from here, a handful of blocks from Lake Superior, Leila could hear the thunder of the waves, and Jackson's sandy brown hair whipped in the wind.

It was long enough now to showcase loose curls she'd never known existed before, and she wondered if they were as soft as they looked.

"What are you doing here?"

She bit down on her lip and shook her head. "I don't know," she answered honestly.

He chuckled. "Want to come in a second?"

Nodding, she shut off her engine, and together, they walked in silence to his front entrance. When he turned the handle without producing a key, she gave him a startled look. "You don't keep it locked?"

He shrugged. "This is Nicolet."

"Yeah, but still."

He *tsked* twice. "Once a city girl, always a city girl, I guess. I wanted to keep it unlocked in case you finally stopped on one of your many trips past my house." He flipped on the lights inside and shut the door. Noticing her burning cheeks, he smiled. "Don't be embarrassed. I liked it. I even started watching for you." He shrugged. "I figured you'd stop eventually."

She glanced down. "Well, I *am* embarrassed."

He leaned forward and sweetly kissed her cheek. "I know, but it's just me. Just you and me." He took her coat and purse and hung them on the coat tree next to the door. "Can I get you anything? Coffee, soda, water?"

Leila noticed he hadn't said wine, and she sheepishly wondered if she'd have to give up her habitual nightly glass if they got back together. It would be a small price to pay, she decided.

Jackson read her mind. "I'd offer you wine, but I don't keep any in the house. It's not that I mind being around it, not at all. Just tonight at my sister's, everyone was having a glass, well, except Lizzie. She's expecting."

"I know. I saw her the day she and Virginia came by ... after the accident. Twins, she said."

He beamed. "Two boys. They'll be here next month."

"And you'll be an uncle," she pointed out. Somehow, that made him even more appealing than he already was. Uncle Jackson. She pictured him holding a baby and could have sworn she felt a surge of activity in her ovaries.

She coughed.

"That I will. I can't wait. Anyway, how about a cup of coffee?"

"Only if you're having some," she answered.

"Sounds good to me. Make yourself at home in here." He gestured toward the leather sofa. "I'll be right back." Leaving the living room, he passed through a small, curved archway that presumably led to the kitchen.

Leila sat and took a deep breath as she watched him leave. It felt surreal. Grown-up Jackson and grown-up Leila about to sip coffee together like a couple of, well … grown-ups. On the one hand, it felt like an eternity had passed, but on the other, it felt like she was right back in high school again.

Nerves aside, they had already settled into a familiar sort of rhythm with each other, but maybe it wasn't real. Could two people really pick things up where they left off after more than a decade apart? She supposed she'd find out.

Looking around, she took in the details of Jackson's living room. It was a cute space. The walls were painted an almond beige, and white trim gave it a clean, crisp feel. She stood and walked over to the console table on the far wall that was made out of natural, reclaimed wood. On it were several framed photos including one of Jackson and Freddy Loma on kayaks and a sweet one where Jackson was being kissed simultaneously on the cheeks by Virginia and Lizzy. Jackson looked truly happy in it, and Leila found herself profoundly thankful that he'd at least had some good people in his life over the years to counter whatever damage Philip had done. She tried not to think about the fact that she hadn't been one of them. For a time she had, yes, but only a very short time.

She swallowed down her shame.

After seeing Jackson that night, and after Amelia's victory stare, she'd rushed home to her parents in tears and had spent the weekend in her room with the shades drawn. Her parents had tiptoed around her, and dutifully, Atticus had lain beside her in her bed. Instead of demanding romps in the woods, he seemed to know she needed his snuggles instead, and he'd allowed her to repeatedly soak his fur with her tears.

By the time she made it back to campus, her grief had turned to anger, and Jackson was right. That anger was fueled by Caitlyn. Oh, she wasn't blaming her crazy roommate, at least not fully. She'd given Leila bad advice, but Leila had taken it, stubbornly refusing to hear Jackson's side of the story and deciding to believe the worst about what she'd seen. She wondered for the umpteenth time if things would have turned out differently if she had just talked to him.

Jackson reappeared holding two steaming mugs of coffee. "I gave us each a shot of cream and sprinkle of cinnamon in honor of the holidays," he said.

Leila thanked him and asked about the picture with Freddy. "It looks pretty recent."

Jackson invited her to sit and seated himself across from her on the other side of the coffee table. "It was taken last summer on Isle Royale."

"Who took it?"

"Peter."

Leila nearly choked on her coffee. "Peter Lindberg?" she asked in shock.

Jackson laughed. "We made nice a long time ago."

"Wow, just ... wow! "I can't believe that."

"Turns out our dads must have read the same parenting book. It'd make anyone mean."

Leila didn't say it out loud, but it hadn't made Jackson mean. Not really.

"He and Freddy work together over at Four Peaks Bank. They're the ones Lizzie and I went to for our business loan."

"A business loan?"

He filled her in, and when he was done, Leila had caught his enthusiasm. He and his sister had the savvy, the name recognition, and the expertise, and if that wasn't enough, the town had a real need for what they were offering. She had no doubt their business would be a success.

"I was just over at Lizzie's to celebrate the finalization of everything," Jackson continued, "because I put in my notice today. It feels real now. Three more months, and I make the switch."

"Was it hard?"

"Giving my notice? A little. Only because I really like Sean LaCombe, the head coach. He's a good guy."

"He's a terrific guy."

Jackson smacked his forehead. "That's right. I heard you're kind of part of that crew now."

Leila smiled. "Yeah, I guess I am."

"So is Brian Benninger. Who'd have thought? But I guess he goes by Benny now."

"He dates my friend, Sarah."

"I was a real jerk to him growing up."

"I remember you saying that. I'm sure it's water under the bridge. Kid stuff."

"Maybe," he said doubtfully.

They sipped in silence, but he watched her over the rim of his mug.

She couldn't hold his gaze, but she heard him set his mug down. The creamer from the coffee curdled in her stomach as she sensed the time for small talk had come to an end.

He spoke her name, and his voice was so impossibly tender, she had the horrible feeling she might cry. She couldn't look at him.

"Leila, what made you stop here tonight?"

She took a deep breath and spoke to the floor. "Jackson, it was—" she shook her head and tried again. "Jackson, I'm sorry. I'm sorry I never let you explain. It was ... wrong of me."

She looked at him then, and his turquoise eyes stared intently back.

She wet her lips before continuing. "It was wrong, but I was hurt and angry, and I let my insecurity and pride ruin everything. I guess I—I'm just really sorry for everything," she repeated.

He nodded. "I'm sorry too. I wish we could both go back and do it all different, but we can't. I guess for me the question is, where does that leave us now?"

"Um," she hedged, afraid to ask for what she wanted, "I don't know."

He waited, and when Leila realized he wasn't going to let her off the hook that easily, she laughed nervously. "This is where I start to feel all awkward and embarrassed, like I'm seventeen years old again."

Jackson stood and moved around the coffee table to seat himself beside her. A whole cushion separated them, and he was simultaneously too close and too far away.

"That's not so bad, is it? Feeling seventeen?"

"Except that I'm not. I'm a thirty-year-old professional now. I've been on my own a long time, and I don't know how to go back in time to the way things were."

He cocked his head and looked at her curiously. "But we don't have to go back in time at all, and we couldn't even if we wanted to. Sure, we have history, but that only makes this even better. We're connected, the two of us. Bonded together, and what we have is right here in front of us. It's not in the past, it's the future. It's now."

"But Jackson, are you sure that's what you want?"

"You know it is," he answered quietly. "The question is, do you want it?"

She looked into those blue-green irises that had always beguiled her and said out loud what she'd been so afraid to admit, even to herself. "I do."

He let out a relieved chuckle. "That's really good because I have a surprise for you that wouldn't work out real well if you'd said no."

"What surprise?"

"It's a Christmas gift, so you'll have to wait."

He'd been so sure they'd get together that he'd already bought her a Christmas gift? That meant that three whole people knew her better than she knew herself: her mama, Elena, and Jackson. They'd all known she'd end up on this couch, in this house, admitting these things, eventually.

She smiled.

Jackson reached for her hand, and when he spoke, his voice was husky. "I do have something I can give you right now, though, but it'll mean skipping into second-date territory."

Leila wet her lips again. "I guess … I guess that'd be okay."

Without closing the space between them, Jackson touched her hair, running his fingers through it. "I've missed this," he whispered. "It always felt like this, like pure silk." He moved to touch her face. "And here too. Kitten-soft."

Leila stopped breathing when he touched her lips.

"And your mouth. How I've missed this mouth."

Their eyes met and held, and a jolt of heat settled in Leila's stomach. Neither one of them spoke. They only stared, and in the silence, Jackson brought her against him slowly. Her arms crept tentatively around him, and she willed herself to relax. She was all fast-breathing tension and locked muscles as he brought his lips to her neck.

"Easy now," he whispered before placing a kiss in the hollow behind her ear that sent shivers up and down her spine. He moved lower on her neck, sprinkling kisses as he went.

It tickled in the best kind of way, and Leila sighed as she relaxed and let her head fall back.

A minute later, he pulled away to see her face, placing his fingers beneath her chin to bring her gaze to his.

She felt a little like a boiled noodle and smiled at him. A feeling of peace flowed through her like a quiet stream.

The corners of his own mouth lifted. "Do you know how many times I've dreamed of this?"

"Hmm. I wonder if we ever dreamed of each other at the same time."

"I'm sure we must have." Stroking her cheek, he whispered, "I don't want this to be a dream, Leila. I don't want you to disappear by morning."

"I won't."

"I need you."

"I need you too," she whispered back.

He dipped his head and drew her into a firm and loving embrace. "You're so beautiful. You're so beautiful to me."

She closed her eyes and felt his breath on her lips. She parted them in anticipation. And then he was kissing her, a slow and gentle caress, very different from the frantic one in the shop a few weeks ago. It spoke of promises, of the care they would take with one another's hearts. It was one soul speaking to another. Words weren't necessary. They were going by feel and by memory.

Jackson's embrace and the touch of his lips to hers sheathed Leila in a warmth that even the chill of the winter night couldn't have penetrated. She revelled in the closeness of his body to hers, her heart bursting with a love for him that had never really stopped. She knew that now. And she knew it never would stop. She needed him the way the sky needed the sun, moon, and stars. She wasn't complete without him.

Any fears she'd had slipped away as she matched him kiss for kiss. There were no guarantees in life. Loss was real, grief was real, pain was real. She knew that well. But love was real, too, and Leila recalled something her papa had told her once. He'd said that there was no fear in love. That perfect love casts out fear.

She broke off the kiss.

"What is it?" Jackson asked.

"I was just thinking of Papa."

"You were thinking about your dad while you were kissing me?" Jackson asked with a joking grin. "I must not be doing it right. Here, let me try again."

Leila laughed and planted a swift kiss on his mouth. "I'm sorry. I'm just so happy, Jackson. I'm not afraid anymore."

"Of what?"

"I'm not afraid to love you."

He shook his head in wonder and reached for her. "Oh, Leila. I love you too."

Chapter 23

Three days before Christmas, Jackson sat with Leila in her darkened living room with only the light of the tree to see one another. He sipped a ginger beer while Leila nursed a small glass of Merlot. They'd been talking about Leila's work when Jackson noticed something on the mantel.

"What's that?" he asked, pointing at the small white box. It was roughly the size of a book, and it had their names on it.

Leila set down her wine glass and retrieved it. "I don't know, but this is Mama's handwriting. She said she was coming by earlier today to grab some of Papa's things from the attic."

Jackson looked on as Leila coaxed it open. Inside was a folded letter and a smaller box. Leila looked at him. "Go on," he prompted.

Leila opened the paper with the bookstore letterhead at the top and read aloud.

Dear Kids,

I know it's not quite Christmas yet, but I wanted to give you this gift in a setting where you could have some privacy instead of in front of all of us during the gift exchange. This is a gift for you both from Samuel. Please open the box now and come back to this letter once you do.

Leila looked at him in bewilderment. "I don't understand. From Papa to both of us?"

Noticing that her hands had begun to shake, he asked, "Do you want me to do it?"

She nodded and gave him the smaller box. It was roughly the size of a deck of cards, which was fitting because inside was the 1952 Bowman Mickey Mantle Samuel had shown him all those years ago.

His best card.

"No way," Jackson breathed, lifting the card out of the box and holding it reverently. He flipped the protective sheath over to look at the back and then at the front again. It was just as he remembered it, and for a moment he was shuttled back in time.

Emotion rolled over Jackson in waves, and he swallowed several times before speaking. "This is his best card. He told me. He gave us his best card, Leila."

"I still don't get it."

"There's something else in here." He reached into the small box with his thumb and forefinger and pulled out a black velvet pouch. It was tied closed with dainty black ribbon. He gave it to Leila.

It took a few tries, but she finally unworked the knot in the ribbon and carefully flipped the pouch over, shaking out a ring into the palm of her free hand.

Jackson recognized it immediately.

She gasped and looked at him. "It's the promise ring you gave me."

Wordlessly, Jackson picked up the ring and examined it. He remembered how proud he'd been the day he'd given it to Leila. How proud, and how nervous. "I thought you said you threw it away," he murmured.

"I did! One of them must have gone after it for me and then kept it all these years." She took it back and fingered it reverently.

The creaking of the steps signaled Elena's descent, and both Jackson and Leila turned to look.

Leila's cousin wore fluffy red slippers and a pair of faded Christmas pajamas. With her hair up in a bun and her face scrubbed of makeup, she looked more like a teenager than a teacher of teenagers. Jackson had gotten to know her the last several days, and he liked her immensely. She was an interesting combination of fire cracker and delicate, fragile porcelain.

"I'm just getting a quick glass of water," she said, as if she needed to apologize for coming down the stairs while he was there.

Leila popped up. "What happened? I thought you were going out with your millionaire tonight."

"He canceled me."

"Why?" Leila demanded.

Elena shrugged. "I don't know."

Leila put one hand on her hip. "This is the third time he's done that, Elena."

Jackson watched Elena stiffen. "He's a very important man. Things come up with his business all the time."

Leila treated him to a swift glance before turning back to her cousin. She lowered her voice and spoke in Spanish. Elena must not have liked what she said because she started gesturing wildly with her hands as she, too, spoke in Spanish.

It went on like that for a full minute, two beautifully stubborn Latinas, until Elena finally sighed and said in English, "You make me so crazy sometimes." She reached for Leila.

Leila let out a tortured groan before hugging her back and saying, "Go get your water."

When Leila sat beside him on the couch again, Jackson pulled an *uh-oh* face. "What was that about?"

"Just Elena not valuing herself the way she should." She shook her head. "Nothing new."

Leila had already filled him in on Marc Ghetty. She'd only met him the one time, but it had been enough for her to form a strong opinion of the guy. Jackson didn't know a lot about him, but he was rich and powerful and sometimes that alone could ruin a person. He knew about that first hand.

She leaned in and spoke close to his ear. "I think this guy's toying with her, and I can't stand it. She always shuts down the nice ones and goes after the jerks. I don't get it."

Jackson cared about Elena, he really did. But right now he was more interested in the ring Leila held in her closed fist and getting back to the letter that would explain it all.

"*Buenas noches*, you two lovebirds," Elena said as she breezed through with her glass of water in hand.

"*Buenas noches*," Leila called after her. She turned her attention back to Jackson and the ring.

"Can I see it again?" Jackson asked.

Leila handed it over. First, he tested the weight of it in his hand, and then he examined it more closely. Back then, he'd wondered if she would mistake it for an engagement ring, which seemed laughable now. Yes, it had a diamond in it, but it was only the tiniest of chips—all he could afford back then. One blink and a person would miss it completely. At the time, though, he'd been so proud to buy it for her, and even prouder when he slid it on her finger.

The stairs behind them sounded and Elena appeared once again.

"I'm sorry you guys, I left my phone in the—Whoa, is that a ring?" Within seconds, she was standing behind the couch and peering over Jackson's open hand. She leveled him a look. "Jackson, *please* don't tell me you're proposing to Leila with that."

Leila cupped her face in her hands. "Elena!"

Jackson chuckled. "No, it's okay." To Elena he explained, "I gave Leila this ring when we were teenagers ..."

By the time he'd finished the story of the ring and what they were doing with it now, Elena had seated herself in the rocking chair across from them.

"And they saved it all these years? Did they somehow know you'd get together again?"

"I don't know." Leila reached for the letter she'd set down on the side table. "We need to read the rest of this letter."

Jackson played with the ring as she resumed reading Carmen's tidy cursive.

Samuel couldn't read the future, but he did hope the two of you would end up together in the end. It's why he fetched the ring out of the trash. He saw Leila walk to the end of the driveway and throw it in the bin that night, and he knew she would regret it. You see, it was a piece of your history he thought you'd want to have.

As for the baseball card, Samuel wanted Jackson to have that specific card regardless of whether you got back together or not. He'd always planned to give it to Jackson himself once he worked out how to accomplish it, but then he passed on, and I didn't honor those wishes right away. Now I am.

Samuel loved you, Leila. I know you never could have doubted it. Fervently, he prayed for you. Every day he prayed blessings over you. You were his sunshine, even in our darkest days.

But he loved you, too, Jackson. You were special to him in a way I'm not sure you ever realized. He knew you needed a strong and good man in your life, but Jackson, Samuel needed you too. You were an important part of his healing after we lost our boy. In some ways, he felt he'd gained a son in you. He would be so pleased to know you and his Leila are together again at last and that you now have these gifts. I wish he could have given them to you himself.

Merry Christmas to you both from Samuel.

Love,

Mama

Leila dropped the letter to her lap and let out a long, deep breath. "I just—I can't believe he did that. I don't even know what I feel right now."

Jackson watched Elena swipe at a tear trailing down her cheek. "Samuel was the greatest man I ever knew," she whispered. "He was so good. You were lucky, Leila."

"I know," Leila answered in a voice that broke. "I know I was." She turned to Jackson. "Are you okay?"

Jackson cleared his throat and nodded.

"I'm glad he left you that card. He liked showing you all his treasures." They shared a nostalgic smile.

"Put it on, Leila. See if it still fits," Elena broke in.

Leila started. "The ring? Oh, gosh, I don't know if ..."

She looked at Jackson, and he could see the question in her eyes.

"Put it on, Leila," he echoed in a gentle but firm voice.

Elena froze as she became aware of the magnitude of the situation she'd just created.

"Jackson, are you sure? I mean, it's not an engagement ring, but it's still, you know ..." Leila trailed off helplessly.

Jackson cast a brief glance at Elena who had settled into her chair and now watched them like a movie. All she needed was a bag of popcorn, and she'd be set.

Her eyes turned haughty as he sent her a pleading look.

"No way." She shook her head. "Don't you dare ask me to leave."

"Elena—" Leila began in warning.

Jackson put a hand on her arm. "No, it's fine. You tell her everything anyway."

Elena beamed at him. She was an interesting one, that was for sure, and Jackson had better get used to a certain comfort level with her because it seemed wherever Leila went, Elena was there too.

Resigning himself to the fact that a woman he hardly knew would be listening to the retelling of the most deeply personal and consequential event of his life, Jackson began the story that would help Leila understand why he had no qualms whatsoever of her wearing this or any other ring he would give her. He knew they were meant to be together. "Leila, I need to talk about that day in the lake."

At her nod, he continued. "I know it seems strange after so many years, but I need you to know that you were the one I thought of as I got into the water. I knew I might not survive, and I had so many things I wanted to say to you. So many things I was afraid would never be said.

"When I started swimming, you were all I could think about. I prayed over and over that I could see you just one more time. And then, like magic, you were there. For a second, I thought I'd died, but then I knew he sent you to me. To rescue me."

"Who?"

"Samuel."

Elena covered her mouth with her hand, her eyelashes fluttering with each rapid blink.

Leila placed a gentle hand on his knee and stared at him in wonder. "What do you mean?"

Jackson ran a hand through his hair. "It sounds crazy, and I don't really understand it, but ... so ... Well, I'm just going to say it. I heard Samuel's voice. In the water. I heard him, I know I did. He even called me 'son,' just like he always used to. I always really liked that, and I think he knew. He knew I needed to hear it sometimes." Jackson paused to wipe at one of his eyes.

"Jackson," Leila said shaking her head, "I don't understand."

"It happened when I stopped swimming. My arms and legs got to be too heavy to move, and I think I might've fallen asleep or something. But I heard him as I floated there in the water. I swear it. It wasn't a dream. It's what woke me up. He said my name, twice, and then he said, 'Swim, son. She's there.'"

Elena went back to covering her mouth, but Leila gaped at him.

"He meant Leila," Elena finally whispered.

"What else did he say?" Leila demanded.

Jackson shook his head and sniffed. "That was it."

Elena hopped out of the rocker to grab a box of tissues from the adjoining dining room. She held out the box to Jackson first, and then to Leila. Then she took a tissue for herself.

"I know it sounds crazy," Jackson said after putting the tissue to good use, "but I wouldn't make something like this up."

Elena looked at Leila and then back at him. "We believe you."

With bright eyes, Leila echoed her. "We believe you."

Jackson swallowed before continuing, "So to answer your question about the ring, I want you to wear it, but only if you want to, and only until I can do it right and get you the real thing."

Elena squealed while Leila smiled through a fresh set of tears. "Here," she said, handing him the ring. "Put it on me." She presented him with her right hand. "Maybe by summer I'll have one for my left hand."

Jackson grinned and took the ring. "Maybe you will."

"And that one will have a *much* bigger diamond," Elena declared.

While there would be no holiday proposal, Jackson had something planned that was almost as good. An idea had come to him the night of Leila's fourth drive-by of his house, and like most good ideas, it came smack dab in the middle of the night when he couldn't do a darn thing about it.

It would be the "Grand Gesture." The one that would show Leila just how much he loved her. Once the idea had solidified in Jackson's mind, there was no going back to sleep, and he'd restlessly awaited the hour when a phone call would be acceptable.

Five hours later he was on the phone with the mayor, and an hour after that, he stood in the man's kitchen and contemplated the squirming contents of a large kiddie pool.

Chapter 24

After a long twelve-hour shift, Leila walked into the foyer of her mother's complex and was immediately engulfed in the aroma of hot caramel. Sure enough, when she opened Carmen's unlocked door, she found her mama in the kitchen pouring the sugary liquid into a large mixer bowl while she sang along to Eartha Kitt's *Santa Baby*.

"We're all going to get cavities," Leila joked with a laugh.

"*Hola, mija.*" Her mama greeted with a cheerful smile.

While Eartha asked for yachts and platinum mines, Leila set her purse down on the small table near the door and kicked off her shoes. Before removing her coat, she entered the kitchen and gave her mama a kiss on the cheek.

Carmen turned down the volume of the bluetooth speaker. "Don't worry. Your teeth are safe. I'm making it for my neighbors. I gave them each a small bag as a gift, and they are all clamoring for more. Here—" She handed Leila a wooden spoon. "Give me a hand."

For the next hour, Leila helped pop the corn, stir, measure, and pour, until they'd filled ten gallon-sized bags. It was nearly nine o'clock when they finished, and Leila was dead on her feet. As a reward, Carmen poured them each a glass of Merlot, and they headed over to the sofa together, where they promptly kicked up their feet.

"You said Elena has a date tonight?" Carmen inquired.

Leila took a sip of her wine. It was deep and rich and bold. Perfect for a cold winter night. Immediately, she felt her belly warm.

"With that investor man?" her mother prompted.

Leila nodded. Marc Ghetty threw a lavish Christmas party at his estate every year, and this year, Elena had the great honor of being his date. She wondered who next year's date would be. "I don't have a great feeling about this one," she admitted.

"You didn't like the last one, either."

"Neither did you," she pointed out.

"True." Carmen sighed. "What will we do about Elena, Leila?"

Resting a head on her mother's shoulder, Leila smiled. "You do Auntie Marivi proud."

"Well, someone needs to look out for Elena. Without my sister, she has no one else."

Leila lifted her head. "Hey, she has me too!"

Carmen patted Leila on the knee. "Of course she does, but you know what I mean. She still needs mothering. So do you, even though you might not know it."

"Oh, I think I've come to the realization." Leila chuckled. "You can interfere in my love life anytime. I'm so happy, Mama."

Carmen gave her another pat. "Where is Jackson tonight?"

"The head coach of the Nicolet hockey team wanted to take him to dinner. He has a list of candidates for Jackson's replacement, and he wanted Jackson to weigh in on them."

"He must value Jackson's opinion."

"I think he does, and it sort of shows that there aren't any hard feelings about him leaving. At least not by Sean."

"Hmm. That's good. There shouldn't be hard feelings or worry about hard feelings over the holidays. It's too magical a time." Carmen took a slow sip from her glass. "Have you been to confession lately?"

Leila winced. "It's been a little while."

"Tomorrow is Christmas Eve," Carmen reminded her.

"I'll go in the morning," Leila promised.

"Take Elena. I happen to know she hasn't gone in months."

Leila fought a smile. "I'll try."

They listened to several bars of *Silent Night*, and for a moment, Leila considered telling Carmen about Jackson's story. About how Samuel had spoken to him, but she decided to wait. The timing needed to be just right for that conversation. Instinctively, Leila knew there would be some tears, and now wasn't the time for tears, even if they would be mostly good ones.

"Thank you again, Mama, for the gift. It was such a beautiful thing you and Papa did. We'll never forget it. And your letter, I'll keep it forever."

Carmen pet Leila's head lovingly. "Samuel would be so proud of you, my Leila. Of Jackson too."

Playing with the ring, Leila wondered again how her Papa could have had the foresight to know she would want it back. There were so many questions she wanted to ask him. He'd always given such thoughtful answers, and she missed his insights. One day, she'd ask him about the ring. She'd ask him how he'd known Jackson was in danger in the water and how he'd managed to speak to him. She wondered if he would ever speak to her.

In the end, the answers to those questions didn't really matter. It was enough to know that her steps were being guided, just as her papa had always told her. Her whole life story, from the time she came to be until this very moment sitting here with her mother, had all been known in advance. She believed that. She had faith in that, even if she might not understand all the twists and turns her path had taken or where they might lead her in the future.

"Hey, Mama?"

"Yes, *mija*."

"I've been thinking about something for a while."

Carmen adjusted her position on the couch to better see her.

"I need to make some changes."

"What kind of changes?"

"Well, for starters, I've been thinking I might want to cut back my hours at work a little."

Carmen lifted her brows.

"I always take the extra shifts because ..." She shrugged. "I don't know, I've been striving for some kind of elusive perfection for a long time."

Carmen nodded knowingly. "Ever since Luca was born."

Leila blinked. "You noticed the timing?"

"Of course I noticed. I'm your mother. Oh, you were so high-strung, and you put so much pressure on yourself. I worried you would have ulcers by the time you hit twenty. Your senior year was different, though. You were more relaxed then. I remember you got an *A* minus in trigonometry that year, and you didn't even cry."

Leila smiled sheepishly. "I have put a lot of unnecessary pressure on myself. I haven't always told myself the kindest things. But lately I feel like I'm ... I don't know ... ready to grow up, I guess. I'm ready to stop pushing myself so hard. I'm ready to leave all my insecurities behind."

"Oh, *mija*. Insecurities have a way of plaguing us our whole lives. You will always have to fight them, or pray them away like I do. But I'm glad you're ready to do battle with them. I think you have all the armor you need. And as for demanding so much of yourself, you have nothing to prove, Leila. You are already a success. Such a wonderful daughter, and so very lovely."

Leila leaned into her. She hadn't even made any changes yet, and already she felt a weight had been lifted. "I love you, Mama."

"I love you too, *mi amor*."

Leila woke up Christmas Eve morning to at least six fresh inches of snow and Jackson out in the driveway running the snowblower. She giggled as she watched from her bedroom window. The abominable snowman was clearing her driveway. White powder clung to his outerwear, including the dark balaclava that covered his head and face, and the snow he kicked up hung in the air around him like a heavenly dust storm. Leila looked around the yard at the pristine drifts of white that sparkled like so many diamonds in the morning sunlight.

Today was Christmas Eve, and it would stay Christmas Eve all day long. It made her feel all warm and snuggly just thinking about it. She'd kick off the holidays with a mug of hot coffee in front of the fire she'd build in the fireplace, and end it with midnight mass at St. Peter's. To keep her word to her mother, she'd have to squeeze a trip to confession in there too.

Tonight she was hosting a dinner—her first one. Olivia and Sean Lacombe had been invited, along with their little girl, Nora, and of course Carmen and Elena would be there, as well as Jackson. Jackson's mom, sister, and brother-in-law were also coming. Elena's fancy man had been invited, but he'd declined at the last minute, the jerk.

Nobody in her family had ever been a fan of ham, so Leila was serving Cornish game hens along with twice-baked potatoes, stuffed acorn squash, and green beans. Dessert would be apple pie a la mode and *tembleque*, the only deviation from an otherwise very American meal. *Tembleque* was a type of wiggly coconut pudding that was supposed to go down rich and smooth. Leila had never been able to stomach it, but it was a favorite of both Carmen and Elena. That and the *coquito*, Puerto Rico's version of egg nog, would give both women a small taste of home during the holiday meal.

Leila headed downstairs to make the coffee and build the fire, stopping first to open the door and blow Jackson a kiss, which he hilariously returned from behind the snow-caked balaclava and a gloved hand. She'd just finished pouring out both their coffees when she heard a distant sound she recognized as Jackson's ringtone. Thinking it could be Lizzie or Virginia calling about the dinner, she moved into the entryway where she found his cellphone face-up on the wooden bench. A quick glance at his screen told her it was neither of the other two women in his life.

It was Amelia Channing.

Leila felt the blood rush from her face, carrying all her joy with it.

Chapter 25

"**M**an, it is *cold* out there!" Jackson exclaimed, stomping his feet on the welcome mat in the entryway. He could hear Leila moving around in the kitchen. "Can I throw my stuff in your dryer? It's all caked in snow."

"That's fine," she called back.

Once he'd gotten everything off, he came into the kitchen, a bundle of winter wear in his arms. He stopped and gave her a small nuzzle on the side of her neck. "Be right back."

"You didn't have to clear my driveway," she said, not looking up from the hard-boiled eggs she was peeling.

Was it him, or did her voice sound a little stiff?

"I wanted to."

"Well, thank you."

She looked at him then, and he felt a sharp stirring of desire. Sleep-rumpled, Leila was far more enticing than she had a right to be.

"You're welcome," he replied before placing a long, lingering kiss on her lips. She sighed and leaned into him. The wet clothes compressed between them, and he reluctantly pulled away. "Let me get rid of these."

The laundry room was downstairs in the basement, and Jackson made quick work of loading his wet things into the dryer so he could get back upstairs and into the arms of the woman he loved. She'd started a fire—he'd seen and smelled the evidence of that from the chimney outside—and he wanted to sit and linger with her there for a while before the flurry of activity began. He wouldn't have her to himself for long.

Elena would be waking up anytime, and Carmen would be there soon to help prepare for the party. Jackson could hardly wait until the dinner was over. He'd filled Leila's mother in on the surprise, and he didn't know which of them was more excited to witness Leila's reaction.

The fire was well established by the time he and Leila sat. They talked of the day's plans as they watched the flames dance and flicker, and they listened to the wood crack and pop once the conversation lulled and they were left to their thoughts. Jackson had a bit of work to do to ready Leila's present, and he still had to shovel his own walkway. He figured he'd get back to the Victorian around four o'clock, in time to help put dinner on and visit with everyone.

"You missed a call while you were outside."

Jackson reached and patted his empty back pocket. That's right. He'd left his phone in the entryway and forgotten all about it. "Thanks. I'll check it in a minute."

"Were you expecting someone to call today?"

He was, but he couldn't tell her that. "Uh, not really."

Leila studied him, and he saw some mysterious emotion flit across her face. "What?"

"Nothing," she muttered.

"No, what?" he insisted, reaching for her.

Leila gazed at him for a long moment and then visibly relaxed. "I'm sorry. I'm being ridiculous. It's just that I looked at the screen and saw it was Amelia Channing who was calling you, and it brought back the past a little. But I do trust you; don't think I don't." She bit down on her lip. "But, Jackson, why was she calling you?"

Ah. He hadn't been imagining what he'd heard in her voice back in the kitchen.

He pulled her against him and kissed her hair. His voice was husky when he murmured, "Thank you for trusting me."

She nodded, and the movement tickled his face.

"There's nothing at all to worry about. I'm just ... figuring out some logistics with Amelia for some ... business we have."

Leila looked at him askance. "Logistics? For business?"

He grinned. "You're going to have to keep trusting me."

With a rueful smile, Leila sighed. "You're really not going to tell me."

"Not yet. It's a surprise."

She groaned. "I hate surprises."

"Well, you're going to love this one," he promised.

Three hours later, and Jackson determined he would never be able to keep up with the snow blowing and shoveling. Fresh snow continued to fall in fat, languid flakes, and although it seemed to be coming down slowly enough, it was accumulating quickly.

He made a mental note to buy another bag of salt to take to Leila's. The last thing he needed was Lizzie—or anyone—slipping on ice.

Jackson was glad Sean and his wife would be joining them tonight. It was good to know he hadn't burned any bridges there. Sean was one of those guys who was universally liked and respected. Jackson would miss working with him, but he supposed he'd still be seeing him from time to time socially. He'd probably be thrust together with Brian—Benny—eventually too. His stomach gave a small flip at the thought. He'd need to apologize for the past.

It was becoming a habit—apologizing. Just yesterday, he'd exchanged an "I'm sorry" with Amelia. She'd been a piece of work back in high school, but then he hadn't been a saint himself either. He'd used Amelia for years, stringing her along and taking advantage of her need to be with him. He'd known at the time exactly what he was doing, and he was ashamed of it now that he had a fully formed frontal lobe and a set of morals.

For her part, from a place of hurt and jealousy, Amelia had tried to make Leila feel as unwelcome and uncomfortable as possible senior year, and then she'd executed one final twist of the dagger that night in college when Leila had stumbled upon them, allowing her to believe the worst.

She still lived in town, and he'd seen her around here and there over the last several years. Usually, they acknowledged each other with a brief smile or a casual wave, but they hadn't spoken since college. Through the grapevine, he'd heard that she'd married and had two kids already. It had kind of blown him away. He never would have pegged her for the settle-down type.

So when he'd gone to her home yesterday, at her request, he hadn't been sure what to expect. What he'd found were those two kids and her husband—an older guy he didn't recognize—playing on the living room floor with blocks. They greeted him with friendly smiles before Amelia had drawn him back to the kitchen, where she'd immediately launched into an apology for her past behavior. It was easy to see she was sincere, and it was just as easy for him to express his own regrets.

"I've been ashamed about all of it for a long time, Jackson," she'd said. "It's hard living as an adult in the town you grew up in, especially if you have the kind of past I do. But I'm a different person now than I was back then. When you called, I felt like this might be a way to make amends."

"I feel a little bit like I'm stealing from your children, Amelia," Jackson had admitted.

"You're not. Please don't feel that way. I've already explained to them that this is what will make Mommy happy. There will be other opportunities."

"I'm really grateful. Without you, I wouldn't have been able to pull this thing off."

"She's lucky to have you, Jackson."

Jackson had shaken his head in denial. "I'm the lucky one."

Amelia conceded the point. "Give her my best, okay? I don't imagine she has much good to say about me, but still. Merry Christmas to you both."

He'd thanked her and followed her to the door, promising to drop off the check the following day on Christmas Eve.

After having done just that, and driving away from Amelia's a thousand dollars poorer, Jackson had to admit: Life was completely unpredictable.

An hour earlier than planned, he arrived back at the Victorian. First, he'd taken care of the newly fallen snow outside and thrown down enough salt to cure a dozen hams. Then he'd run out for the bag of onions Leila had forgotten. Carmen had called immediately after he'd checked out and asked him to grab two more poinsettia plants for the dining room, and just as he'd been getting in the car, Elena texted asking him to grab her some tampons and Midol.

That was a first and an experience he would prefer not to repeat.

Once Jackson unloaded all his purchases in the kitchen, Carmen handed him a key and asked him to bring down three more chairs from the attic.

It was like stepping back in time. The space looked just as it had the last time Jackson had been up there. Sure, things had probably been moved and reconfigured, but the overall feel was the same.

Over the course of his senior year, he'd helped Samuel get things organized, and together, they'd reassembled his old train table, placing it in the center of the room. Jackson walked over to it. It was covered in a thick layer of dust, but it was all set up and ready to go.

Having sold off his entire collection of HO-gauge train sets, Samuel had been left with only his standard-gauge trains, and he'd spent hours building intricate environments—or layouts—for them on that eight-by-five table. He'd more than achieved the degree of realism he was looking for in his layout. Back then, Jackson would never have admitted to any of his friends that he'd caught the model-train bug, but he had.

He'd loved every minute of his time spent in the attic with Samuel.

Watching those trains emerge from tunnels or climb around the perimeter of the pine-covered mountains had tickled something awake inside of him. He'd felt like a young boy in those moments, or at least the way he wished he'd felt as a young boy. It was pure magic.

Jackson moved around, surveying the layout from all directions, lifting a train car here and there to secure it more fully to the ones in front and behind. He righted a fallen tree and snapped together a section of separated track, and then he froze.

Goosebumps broke out on his skin as he slowly lifted his head to look across the table. Nobody was there. Of course nobody was there, but for a second, he could have sworn he wasn't alone. For a second, Samuel was there, just like always, smiling in that way he had that told Jackson he knew just how he felt. Every time he lit up the track, they shared in the magic.

Jackson flipped the switch and heard the familiar buzz before shutting it off again. And there, alone in the silence, Jackson felt the loss of Leila's father so acutely it hurt to breathe.

"I'll never forget what you did for me," he whispered. "You were the father I never had, and I loved you. I never said it, but I did. I hope you knew."

Many times, Samuel had said of his trains, "These are more than just toys, son, these are masterpieces of mechanical science. Play with them and enjoy them, but don't forget that." Jackson hadn't, and he never would.

He wiped his eyes with the back of his hand and took one last look around. He'd come back to clean things up as soon as he could, but for now, it was time to grab those chairs.

As he made his way back downstairs, gradually the voices in the kitchen floated up to greet him, and as the women laughed and chattered away in the kitchen, Jackson was overcome with an intense feeling of well-being. It was Christmas, and he had a full and loving circle of people to spend it with.

Chapter 26

L eila surveyed the guests around her dining room table. So far, the evening was everything she'd hoped it would be. The food had everyone sending compliments her way, and she imagined her pleasure over their praise was obvious.

Sean and Olivia had brought Nora's booster seat along, and the young girl sat between them, eating a small bite of everything off her plastic, purple plate. She was a very well-behaved child, and Leila was impressed. She wasn't the only one.

"How old is she?" Lizzie asked.

Olivia set down her fork. "Just over eighteen months."

Chuckling, Matt said, "I'm going to have to get used to these units of time." At Lizzie's confused glance, he clarified, "She can't be a year and a half. She's got to be eighteen months."

"Well, that's because you need to be precise," Lizzie instructed. "A lot of changes can happen in a month when you're just a little kid. One month they're crawling, and the next month they're walking and talking."

"Terrifying," Matt said through a mouthful of food.

Leila shook her head. "She's so good. She's like a little adult over there spooning up her squash."

"I wouldn't have touched the stuff at her age," Sean admitted, tousling the girl's hair.

"Me neither." Matt grinned. "It took me until I was ten years old to eat a vegetable."

"It really stunted your growth," Jackson joked.

"Your boys won't be following suit," Virginia warned Matt. "My grandbabies will be the healthiest babies around, especially with Lizzie making all their food herself."

"You're really going to make their food?" Olivia asked Lizzie.

"I'm going to try. I have an entire book on how to do it."

"I predict it lasts a month," Jackson joked.

"Hey, I can do it," Lizzie insisted.

"Two babies, two businesses, one husband ... Sure, you'll have plenty of extra time," Jackson said.

Elena, who'd been unusually quiet through dinner, finally chimed in. "Enough ganging up on the pregnant lady."

"Yeah, tell us about the business," Sean prompted.

"Which one?" Lizzie asked.

"I'd love to hear about what it takes to run a brewery, but I meant the sporting goods store."

Jackson and Lizzie filled Sean in on the latest developments, which Leila already knew. She let her mind drift. Something was definitely up with Elena. She'd have to ask her tonight, although Leila was fairly certain she could guess the gist of what was going on. It was time for her cousin to give Marc Ghetty the boot.

Jackson spoke beside her, filling them all in on the last minute addition of a small hunting section after their firearms license had been unexpectedly approved. "We didn't think it would come through so fast ..."

Leila's thoughts turned to the phone call that had come through earlier. She trusted Jackson, she really did, but she still didn't like it. "Logistics" for "business," and it was a "surprise." That's what he'd said. She wracked her brain to think of what Amelia Channing could have to do with business, or a surprise, for that matter.

There was nothing to do but wait, Leila supposed. She tuned back into the conversation. Lizzie was talking now.

"... and we've talked about the potential to branch out or even franchise down the line, depending on how things go."

Sean raised his eyebrows, and Olivia stared open-mouthed. "No way," they said at the same time before looking at one another and laughing. Sean wrapped his arm around her and placed a brief kiss against her temple. "That's exciting, you guys," he finished.

Virginia beamed proudly at her two children. "The sky's the limit. It can be scary to take that step, but we've done it before."

Perhaps catching the word *we*, Carmen addressed Virginia with a carefully placed smile. "Will you be working with them on this, Virginia?"

"Mom's just our consultant," Lizzie chimed in. "We tried to bring her on board all the way, but she's happy with you at the bookstore."

Carmen swiped at her forehead dramatically. "Phew."

"We'll need to add her to the payroll with as much advice as she's already given," Jackson said as he scooped up another twice-baked potato for himself.

Leila couldn't tell if he was joking or serious. "Don't sign onto anything until you've negotiated a good rate with him, Virginia," she warned.

Virginia smiled at Leila and Jackson. "I don't need money. You two can pay me in grandbabies instead."

The table fell silent, and Virginia grinned. "Oops."

Leila felt herself go pink, but she smiled.

Jackson reached for her hand under the table and made a promise to his mother. "When the time comes, we'll do our best."

Everyone but Elena laughed.

"If it's payment in grandbabies you want, Virginia, I'll continue to do my part with that," Matt vowed solemnly, though his eyes sparkled.

Lizzie gave him a playful swat. "Speak for yourself. Have you seen how huge I am? I'm not letting you near me for a good, long while, buddy boy."

Jackson gave Leila's hand a final squeeze before letting go and tackling his potato with his fork. He glanced at her before lifting his knife, and she smiled. There was a promise in his eyes, and Leila knew he was thinking about their future.

"Everything is so delicious, Leila," he told her again.

"Thank you."

"It really was," Olivia agreed. She and nearly everyone around the table had already eaten their last bite.

Elena pushed her chair back. "Wait till you have dessert."

Olivia looked at Nora and gave an exaggerated gasp of excitement. "Did she say dessert, Nora?"

The baby grinned, revealing several perfect little teeth. She kicked her legs excitedly and pressed her lips together. "Mmmm!"

"How sweet!" Carmen exclaimed. "She knows the word dessert."

"I think that might have been her first word," Sean said with a grin.

"Well, just wait till you try the *tembleque*," Elena informed him. And with that, she was off to the kitchen.

The Costa Rican dessert wasn't quite the hit Leila knew Elena had hoped for, but everyone tried a bit of it and remarked that it was very "interesting" and "unique" before moving on to the pie. Carmen, on the other hand, ate her portion with exaggerated enthusiasm to soothe Elena's hurt feelings.

It didn't work.

Leila watched her cousin's mood sink further, and not even Carmen's request for seconds could snap her out of it.

They lingered around the table long after finishing dessert and sipped the *coquito*, which was such a hit that it almost made up for Elena's disappointment with how they'd received her dessert. She promised everyone the recipe and lamented that she hadn't made more.

Carmen and Virginia insisted on handling the cleanup themselves, so all the guests—minus Lizzie, who was resting in the family room—moved into the living room. Leila tried to get into the kitchen several times, but with no success. Only Jackson and Elena were allowed to help the two matriarchs.

Accepting defeat, Leila gave up and sat down on the floor next to Olivia. She'd brought some toys over for Nora to play with, so as Matt and Sean talked over them, the two of them visited while the baby played beside them.

"Listen," Olivia said at one point, "thanks for having us over. It was nice to be in a big family setting again." Leila knew Olivia and Sean were only children, and they had each lost both of their parents several years ago. Olivia had also lost a husband, who'd been Sean's best friend.

But the petite, red-headed spitfire had made her peace with the tragedies of her past, and Leila knew that although a certain amount of sadness must still linger, her friend had found contentment and fulfillment. She and Sean had a powerful love that bound them tightly together, and their story was swoon-worthy enough to be made into a movie.

While Dolly and Kenny continued to sing in the background on a loop, Leila thanked Olivia for coming and asked what the rest of their friends were doing for the holidays.

That's when they heard the scream.

Chapter 27

Leila's refrigerator had run out of room, so Jackson hauled leftovers out to the garage and placed them out there on a shelf. It had been Carmen's idea to use "Mother Nature's freezer," and why not? It was definitely cold enough outside—all of fifteen degrees and dropping. The wind whipped and howled, and Jackson wondered how the roads would be as he picked up Leila's surprise. A glance at his watch told him he was due to meet the mayor in less than an hour.

He'd just come in from his last trip to the frigid garage when he noticed his sister sitting upright on the sofa in the family room where she'd gone to lie down. After dinner, she'd found him and asked where she might take a quick rest, so he'd set her up on the couch with a blanket. But instead of looking rested, her face was panic-stricken and she clutched her belly.

Jackson hurried to her side. "What is it?"

"My back hurts. It's hurt all day, and then before dinner I started getting those Braxton-Hicks contractions again. But now, it's different. Something's—"

Lizzie grabbed his arm with one hand and tried to finish, but all that came out was a deep moan of pure anguish.

"Are you in labor?" he demanded.

She stared at him in fear. "Jackson, I have to push," she managed to say before another moan was ripped from her throat.

"Don't do *that*!" Of course, he had no idea at all what he was talking about, but he thought he had enough sense to know that pushing out twins in Leila's family room during a snowstorm might not be the best idea.

"I'm going to get Matt and Leila, okay?"

But she couldn't answer, and she wouldn't let him go. Lizzie gripped him even harder around his forearm and let out a guttural scream that lifted the hairs on the back of his neck.

Adrenaline shot through him, and he turned his head to shout across the house for Leila, but having heard Lizzie's scream, she and the rest of the household were already on their way.

Leila was the first one through the kitchen, taking the two steps into the family room at a run. Matt and Virginia followed closely behind her, while everyone else kept a respectful but concerned distance on the landing between the family room and the kitchen.

Those gathered around Lizzie talked all at once until Leila hushed them.

Lizzie was panting with her eyes squeezed tightly shut, so Jackson spoke for her. "She says the babies are coming, and she needs to push."

"Call an ambulance," Leila ordered Virginia, before moving the blanket off Lizzie's lap and revealing wet pants and a saturated sofa cushion.

Jackson watched his mother's face drain of all color, but she turned and did what Leila asked even though he knew she wanted to stay beside her daughter.

From there, everything seemed to happen at once. Lizzie screamed again, and behind him Nora began to cry.

Jackson was filled with such terror, he saw spots in his vision, and as he glanced at Matt, he could see his brother-in-law wasn't faring much better. Only Leila looked calm as she gave orders to everyone.

Intently, he focused on her voice and followed her directions over Lizzie's moans and cries.

As he and Matt moved Lizzie to the floor, Leila gave Virginia information to relay to the dispatcher. Carmen fetched her the requested latex gloves and a bowl of warm, soapy water. Elena boiled water and rounded up towels, sheets, and blankets, and Matt removed Lizzie's pants as Jackson held up a sheet to shield her, not that his sister seemed to give any thought to her privacy.

He watched Leila scrub her hands over the bowl of soapy water, but it wasn't until she called for throwing the kitchen scissors and other items into the boiling water on the stove that Jackson understood. Leila planned to deliver his nephews right there on the Berber carpet next to the sofa, and she was going to cut their cords with the kitchen shears he'd used three hours ago to open the bag of onions.

He thought he might faint, and he looked away as Leila reached under the sheet.

Lizzie squirmed in obvious discomfort, and a long moment later, Leila addressed his sister. "Lizzie, these babies may not want to wait for the hospital." She turned to Virginia. "How far out are they?"

Virginia removed the phone from her ear. "They just left. They say the roads are bad, but they should get here in ten to twelve minutes."

As if on cue, Lizzie screamed again, squeezing Jackson's hand like a vise as a contraction took over. When it passed, she gasped, "I have to push now, I *have* to!" Wild eyed, she lifted her head and looked at Matt. "I'm so sorry." And then she moaned as another contraction came on.

Matt reassured her. He told her everything would be alright, and that she was doing great, but Jackson could see the fear in his eyes.

Leila saw it, too, and she reassured him. "I've done this before, Matt, and the ambulance is coming. We'll have help soon." To Elizabeth, she said, "Your body is ready to push now, Lizzie, and I want to get these babies out sooner than later, okay? I have no way to check on them while they're still inside, and the first little guy's head is already in the birth canal. A few good pushes, and he'll be out. Okay?"

Lizzie whimpered, but she nodded.

Matt moved up, kneeling by his wife's head and stroking her face. "I'm here, baby. You've got this." He nodded to Leila, and she looked around them, giving further instructions. Everyone moved into position. Only Olivia, up in the living room watching Nora, was left out of the equation.

Jackson and Matt each took a leg, and what happened next was the messiest, most violently beautiful experience Jackson had ever witnessed. Six contractions later, and Lizzie had delivered a purple little human covered in slime. There was some suctioning with a bulb syringe, as well as intense rubbing of the little guy with towels before his lusty cry pierced the silent room. He was in good company. Jackson didn't think there was a dry eye in the room as Leila carefully wrapped the screaming, clench-fisted baby in a blanket and placed him on his mother's chest.

Jackson expected the next baby to launch out of the birth canal immediately, but Leila said it was normal for contractions to stop briefly between births. And as they waited, the paramedics arrived, led into the house by Sean, who had been waiting for them at the end of the driveway.

After that, only Leila, Matt, and his mother remained in the family room with Lizzie and the paramedics. It was an eternity of tense waiting, but when the sound of a second crying baby reached Jackson's ears, he let himself go, and everyone with him in the living room laughed and cried together. Even little Nora.

⁂

Later that night, after excusing himself to make a quick phone call to the mayor, Jackson made the treacherous trip to the hospital. With Leila by his side, he held his first-born nephew and fell in love for the second time in his life. His mother had already been there and warned him not to stay too long. Lizzie was exhausted and getting some well deserved sleep.

"Meet Miles Jackson Maki," Matt said with red-rimmed eyes and a proud whisper once he'd transferred the baby into Jackson's arms.

Jackson glanced at him. "His middle name is Jackson?"

"For both of them. Not my idea."

Jackson grinned. "I love it. Thank you."

Matt nodded, the corners of his lips turning up. "It's a good, strong name."

Leila gave them a moment before saying, "We saw little Matthew in the NIC-U. He looks good."

Matt nodded. "Lizzie was worried at first, but they say he'll only need to stay there about a week, so long as he's feeding okay."

"How big is he?" she asked.

"Four pounds, nine ounces. They want him to hit and hold five before he goes home."

Relieved to hear that his other nephew was doing as well as he'd looked, Jackson gazed down at the sleeping, scrunched-up face of the baby he held. "He's so tiny," he whispered.

Matt chuckled. "He's our big boy. Over six pounds. We're going to have to watch him. Apparently, he steals food from his little brother. Lizzie felt so bad about that, she insisted we give the younger one my name to make up for it."

Jackson chuckled softly and then sobered, looking between his sleeping sister and his sleeping nephew. "I'm glad everyone's okay."

Matt took a step and folded Leila into his arms, burying her in his embrace. "Thank you for what you did, Leila. That was the scariest damn thing that's ever happened to me. My entire universe was in your hands, and if anything had—" He thumped Leila on the back several times before releasing her.

She grinned. "You're welcome. I'd say 'anytime,' but I'd rather not do that again."

He returned her smile. "I hear ya."

"I wonder how many of us you're going to rescue," Jackson mused.

Leila held up her hands. "I'm done for a while. I'm wrapping you all up in bubble wrap and putting you under house arrest until summer."

Matt looked Jackson in the eye. "She's family to me now, man, so you better make it official."

Jackson shifted his gaze to Leila. "Oh, I plan to."

By the time Leila finally got back home, the house was dark except for the Christmas lights, and Carmen's car was gone. Jackson saw her to the door, just as he had when they were teens, and he kissed her goodnight.

"I'm sorry you didn't get your surprise tonight," he whispered between kisses.

"Hmm. Tomorrow's better anyway. It'll be Christmas day," she murmured as his lips found her throat beneath the scarf he'd loosened. The cool air of the wind competed with the soft warmth of his mouth, and she shivered.

"It already is," he replied. "It's after midnight. Merry Christmas, Leila." He wrapped her in his arms and held her close.

She buried her face in his neck and breathed in the scent of him. A sense of rightness washed over her, bathing her in a contentment so perfect, she was sure she'd never experienced it before. It was Christmas day, and she was in the arms of the man she loved. Just hours ago, she'd helped bring a precious life into the world, and now she was held, safe and warm, by the man who would be the father of her own children one day. "Merry Christmas, Jackson," she whispered.

He pressed one last kiss to her lips before stepping back. "Here," he said, moving the scarf back in place and rubbing her upper arms. "Better get inside where it's warm. I'll be back in the morning."

"Nine o'clock?"

He nodded. "In the meantime, I'll see you in my dreams."

Leila nearly melted into a puddle right there on the porch. "I really love you, you know."

Smiling, he shook his head. "There's no one like you, Leila." He touched her cheek in a soft caress, and in a husky voice he added, "I love you too. Merry Christmas, sweetheart."

Leila entered the house through the door near the garage and turned on the lights to the family room. Two of the couch cushions were missing, and a large box fan blew over the area of the carpet where Lizzie had delivered her babies.

At this point in her career, smells didn't faze Leila all that much, but she was pleasantly surprised to find that the scent filling her nostrils was that of freshly shampooed carpet and not the byproducts of labor and delivery.

"You're home," Elena announced from the landing.

Leila jumped, and her hand reflexively pressed against her chest. "You scared me."

"Sorry. Here," Elena said, taking her coat and hanging it on the hooks above the bench where Leila sat to remove her boots. "Your *mamá* just left not that long ago. She stayed to help me clean. How are the babies? How is Lizzie?"

"Everyone is healthy and doing well."

"Oh, good," Elena said on an exhale. "Leila, I was so—I'm just so—" She threw her hands up over her face and sobbed.

"Elena?" Leila stood, reaching for her cousin's hands, but she wouldn't allow Leila to move them. "Oh, come here." Leila put her arms around her, and Elena allowed herself to be held. Eventually, she wrapped her own arms around Leila and held on for dear life.

Once she'd calmed down some, Leila led her cousin up to the window seat in the living room.

"Climb up here, and I'll be right back. We'll get all snuggled up and talk."

Elena nodded and sniffled, her body still trembling from the surge of raw emotion.

It took Leila only a few minutes to pour each of them a small glass of *coquito*—finishing off the bottle—but by the time she got back and climbed into the seat with Elena, her cousin's after-shudders had disappeared.

Silently, they tapped their glasses together before taking their first sips. Leila watched her, but Elena kept her eyes downcast. "You really helped me tonight."

"I was terrified."

"So was I."

Elena looked at her then. "You were?"

"I've learned how to hide it pretty well."

Elena accepted that with a nod. "Marc's with a woman tonight. He posted pictures."

"I'm sorry."

"I slept with him."

Leila sighed. "I'm really sorry. That's hard."

"Yeah." She chewed her lip. "But even without that, and even without Lizzie going into labor and scaring us all out of our minds like that, tonight would have been hard."

"Are you missing Auntie Marivi?"

Elena nodded. "Of course. And I know you miss Luca and *Tío* Samuel." She crossed herself, and Leila followed suit. "The holidays are always the hardest. But that's not what I mean."

Leila took a slow sip. "What do you mean, then?"

"Lizzie was glowing, so beautifully pregnant and with her handsome husband there beside her, and Olivia and Sean sat across from me with their beautiful daughter between them, and now you have Jackson—your *media naranja*—and his mom is teasing you about grandbabies."

She wiped at her eyes with the back of one hand. "Listen, I know how I sound right now, and I hate it, okay? I tell myself all the time that I don't even want children. I'd mess them up and never be able to forgive myself. It's pathetic, I know, and I really don't want to be jealous of you, Leila, but it's like you have this future family already with a ready-made husband, and I don't have one and I probably never will. I've never had what you've always had. I can't find anyone to love me, Leila. I can give my whole self to them and they *still* can't love me."

Elena looked at Leila with misery in her eyes, and Leila held her gaze. This is what her cousin always worked so hard to conceal. There was so much more to her than she let other people see. So much hurt inside. Leila wanted to find just the right words that would help Elena realize how much she was worth to the right people. How valued and valuable she already was.

The problem was, Elena was blind in two ways. First, she was blind to the fact that she was more than worthy of being loved. Having a father who'd left her during her formative years had destroyed her ability to see that. Second, she was blind to the fact that she continued to choose the wrong men. She couldn't see that she deliberately chose the cruel ones. And apparently there was a third blindness. She *did* want children. She did want a family. She was just afraid to admit it.

Leila didn't know how to fix any of those things. So instead of searching for just the right words, she spoke what came to mind and kept it simple and truthful.

"Elena, I love you as if you were my sister. Mama loves you like a daughter. Papa loved you that way, too, and still would if he were here. You got a really bad deal growing up. Your father was a loser, plain and simple, and Auntie Marivi, as much as I loved her, was not the most attentive of mothers."

Leila leaned forward.

"But not all dads leave, not all moms check out, and not all men are shallow cads. There are good ones out there, but here's the thing, Elena. You don't want them. So, I think the better question for you to be asking yourself is *why*. Why do the good men turn you off? Why aren't you attracted to them? You say maybe you do want children? Good, you'd make an excellent mother. You are *not* your parents. So, maybe start looking for a man worthy of being the father of those children. Find a man like Papa, like Matt or Sean, or even Jackson. Don't choose them for how they look or how much money they have, or how fast they make your heart beat. Choose them for *their* heart. For the goodness that's in them."

Leila ignored Elena's raised eyebrows and continued. "If you're not going to do that, then you're right, you shouldn't be thinking of having children at all, because those future kids deserve to have a good man for a father. But if you want to be unattached and just have fun for the moment, keep picking the guys you've been picking. If you want something deeper, then look deeper."

She shook her head, finished with her rant.

Elena was silent a full minute before she finally spoke. "You never said that before."

Leila wiggled her toes under the red flannel blanket that covered them. "Trust me, I've wanted to."

"You should have."

Leila scoffed. "Would you have listened?"

"Probably not," Elena admitted, "but I'm listening now."

Leila wiggled her toes again, and Elena looked down to watch the movement.

"What are you doing?"

"My socks are wet from the snow, and my toes feel sticky."

"Gross."

"You just helped me deliver two babies, and then you cleaned everything up after. How can wet toes be gross?" Leila laughed. "Remember when we used to give each other pedicures?"

"Yes, but I'm not touching your feet anymore, so don't ask. I'm still traumatized by the wart."

"It's gone now," Leila said with a grin. "It only took two years to clear. I threw everything I had at that thing. Nothing worked."

"You could have told me about it. Given me some warning. But no, you let me discover it on my own."

Leila laughed again. "You were so mad."

"I scrubbed my hands for fifteen minutes."

With a smile, Leila thought back to those days back in Puerto Rico. "Do you miss it there?"

Elena was quiet for several beats before answering. "Yes and no. Puerto Rico will always be in my blood, but there was so much sadness in that little house. After you moved, everything kind of fell apart for me."

Leila patted the blanket over Elena's knee.

"Mama was always happiest when *Tía* Carmen called or came to visit. I never heard her laugh any other time the way she did with her big sister."

Leila smiled. "I always knew when they were on the phone together. Peals of laughter would fill our house too."

"Sometimes I wonder what she would have been like if *Papá* hadn't left."

"She never got over it."

"No."

Neither had Elena, obviously. What child would be able to recover from their father getting up one day and just leaving? He'd abandoned his family, and he'd never looked back. Elena had been just eight years old.

Nobody seemed to have any idea where he was. Since he and Elena's mother had never actually divorced, they'd all tried to find him when Marivi was diagnosed with pancreatic cancer, and they'd tried again when she'd succumbed to the awful disease seven short months later, but it was as though he'd simply disappeared. Poof. Leila knew Elena still looked from time to time. "You'll always have me," Leila reassured her cousin.

Elena smiled softly. "I know."

Shifting her body, Leila sat up higher against the pillows. "Now, let's rehash everything that happened earlier, because you were a rockstar. Anyone would have thought you sterilized surgical instruments from your kitchen every day of the week. You may have missed your calling."

On Christmas morning, Jackson arrived at the mayor's house promptly at eight o'clock. Robert Taylor really was a good man. He didn't deserve to be spending Christmas alone with only his dogs for company, and it had been nice of him to go with the flow on Jackson's plan, especially considering the change last night.

"How are your sister and those babies?" he asked, as he led Jackson to the kitchen.

"Everybody's doing great."

"Oh, good. That's good to hear. And everyone's doin' great here too." He squatted down next to the oversized kiddie pool and reached in. "Here's the boy," Robert said, handing him a small, dozing yellow lab. "And the girl is over there biting the tail of her littermate. You're lucky. Only three yellows, and you got two of 'em."

Jackson, petting the pup in his arms, observed the rest of the litter. There were ten total, and they'd all be heading to their new homes tomorrow. Robert knew of Jackson's plan, so he had agreed to let him take his two pups early.

The parent dogs had both been black labs, but their litter contained three yellows and two chocolates along with the other five, which were black like their parents. The last time he'd been here, Jackson had made the mistake of asking how two black labs could produce anything other than more black labs, which had prompted a long lecture about genetics, something about *B*s and *E*s, big and small. Jackson vaguely remembered learning about dominant and recessive genes back in high school biology, and he got the gist of what Robert told him, if not all the nuance.

He couldn't have focused on the details even if he'd wanted to; he'd been too wound up. His entire plan for the "Grand Gesture" had hinged on his ability to talk Robert Taylor into revealing the owner of the female yellow lab. One look at the feisty puppy, and he'd been determined. He had to have her. He had to have two of the yellows: boy and girl.

It turned out it hadn't been all that hard. All he'd had to do was be honest. Robert had asked him why he needed two yellow labs, male and female specifically.

The words had come to him immediately. "For the love of a girl, Robert," he'd said. "For the love of a girl." A minute later, he had Amelia's name and phone number in hand, and the rest was history.

Looking down at the playful and energetic puppy and then at the one dozing in his arms, Jackson felt a deep gratitude to both Robert and Amelia for making this happen. He couldn't have shown up to Leila's with Jem only. He needed Scout—the dog Amelia had purchased—too. He had to have them both for the meaning to be clear. He and Leila were building their future together the way she had always dreamed they would.

Jackson smiled. "Who doesn't love a puppy?" he asked rhetorically.

"My ex wife, Marjorie, that's who, and that should have been my first clue." Robert gestured at the black lab sleeping on the dog bed in the kitchen's corner. "I got Bella here when I started to suspect Marjorie was carrying on with that no good, scum sucking—"

He turned red to the tips of his ears.

"—with your father," Robert amended hastily. "Childish, I know. Mostly I did it for the dog since I went without one for close to thirty years, but heck, I admit it. It was a delight, and I mean *a delight*, to piss that woman off."

Jackson cleared his throat. Between this visit and the first one, he was finding out a lot more about Marjorie and Robert Taylor's marriage than he'd bargained for.

Dismissing the topic with a wave of one hand, Robert went on. "Anyway, you don't need to hear about all that. The long story short is that for years, I wanted to own and breed dogs, like my family did when I was a young boy. Now I can."

"Good for you, sir," Jackson said sincerely. And then, for good measure, he added, "My dad doesn't like dogs either."

Robert clapped his hands and rubbed them together gleefully. "Ha! A perfect match! They'll make each other miserable."

Jackson grinned. "Probably."

Robert lowered his voice to a conspiratorial whisper. "Word is they had a big spat a few weeks back after the tree lighting ceremony at Nicolet Harbor. I was there, of course, but I missed it completely. They drank too much and embarrassed themselves but good, they did."

Jackson rolled his eyes. "You know what they say about karma."

The mayor treated Jackson to a wide, approving grin, and clapped him on the shoulder. "Anyway, let's get these two pups loaded up in the carrier, and they'll be ready to deliver. I already stuck on that red bow you left here yesterday morning, so it's all set. But first, we'll let my Bella say goodbye."

All the way to Leila's, the dogs whined pitifully from the back seat. Poor things. They already missed their mother and siblings.

In the back of the Blazer, Jackson had all the other things Leila would need for the dogs, although he wasn't sure whose house they'd be staying at initially. Her job required her to be away from home for long stretches, so he figured they'd share them between their two places for a time. If he had his way, bouncing them between two houses would be short-lived. He had it all figured out in his mind. If Leila would have him, and he knew she would, they'd be engaged by spring—summer at the latest.

Excitement for the future made his heart race as he drove back to Leila's. It was Christmas, and Jackson felt like a kid again. A kid in love. A kid about to take one of the biggest steps of his life and couldn't wait to do it.

Chapter 28

I t was five minutes to nine, and Leila was showered and ready for the day. It was Christmas, and she had nowhere to be except right here in her house with her favorite people. Mama was coming over with donuts at ten, and she figured that would be right around the time Elena woke up.

They'd eat donuts, drink coffee, and exchange gifts. At some point in the day, she imagined she and Jackson would pay Lizzie and Matt another visit, and Elena had mentioned wanting to drive around with hot chocolate and look at Christmas lights around town once it got dark. But other than that, it was a day to sit and spend time together.

Leila stopped in the kitchen to light a cinnamon-scented candle before heading into the living room to look at the tree. Even without a fire going yet, the space was cozy. Presents wrapped in reds and greens and golds rested under the decorated Douglas fir. Adorning the branches were all the ornaments Elena had selected. Many of them, Leila had hung each Christmas since she'd been a young girl. Her family's history was written all over this tree. Until Samuel's death, every year, they'd each given one another an ornament for their stocking, and every Christmas Eve they'd add it to all the others hanging on the tree.

Smiling, Leila spotted Luca's favorite—the Frosty the Snowman she'd gotten him when he was just four years old. Next to it was her favorite, an ornament with a picture of Atticus framed inside it. She thought of her old, faithful dog often, sometimes missing him with an intensity that made her want to run out and buy another one just like him. And why shouldn't she? Having a dog in the house was one of life's most underrated pleasures, and she knew that for her, no home would ever be complete without at least one underfoot.

Hearing a commotion at the far end of the house, Leila turned and headed toward the kitchen.

"Jackson?" she called.

"Yeah, it's me."

She passed through the kitchen, which already smelled of cinnamon. Hearing whimpering, she hurried along. "Are you okay? Are you—"

She stopped above the steps down to the family room. There Jackson stood, holding a dog carrier with a giant red bow stuck to the top.

He met her eyes with a wide smile. "Merry Christmas, Leila."

Leila's heart jumped up into her throat. "What is this?" She moved, drawn like a magnet to the door of the carrier where two smooshy-faced yellow lab puppies gazed out at her. She crouched down to see them better. It was love at first sight. "You got me puppies?" She stood, briefly taking her eyes off the dogs.

Jackson nodded, a pleased flush pinking his cheeks. "Let me set this down and introduce you to Jem and Scout."

"Jem and"—Leila's jaw went slack—"You *remembered?*"

Jackson chuckled before setting the carrier on the floor. "I remembered."

She brought a hand to her mouth and shook her head. "Jackson, I can't believe you did this. I can't believe you remembered."

He opened the door and carefully removed one puppy. "Here, you take Scout"—He transferred the dog carefully from his arms to hers—"and I've got Jem." He popped back up, cradling the male.

Leila brought her warm, sweet bundle up to her face so she could plant a kiss on Scout's soft fur. The puppy lifted her head and licked Leila's nose.

Leila laughed, and once she started, she couldn't stop. "Oh my gosh! I'm so in love, just like that!"

"Me too," Jackson said, his voice serious as he pet little Jem. "Just like that. Forever. I love you, Leila."

Leila grew quiet. "Jackson, I can't believe you remembered this after all these years. Jem and Scout. She started laughing again, but this time, tears fell too."

He transferred Jem to one arm and reached out to touch her. "You're crying."

She laughed harder. "I'm sorry, I'm just ..." She shook her head, looking for words. "Jackson, I'm just so happy."

Relieved, Jackson smiled and pulled her close. "I'm so happy too. Merry Christmas, sweet Leila."

He kissed her, and all laughing ceased as his lips moved over hers. Pressed together between them, the puppies wiggled and yelped in protest until Jackson and Leila reluctantly separated.

Jackson gazed at her, and the tenderness in his eyes warmed her heart. His voice was husky with emotion when he said, "You know this is just the beginning, right? This is the start of our life together."

Leila nodded, but she knew their life together had started a long time ago that warm summer day in the woods. They'd been given the gift of a second chance, and that was the best Christmas present of all.

About the Author

For Charlotte, few things are more relaxing than an escape into a cozy, little story, and that's what she hopes you'll experience within the pages of her books. An author of contemporary women's fiction, Charlotte writes about small-town women and their families, sprinkling in just the right amount of sweet romance for all the feels. She lives on the Lake Superior shore with her husband and three children, and like most of her characters, she can't imagine ever living anywhere else.

Visit her website or follow her on Facebook or Instagram. You can also join Charlotte's monthly newsletter to receive bonus material and other news by clicking here.

Website: www.charlotteeverhartbooks.com
Facebook: @CharlotteEverhart.Author
Instagram: @charlotte.everhart.author

Acknowledgements

Thank you to my uncle, whose real-life boating emergency in Georgian Bay has always left me in awe of his strength and his faith.